PROTECTION

By

Linda Rettstatt

PROTECTION
Copyright © 2014, Linda Rettstatt

Cover Art Design – Trisha FitzGerald

Published March, 2014

by

Linda Rettstatt

www.lindarettstatt.com

Acknowledgements

No writer writes in complete isolation. We are surrounded by family and friends who both interrupt and encourage. And though I sometimes grumble about the interruptions, I know how lonely I would be without them. I am so very grateful for my family and my friends who give me encouragement and believe in me. I'm also grateful for those interruptions when you remind me that I don't exist in a vacuum and you invite me out of my cave and into life, love and laughter.

With thanks to my friend and fellow author Kimberley Koz who not only cheered me on through this endeavor but gave hours of her time and her talent to critique and edit this book. It is better because of her efforts and I am better because of her friendship. Much gratitude also to my cousin and first-reader, Lisa Hennessey Allison for taking the time to read the very rough draft of this book and provide invaluable feedback.

To my readers who are my reason for sitting down at the keyboard and asking the question one more time—"What if…?" And so begins another story. You give me the drive to keep asking and answering that question. A writer writes, first, for herself. But without readers who are touched by her words, those words are hollow. Thank you for reading my stories and for loving and—when appropriate—hating my characters. And thank you most of all for continuing to ask, "So, when's the next book coming out?"

Linda Rettstatt

Chapter One

The blare of a car horn dragged Jake from a sound sleep. He lifted his head to listen, then sat up and looked out the window. A bluish white glow shone through thick fog beyond the slope of ground at the base of his driveway. He grabbed for his jeans and a shirt. Drivers, mostly kids, often misjudged their speed and missed the hairpin turn on the narrow road below. He shoved his cell phone into his hip pocket and tugged on his boots.

When he reached the bottom of the gravel drive, he saw the car rammed into the oak tree that sat at the curve. He ran to the vehicle to find a woman slumped over the steering wheel and the crumpled airbag. As he reached through the open window and pressed fingertips to her neck, checking for a pulse, she moaned and lifted her head, leaning back against the seat. The blaring stopped. From the backseat came a weak whimper.

"Bailey," the woman struggled to speak. "My baby."

Jake reached inside to unlock the rear door and pulled it open. A baby lay in a car seat facing the back. When he leaned over her, she flashed a broad grin and kicked, big blue eyes locking on his. "She seems to be fine." He turned his attention back to the woman. "You shouldn't move. You're bleeding."

But she ignored him, fussing with the seatbelt buckle and freeing herself. "I'm okay."

"You could have a concussion or broken bones. Let me call for help."

"No!"

The vehemence of her response brought him up short. "Okay, at least move slowly and let me help you."

She turned gingerly in her seat and let him help her to stand. "I'll be fine. Can you get Bailey out of her car seat please?"

"Sure." He fiddled with the snap locks and, once the baby was freed, picked her up and removed her from the car. "See, she's fine." He reached back and picked up a small blanket, handing it to the woman. Press this against your forehead.

She did so, then paled at the sight of her own blood. "I'll take

5

her." The woman stretched out trembling hands.

"Maybe I should carry her. You're shaking. Can you walk? I live right up the drive."

She took a halting step, then two. "I think so."

"Here, hang on." He secured the infant in his left arm and slid his right around the woman's waist to steady her. "Slow and easy."

She staggered against him as he guided her up the rough driveway and the few steps to his log cabin. He flung the door open and directed her to the sofa.

The woman dropped down and reached for the baby. "Give her to me." She lay the child in her lap and began to inspect her for injuries.

"Your head's still bleeding. I'll get a towel. Don't try to stand." He hurried to the kitchen, removing a clean dish towel from a drawer and dampening it with cold water, then grabbed a first aid kit from above the fridge. He returned and knelt in front of her, dabbing at a cut above her left eye.

She winced.

"Sorry. I really should call the EMTs. You might need stitches. And both of you should be checked out. You can have hidden injuries after an impact like that."

"No. We're fine. I just need a Band-Aid." She lifted the baby over her shoulder and rubbed the infant's back in soothing circles.

"At least let me clean this cut and bandage it for you. What's your name?"

"Hea…Shannon."

He continued to minister to her wound, first dabbing it with a cotton ball soaked in peroxide, then applying antibiotic ointment and a butterfly bandage. "I'm sorry, I know that hurts."

"It's okay." She lifted her eyes to meet his. Deep blue that matched the baby's eye color, locked on him. "Thank you. May I use your bathroom?"

"Sure. It's right around the corner." He helped her to her feet. "I'm going to see if I can tow your car up here before someone else takes that curve wide and hits it. You need anything?"

She shook her head, then swayed. "I shouldn't do that." Holding the baby against her chest, she gingerly made her way to the powder room.

Once she was inside and had closed the door, Jake grabbed

6

his keys and headed outside. Before moving the vehicle, he had the presence of mind to snap a few photos with his cell phone in case she needed them for insurance purposes. He used a chain to secure the vehicle and fastened it to his truck. The car groaned and bits of the body fell loose as he tugged the car slowly away from the tree and then up the driveway. He jogged back to the accident site to retrieve the bumper and kick pieces of plastic and glass off the roadway.

The front end of the Chevy was in bad shape. The radiator was clearly destroyed, one headlight broken, and the hood bent. He'd have to inspect it further in daylight to assess the full damage. Good thing she wasn't going very fast.

When he returned to the house, Shannon sat once again on the sofa, rocking and murmuring to the child pressed against her body. Tears now trailed down her face. She sniffled when she looked up at him. "Thank you for helping us. Is there a motel nearby that you can take us to?"

He shook his head as he sat in the chair opposite her. "Not for miles, and not in this fog. You can stay here tonight. You shouldn't be alone, anyway. Not after an accident like that. Your car's probably not drivable, but I'll know more once I see it in daylight." He paused, then added, "I'm Jake Garber."

"Thank you, Mr. Garber, but I don't want to put you out."

"You're not. Give me five minutes to fix up the spare room." He considered her wary expression. "There's a lock on the door, if that makes you feel better. Maybe I can make up a bed for the baby in a drawer or something."

"If you could bring in the car seat, it doubles as a carrier."

"Good, I'll do that. You just rest. Do you need something to eat or drink?"

"No, thanks."

Jake wrestled to disengage the car seat. The floor in the back of the vehicle was filled with plastic bags stuffed with clothing and boxes of diapers. It looked like a hasty packing job.

After placing the car seat in the spare bedroom, Jake put clean sheets on the bed and two fresh sets of towels on the dresser. He descended the stairs and paused, watching Shannon and Bailey— an unlikely Madonna and child. He sat again in the recliner and gazed at her. "Where were you headed?"

She regarded him for a moment before replying, "North."

"How far north? Seattle, Bellingham? Or Canada?"

"Uh...Lynden."

Her hesitation wasn't lost on him. She wasn't very forthcoming. But she had just endured what could have been a serious accident and she didn't know him from Adam. Which was a good thing for him. "Lynden. Just about to Canada. Got family there?"

"No."

"Is there anyone I can call for you?"

"It's just me and Bailey. I'll get the car taken care of tomorrow and we'll be out of your way. I appreciate your hospitality for tonight." She bit her lower lip. "If I could ask just one more favor? There's a small overnight bag in the trunk of my car. Could you get that for me?"

"No problem." When Jake popped open the trunk that was stuffed to capacity, he noticed a briefcase that lay atop several plastic bags. His fingers twitched with the temptation to pop it open and see if he could learn more about Shannon. Instead he snatched up the overnight bag and closed the trunk.

Shannon stood as he entered the cabin again.

He slid the strap of the bag onto his shoulder. "Why don't you let me carry the baby up the stairs? You're still a little shaky."

Reluctantly, she handed over Bailey. The baby had been nearly asleep and snuggled in under his chin. Something loosened in his chest as the warm little body trustingly settled into his. "You go first. It's the bedroom on the left past the bathroom."

He followed her into the bedroom and eased the sleeping infant back into her arms. "She's beautiful."

For the first time, Shannon gave a brief smile as she looked at her daughter. "Yes, she is."

"How old is she?"

"Fourteen weeks."

He set down her bag. "Do you need anything else?"

"Not just now." Then she frowned. "I'll need to make up a bottle for Bailey. She'll be awake soon and hungry. I'll try to be quiet about it." She eased the sleeping baby into the carrier and removed a can of formula and a bottle from her bag. "May I use your kitchen? I need to wash this bottle so it'll be ready."

"Sure, come on."

Jake poured himself a glass of milk and sat at the table,

8

watching while Shannon washed the baby bottle and nipple under steaming hot water. She paused and eyed his glass. "May I have some of that, too?"

He nodded and stood to get a glass from the overhead cabinet above the sink then filled it.

"Thanks." She carried the glass of milk with her back up the stairs.

Jake stared after her, wondering about her story. A woman and baby alone in the middle of the night on the narrow back road that ran in front of his property and heading "north." He didn't even know her last name. He dragged a palm down his face. What if this was a set-up? What if someone had found him?

Chapter Two

Shannon set the glass on the night stand, her hand trembling. She bent over the carrier to check Bailey. The baby slept soundly, her chest rising and falling rhythmically. She lightly pressed her fingers to the baby's cheek and smiled. This was her love. Her life. Nothing else mattered and she'd be damned if she'd let anyone take Bailey away from her.

She wrapped her arms together over her chest. What was she going to do? She had no one to call for help. Her cell phone lay somewhere at the bottom of the Missouri River where she'd tossed it once she realized she could be tracked through its GPS. She couldn't use her credit cards and had a limited amount of cash on hand—as much as she'd been able to withdraw from an ATM. If she used her debit card, her location could be traced. She couldn't take that risk. There was the other cash—the blood money. She shook her head. Using that money made her feel dirty.

And now the damned car was destroyed. Probably just as well. It would only be a matter of time before it was spotted and the license plate traced. The car registration was the last piece of Heather Carlson she had brought with her.

She needed paperwork to substantiate her new identity. She also needed a new job, a new place to live. She needed a new life. How to accomplish that became the question. When she looked up Washington State at an internet café in Salt Lake City, she'd ruled out Seattle because of its size. Lynden looked perfect—close enough to the Canadian border, should she need to move fast. She hadn't thought out any other details, just loaded the car and began to drive.

Her thoughts turned to Jake, her rescuer. For all she knew, she had just taken herself and her daughter from one dangerous situation to another. She didn't know this man who lived in seclusion in the back woods of Washington. For all she knew, he could be an ax murderer.

Shannon shook her head, a motion that caused a painful thrumming above her left eye. The last thing she needed was to let her imagination run away with her. She had to keep a clear head and figure out what to do next. A yawn made her aware of her exhaustion. Her head pounded and she padded down the hall to the bathroom hoping to find ibuprofen. The small wall-mounted medicine cabinet above the sink was sparsely and neatly arranged. Toothpaste and a brush occupied one narrow glass shelf. The other shelf held a metal hand razor, a can of shaving cream and, yes, a bottle of Aleve. That would work. She removed one of the blue tablets and popped it into her mouth, followed by handfuls of water until she'd downed the pill. A thin trace of blood crusted her hairline at her temple. She bent forward to splash water on her face, but the motion made her head throb harder. Removing a few tissues from a box on the counter, she dampened them and dabbed away the blood. A large knot had formed above her left eyebrow and the skin around her eye was puffy and turning black. She'd have a shiner by morning.

She washed her hands and returned to her room after pausing briefly to glance across the hall at Jake's closed door. The thought of being alone in this house at the mercy of a strange man gave her unease. But the thought of being out in the night alone with her baby while she was being hunted made her stomach twist with panic. At least this remote cabin offered protection. For now.

Moonlight sent a bluish glow through the window and across the quilt at the foot of the bed. Bailey had begun to stir and would waken in minutes, ready for a diaper change and feeding. Shannon sat up, propped against two plush pillows. She ran a hand over the soft floral-patterned sheets that had to be Egyptian cotton and at least eight hundred thread count. The sheets, along with the rest of the cabin's décor, hinted at a woman's touch, yet there was no evidence a woman lived here.

Bailey began to whimper. Shannon picked her up and laid her on a towel on top of the bed to change her diaper, shushing her so as not to waken Jake. She snapped up the one-piece sleeper and lifted the baby, heading for the stairs. After preparing the bottle, and with Bailey's demands growing louder, Shannon settled into the large comfy leather recliner. Bailey grabbed the nipple and sucked hungrily, staring up at her wide-eyed.

This was really all that mattered. She let the chair wrap her in an embrace, and watched her baby drain the bottle. With Bailey lying on her chest, asleep again, Shannon lifted the footrest and stretched out in the over-sized chair, closing her eyes.

11

She startled when something covered her. A man hovered over her, reaching for Bailey. Instinctively Shannon reacted, swinging her right foot up hard, directly into his crotch. The man groaned, fell back onto the floor, and curled into a fetal position. Not until the light streaming from the kitchen shone on his face did she recognize her host.

"What are you doing?"

Jake groaned. "Covering you."

Bailey whimpered and Shannon struggled to her feet, soothing the infant. She stared down at Jake. "You scared the life out of me. Are you okay?"

He grimaced, his face ashen. "I will be," he choked. "Just…give me a…minute."

She watched as he gasped and fought to get his breathing under control.

Jake rolled over and struggled to get to his feet. Once standing, he bent, palms on his knees, breathing deeply.

"I'm really sorry. I woke up and you were standing over me. I forgot where I was."

He straightened slowly. "I was just covering the two of you with a blanket. It gets chilly at night."

"I came downstairs to feed her and we both dozed off. Something I should not do when holding her."

Jake nodded. "I guess I don't have to worry about you being able to protect yourself." He walked gingerly toward the kitchen. "I came down to see if you found everything you needed. I think I'll have a drink since I'm down here. I don't have to work tomorrow, so I'll see what I can do with your car."

"Thank you." She headed for the stairs. "I feel terrible."

"Don't. I'll be fine. You need anything?"

"No. Thanks." She climbed the stairs, feeling like a total idiot.

Shannon tugged her nightgown from the overnight bag and laid it on the bed. She pulled her tee shirt over her head and removed her bra, then slid her jeans down and kicked them free. The nightgown slipped over her head and down her body. After checking Bailey once more, Shannon slid in between the soft sheets, sinking into the pillows.

She had just kicked a complete stranger in the groin for trying to help her. All of her life, she had been trusting, never in a situation where she had to question everyone's motives. Now she could trust no one and had to keep an eye behind her at all times. She wondered how far would be far enough to run before she would start to feel safe again.

~ * ~

Jake removed a bottle of bourbon from the cabinet above the refrigerator and filled a small juice glass. Pain still radiated in his nether region and he gingerly adjusted himself. He took a gulp of the whiskey and felt its burn in his stomach. He'd only been kicked in the nuts once before and that was by his nephew while they were wrestling. His heart became heavy, as it usually did when a memory of his former life rose to the surface. Charlie would be ten years old now. Jake wondered if the boy was playing baseball. It had been his passion the last time Jake saw him. But that was three years ago.

Downing the rest of the whiskey, Jake rinsed the glass and set it in the sink. He wondered if his sister and brother-in-law had the second baby they were planning at the time. He wondered if his father had finally moved out of his house and into a senior apartment. They had discussed the matter just a few months before his life as Steve Avery shattered and Jake Garber came into being.

Jake had lived in this secluded cabin in the Snoqualmie, Washington for the past two years. He'd come here with a new name, a new history, and a new vocation—carpenter. This was his one link to his past, a trade taught him by his father and grandfather. It was the only skill he had that he could use in the program and still maintain a low profile.

He dragged fingers through his too-long dark locks. Some days he itched for a neat haircut, but knew that wouldn't be wise. He still sometimes had to take a second look in the mirror in the morning to remember who he was now. A glance at the clock told him the sun would be rising in a few hours. He switched off the lights and headed up the stairs. He'd have to deal with Shannon tomorrow.

Hell. This would complicate things if she had nowhere to go. He couldn't just toss her and the baby out. Besides, her car was going to require a lot of work to get it running again, if that was even possible.

What was Shannon's story? And there had to be a story. A single woman traveling with a three month old in the middle of the night in the middle of nowhere. She'd been vague about where she was headed and offered nothing about where she was coming from. Maybe he wasn't the only one in this house with secrets.

Chapter Three

Shannon opened her eyes and stared up at the ceiling. It took a few minutes to piece together the events of the night before and remember where she was. She pressed a finger lightly to her left eyebrow and felt the swollen tender lump.

After changing the baby, she pulled on her jeans and a tee shirt and went to the window. In the driveway below, Jake examined her wrecked car. From her vantage point things didn't look optimistic. He straightened and walked to the garage, disappearing inside. She used the bathroom, then carried Bailey downstairs to prepare her bottle.

While the bottle warmed, Shannon spied the half pot of coffee. She rummaged for a mug and filled it, then added milk from the fridge. The first savory swallow almost made her groan out load. Once the bottle was ready, she sat on one of the cushioned oak chairs at the farmhouse-style dining table and fed Bailey. The baby ate with enthusiasm, making little sucking noises, all the while her eyes locked on Shannon's face. Sometimes she gazed down at her daughter and the amazement that this child was hers overwhelmed her.

The gravity of their situation once again struck and tears stung Shannon's eyes. What could she do now? She had taken a circuitous route of back roads, deliberately avoiding interstates where her car could more easily be spotted by State Police or from the air. She truly hadn't a clue exactly where they were. She had turned off the GPS in the car for the very same reason she had disposed of her cell phone. Tracking. Would Governor Corinne Baker Hastings track her this far?

"Good morning."

Shannon startled.

"I'm sorry. I didn't mean to scare you." He stopped on his way to the coffee pot and stared down at the baby. "Does she ever cry? She seems so content."

"Oh, she cries. I tried to head her off at the pass last night. I didn't want her to wake you." She tried not to glance at his crotch as she asked, "Are you...okay?"

He poured a cup of coffee and sat down opposite her, studying her face. "Probably better off than you are. That's quite a shiner you have. How are you feeling?"

"Like I went five rounds with a pro boxer. I stole some Aleve from your medicine cabinet."

"Take what you need." He sipped his coffee. "I've given your car a once over. The radiator is shot. One headlight is broken. The hood's bent, and I'm pretty sure some hoses and belts will have to be replaced. And the front bumper is destroyed. You're lucky all you got was that bump on your head. I know a guy in town who can give you a better estimate of the damage. I'm sure he'll come out and look it over."

"Town?"

"Yes, the town you drove through to get up here."

She felt a rush of heat to her face. In the dark and the fog, she'd completely missed the name of the town. "What town was that? I was kind of lost."

"Snoqualmie."

"Are we near Seattle?"

"We're about twenty-eight miles east. Was your GPS broken or were you just sightseeing? Not many people drive through here. Most folks would have stayed on I-90 to Seattle and up I-5 to Lynden."

"I...uh...got off I-90 and then got lost. I figured as long I kept heading north, I'd be fine." She lifted the baby onto her shoulder. "Is there a motel anywhere nearby where you could drop us?"

"Sure, but there's no reason you have to leave. You're welcome to stay here until your car's repaired. I promise you, I'm not a serial killer."

She grinned. "What are you then?"

"A carpenter. I do contract work for a number of home builders and some specialty work that's sold through a few home stores in Seattle. I have a workshop in the garage."

She sipped her tepid coffee and grimaced.

Jake stood and picked up her cup. "Let me get you a fresh refill."

"Did you always live here in Snow...?"

"Snoqualmie. No, I've lived here for a little over two years. It's a great small town and I love the woods, the mountains, the people. How about you? Where are you from?"

She hesitated. If she said Missouri, she'd give away one piece to her puzzle. Then she thought of the small town where her mother had grown up. "Uniontown, Pennsylvania. Ever heard of it?"

"Can't say I have." He paused, then asked, "Do Shannon and Bailey have a last name?"

"Chase." The irony of the name she'd chosen hadn't been lost on her.

He opened the refrigerator and removed a carton of eggs and a package of bacon. "You're not a vegetarian, are you?"

"Oh, no. But you don't have to cook for me."

"Might as well. I'm cooking for myself. I haven't eaten yet. Since Bailey's the only one with a full stomach, I figured it was our turn."

Shannon nodded. "I'm going to take her upstairs and change her clothes, give her a sponge bath. I need a shower, too. You go ahead and eat."

"No rush. If you need anything, let me know." He continued to pull a skillet from a cabinet beside the stove and turn on the griddle.

~ * ~

Jake listened to Shannon's footsteps as she ascended the stairs. He reminded himself to be careful about asking too many questions in case he had to answer those same questions in return. That would be problematic. He dumped the remaining coffee and prepared a new pot to brew, then set the table for two, staring for a moment at the unusual setting. In his two plus years here, he'd only had a guest twice for a meal and never one that stayed over. Particularly not a woman. He knew there were folks in town that stared and whispered and wondered about the hermit-like stranger in their midst. A few of the guys he'd worked with locally and joined for a beer now and then called him Choirboy. They rarely heard him swear and noted his efforts at avoiding the women who occasionally threw themselves his way. He was sure a few of the guys and several of the women thought he was gay.

He was about ready to crack open the eggs when he heard the shower upstairs. Setting them aside, he toasted two English muffins and waited.

Shannon padded down the stairs with Bailey in her carrier. The baby kicked her chubby legs and blew bubbles through her tiny bow-like mouth. Shannon's dark hair, still damp from her shower, curled around her heart-shaped face. Her skin glowed, much better than the sallow look she had the night before. "I didn't mean for you to wait."

"Eating alone gets old. It's nice to have a guest. This'll be ready in a few minutes. The coffee's fresh if you want another cup."

"Thanks. I think I will. It's my one addiction."

She wore a pair of knit pants topped with an oversized tee shirt. She was barefoot. And she was beautiful. Years ago, he'd learned not to notice the way a woman smiled, the way she tilted her head or toyed with her hair when she spoke. He'd learned not to see her womanliness, only to see her as an *other*. But here in his kitchen, in the early sunlight, fresh from a shower and looking so fragile and vulnerable, he *saw* Shannon.

"Is something wrong?" she asked, tilting her head slightly.

"No, I was just thinking. Nothing's wrong." He turned back to tend to the bacon and scrambled eggs on the stove top. Without work to do today, he'd have to keep himself busy in the shop. He needed to get some distance, get a grip. Living between two worlds had been easy as long as he lived alone. Bringing someone else into his world, someone who resurrected feelings he'd long forgotten, created a dangerous game.

Silence hung heavy between them as they sat opposite one another and ate.

"Are you going…?" Shannon began.

"If there's anything…." Jake said at the same time. He grinned. "Sorry. What were you going to ask?" The flush that colored her cheeks made her eyes look almost turquoise. It fascinated him how her eye color could change from an ice blue to the waters of the Caribbean.

"I was wondering if you were going into town or near a store. I'll need to get more baby formula soon."

"We can go after breakfast and stop by Herb Hightower's, arrange for him to come out to look at your car."

"Do you think he'd buy it for parts and maybe I could find something cheap to get me to Lynden?"

"I…uh…don't know. You might want to wait and see what the damages are first. If you're worried about being in the way here, you're not."

Bailey screwed up her face and flailed her tiny fists. "Uh-oh. About time for a diaper change." Shannon stood and carried her empty plate to the sink. "Leave the dishes and I'll clean up after I change her."

Jake sipped the remainder of his coffee. Another piece to the puzzle of Shannon Chase that didn't add up—her eagerness to dispose of her car without even knowing the extent of the damage. Again, he had to remind himself not to delve too deeply into her personal life. Leave the boundaries where they were. Help her get her car repaired so she could be on her way to Lynden. Hell, he'd drive her there himself if need be.

By the time she returned to the kitchen, he had already washed the dishes and was finishing up the frying pan. "All done here. Ready to go?"

"Is there a way to attach her car seat into your truck?"

Jake nodded. "It's an extended cab with a back seat." He picked up his keys from the hutch next to the refrigerator and held the door for Shannon to move past him with the baby. The mixture of her fruity shampoo and Bailey's baby powder made him momentarily lightheaded. It was as if this woman had been dropped into his life to shake loose all of the senses he had worked to secure away. Hopefully, Herb could get her car running in the next day or two and get her on her way.

Again a strained silence accompanied them on the ten minute drive into town. Jake pulled into the parking lot of the IGA. "I'll come with you. I need to pick up some things, too."

Inside the store, Jake was aware of stares following them as he accompanied Shannon and carried the baby carrier. His appearance with an attractive young woman and an infant would no doubt be fodder for the gossip mill before they were back in the truck.

"Hey, Jake. It's been a while."

He turned toward the voice. Carlie Hawk had pursued him long and hard within weeks of his arrival in town. She still kind of lit up around him, even though she was now engaged. "Hi, Carlie."

She smiled and shifted her gaze to Shannon, studying the black and purple bruise around her eye, and then to the baby in the carrier Jake held. "And who's this?"

"This is a friend who…uh…stopped by on her way north.

Shannon—Carlie. And this is Bailey." He lifted the carrier slightly.

"Cute." She glanced at Shannon, then turned her full smile back to Jake. "The baby, I mean. It was nice to see you, Jake." She nodded toward Shannon. "See you around."

Jake watched as Carlie pushed her shopping cart to the end of the aisle and turned from his line of sight.

"Old girlfriend?" Shannon asked.

Jake felt the heat creep up his neck. "No, but not for lack of trying. On her part."

"I could see that. She's still trying." Her mouth quirked up at the corners.

The heat threatened to consume him. "She's engaged. Something she seems to forget now and then." He cleared his throat. "Did you find what you need?"

"The formula. Yes."

"Good. Let's hit the produce and we'll need something for dinner." As soon as the word was out of his mouth, he wanted to draw it back in—'we.' "Do you like steak? I can cook them on the grill."

"Yes, but I'll pay for some of the food. You've been so kind."

He shook his head. "You don't make it easy."

Color drained from her face. "What do you mean?"

"Nothing. It's just... I'm trying to help you here and you keep apologizing and insisting on paying your way."

Now the color returned to her face full force. "I've always paid my way." She reached for the baby. "I'll take her while you finish your shopping." Taking the carrier, she brushed past him and walked ahead.

Jake exhaled heavily. He hadn't wanted to offend Shannon or come across as patronizing. If he were to be honest, what he wanted to do was put an arm around her, reassure her she was safe from whatever she had fled. He wanted, for some inexplicable reason, to take care of her and Bailey. He sighed again and headed for the meat counter. After purchasing two better cuts of steak at a price he rarely spent for dinner, he caught up with Shannon in the produce aisle. She had found a basket and was selecting apples. "I'm sorry if I offended you."

"I'm sorry, too. I guess the accident still has me unnerved and I'm a little touchy."

"Look, I'm not very good at this whole having a houseguest thing. But I do recall that a good host provides for his guest. Please let me pay for the food. Otherwise, I'll feel like I failed, and I don't like failure."

She rolled her eyes and dropped the bag of apples into the shopping cart. "I wouldn't want to be the cause of you having to go to confession."

"Confession?" He hesitated, then asked, "Are you Catholic?"

"I was once." She picked up a cantaloupe and rapped on it with her knuckles. "How do you know if these are ripe? I'm lousy at selecting melons."

He took the fruit from her hand, examined it, and tossed it into the shopping cart. "Beats me. It's always a gamble. I do know this goes well with ice cream." After picking up a few potatoes for baking, he directed her to the frozen foods section. "French vanilla?"

"Oh, yes."

When they reached the checkout, Jake was quick to place the entire contents of the cart onto the belt. Shannon's gaze followed the cans of baby formula, but she didn't rip them from his hands. He slid a glance at her and grinned. She blushed and grinned back. And something loosened in him even more. He didn't know much about this woman, but he liked her. That could mean trouble on so many levels, but he pushed that thought from his mind.

Chapter Four

"Maybe I could call the mechanic later. You don't want the ice cream to melt." She tried to sound casual, reasonable. Inside a flurry of nerves betrayed her anxiety. What if a watch had been issued already for the car? Could that have been done and would this Herb know to look at the make and model or check the VIN?

Jake pulled into the combination gas station and repair shop. "This'll just take a minute." He disappeared into the gaping darkness of the open garage, returning a moment later with another man dressed in oil-stained denim coveralls and wiping his hands on a dirty rag.

"Herb, this is Shannon Chase. She ran into a tree last night at the hairpin curve out by my place. I towed her car up into my driveway to get it off the road. I was wondering if you could come out and take a look, see what you think about the damage."

Herb nodded to Shannon. "That's a bad curve out there. If that bump and black eye's all you got, you were lucky. What kind of car?"

"It's a Chevy Malibu, 2010," she replied.

"I could see that the radiator took the brunt of the impact and is probably finished. One headlamp is broken and the bumper fell off, but I salvaged it. Fortunately, the windows didn't shatter, though the airbags deployed," Jake said.

Herb nodded as he listened. "I could come by tomorrow morning. The kid that works for me called in sick today, so I'm the only one here."

Jake slapped Herb on the shoulder. "Thanks. I appreciate it."

"Glad you weren't badly hurt, Miss." Herb gave Shannon one last nod and turned back to the garage.

After buckling his seatbelt, Jake glanced at Shannon. "Did I overstep?"

"No. I appreciate your help. I wouldn't know where to start, being a stranger around here. I'll see what Herb says tomorrow about my car before I decide what to do with it." If she were on her own, she could just pack her bag, slip out of the house, and head for the highway when Jake wasn't looking. But with Bailey in tow, that was not an option. She would have to wait, see how this played out. She was dying to check her email and her cell phone account for messages. But she couldn't risk being traced. That would put not only herself and Bailey in danger, but now Jake, as well.

On their way back to the cabin, Shannon had a chance to see the town she'd missed the previous night. Small shops lined the main street. An historical marker indicated Snoqualmie was incorporated in 1889. They passed a train depot dating from 1890 that now housed a railway museum. Small-town America—1950. And that suited her just fine.

"Blink and you've missed it," Jake said.

"Pardon?"

"The town. It's small."

Was he reading her mind? "It looks quaint, kind of like a place out of time. It must be so different from living in a city."

"Different, yes, but in a lot of good ways. And Seattle's close enough."

Jake made a turn and wound the truck up the narrow mountain road to the cabin. He carried in the groceries while Shannon handled the baby. He set the bags on the table. "I have a little work to do in the garage. Would you mind putting this stuff away?"

"I'm happy to. I hope I didn't interfere with your work schedule today."

"Not at all. Make yourself at home. There's a computer in the living room if you want to check your email. If you need anything, just open the back door and shout." He removed a bottle of water from the fridge and headed out the door.

Shannon set the baby carrier in the center of the table and smiled at Bailey. "I'll bet you'd like to be out of that carrier for a while so you can stretch. Wait until Mama puts these groceries away, then I'll get you out of there."

His cupboards were well-stocked, as was the fridge. She helped herself to a can of diet soda and picked up the carrier. In the living room, she spread the thick afghan that draped the sofa on the floor and removed Bailey from the carrier, laying her on her back. "There you go, sweetie. Now you can stretch a bit."

The baby grinned, flailing her arms and kicking her legs.

Shannon eyed the computer in the corner. Her fingers

twitched as she imagined opening her email to see what was happening in her former life. It was too risky. What if she opened a new email account under a different name and contacted her best friend, Brooke? She was sure her mother's email was being monitored. But it was unlikely they knew about Brooke.

She hurried to the computer and wiggled the mouse to bring the screen to life. She went to Gmail and set up a new email account under the name of Eve Adams and using the screen name of adamseve1. She had no trouble remembering her friend's email address—babblingbrooke30. Now, how to compose a message that Brooke would understand without identifying herself. They'd sent cryptic messages back and forth all through high school. This wouldn't be much different.

Hey, sorry I missed the movie last Friday. Had a family emergency and had to run. I'll talk to you soon, Babs. Or you can call me Eve.

She was sure the use of the nickname would clue her friend in. Babs was an abbreviation for Babbling Brooke—something Brooke did when she was excited or anxious. She babbled. Shannon also hoped Brooke picked up on the last line and didn't give away her real name in a reply email. Someone else would likely just think she'd forgotten the comma. She stared at the message for a long moment before pressing 'send.' Brooke was the only person besides her own mother who knew what was going on in her life. She could count on Brooke to be cautious.

Leaving her mail open so she'd be alerted to a response, she browsed the book shelves. Jake had eclectic taste in reading—everything from murder mysteries to non-fiction books on religion and spirituality. Just as she began to pull a book from the shelf, the email dinged a message notification. Shannon startled and dropped the book which hit the floor with a soft whump. She hurried back to the computer and found a message from babblingbrooke30.

Missed you on Friday. Hope all is well with the family now. Mom said to say 'hi.' Have a date with W. Give me a call when you can. Babs.

Shannon breathed a sigh of relief. Brooke knew exactly what she was doing. Her own mother was deceased, which meant she had been in contact with Shannon's mom who was saying 'hi.' It was also a signal that she'd let Shannon's mom know she heard from her and that she and the baby were okay. Brooke had been dating the same guy for the past three years and had given Shannon the clue to call her that evening at Warren's apartment. Shannon closed out the email and went to the internet and white pages to look up Warren McDowell in Jefferson City, Missouri, hoping he had a listed number. He did. She jotted it down and slipped the paper into her pocket. She shivered with anticipation, needing to hear her friend's voice and advice.

~ * ~

Jake smoothed the wood with a hand sander, then ran his fingers over the surfaces to make sure there were no rough spots or splintered wood. He had taken a spare, flattened pillow to affix into the bottom of his creation and to serve as a mattress. His first consideration was a quilted cover, but he remembered something about soft bedding being a danger for infants. He grimaced when he stood back to look at what he'd done. It wasn't his finest work, crude and somewhat unfinished, but there was no time to paint or varnish and have it dry by evening. The lined wooden box would have to do as a makeshift crib.

Setting the tools aside, he emerged from the garage, wiping an arm across his moist forehead. Curiosity made him focus on the car, in particular, the glove box. Just as he took a step toward the vehicle, the cabin door swung open and Shannon strode toward him holding out a glass of iced tea. "It's getting warm. I thought you could use a cold drink."

He shifted his gaze back to her, accepting the drink. "Thanks."

"What are you working on?"

"Come on, I'll show you."

She hesitated. "Bailey's asleep in the living room. I shouldn't leave her alone for long."

"Go back inside. I made something for her and I'll bring it in." He handed back the drained glass.

Her eyes widened when he carried in the wooden cradle and set it down. "I can't imagine sleeping in a chair night after night. I don't suppose it's comfortable for her, either."

Shannon ran her hands over the smooth natural wood and pressed her fingers into the bottom. "This is perfect, and the pillow's not too plush." Her eyes filled as she looked up at him. "Thank you."

Jake shrugged, taken off guard by her emotion. "Not the most attractive piece I've ever made, but it'll serve its purpose temporarily. I can finish it off and paint it before you leave."

"No, it's perfect. I love the natural wood." She swiped away an errant tear. "I'm sorry. It's just such a kind thing to do. Thank you." She nodded toward the computer. "I went on to check my email."

"Good. Well, I'm going back out to the shop. Help yourself to lunch or anything you need. I'll wash up around five and get the steaks on the grill. Is there more iced tea?"

"Yes. And, thanks again. I hated having her sleep in that carrier all the time. She couldn't really stretch. I'll get your tea."

She brushed past him, close enough that he could feel the heat of her body and breathe in her scent. It took everything in him not to reach out and take her arm, pull her close. Feel the softness of her against his growing hardness. He followed, snatched the glass from her hand and continued moving toward the door and straight to the garage.

He needed to finish off a set of matching bookcases. His reaction to Shannon had him unraveling faster than a ball of yarn in the paws of playful cat. He had to get a grip. So he tightened his fingers around the hammer and, with one hard whack hit the nail on the head, splitting the wood in two. "Damn." Setting down the hammer, he closed his eyes. Once a man of prayer, he tried to find a way to ask for help, but that part of him had faded away with his former identity.

At first, he'd been confident his God would bring him justice. Then when his life was threatened, he became doubtful. The discussion about placing him in witness protection left him angry, wondering why he'd done the right thing and was now condemned to a prison of a different sort while the real criminals were still out there. Over the past two years, faith evaporated faster than the remnant haze of incense with which he'd once been so familiar.

Father Steve Avery disappeared like that vapor. Jake Garber, a carpenter from Arizona, moved to Snoqualmie, Washington because he'd always wanted to live in the Northwest. Beginning and end of story.

His life had been quiet, peaceful for the past two plus years. It was hard at times to be separated from his family, but it was for their safety, too. He was amazed at how easily and thoroughly Steve Avery had been eliminated, erased from this life. It killed him to think of the pain that had caused his father, his sister and her family.

Sometimes he thought about re-emerging from his exile and taking his chances. But he couldn't gamble with their lives, and his Department of Justice contact kept him informed and told him someone still searched for him and wanted him dead. And that someone would know that the one way to get to him would be through his family.

The FBI kept tabs on the foreign child adoption organizations involved in the scandal Father Steve had so innocently uncovered, implicating a fellow priest, a former priest, and a Catholic adoption agency. Jake was fairly certain his own brother priests presented the greater threat, especially the former Father Louis Crowley. Lou had somehow evaded capture when the whole ugly mess blew up. Steve was viewed as a traitor among his ranks. He had bypassed the step of informing the Bishop first, thus allowing the matter to be handled in-house, and had gone straight to the police.

Jake sighed wearily. If he hadn't gotten that phone call while he was away for a week of retreat and returned early to be with a family from the parish while the husband and father was dying, he would never have suspected anything wrong. Instead, he rushed into the rectory to drop his bags and pick up his stole, holy oils and prayer book to administer last rights to the dying patient.

That's when he heard the child crying behind the closed oak doors leading to the dining room. Then he heard the tight voices of Lou Crowley and the pastor, Father Alvin Martin arguing.

"I don't care. I have to deliver her to the client tonight," Lou said. "She's supposed to be three years old. That one is at least seven."

"What do you want me to do?" Alvin asked. "This is the girl the agency brought to me. The only one. So tell your client there was a mix-up. They want a daughter, they get a daughter. And this child gets a decent home."

Steve's mouth went dry and his heart thudded. He couldn't believe what he was hearing.

"Our client is not going to be happy about this," Lou growled.

Footsteps crossed the room and the child let out a frightened cry.

"Shut up. I'm not hurting you. I'm taking you to your new family."

As someone strode toward the sliding doors, Steve backed up

and slipped into the front office. He peered around the corner to see Lou dragging a little girl with long dark hair beside him down the hall and out the door. *Shit.* He'd left his car in the driveway. He took two long strides across the hall and ascended the stairs. He waited a few moments, then came back down as calmly as possible.

Father Alvin waited for him at the bottom. "Steve, I thought you were on retreat."

The Leandros family called me. Mike's dying. They wanted me to come, so I drove back." He held up the box containing his oils. "Just stopped by to get these." He slipped past the older man and headed to the back door. His hand shook as he tried to slip the car key into the ignition.

A week later, Alvin called him in to say that he was being transferred to another parish in the Diocese. When Steve asked for an explanation, he was simply told it was the Bishop's orders, that the parish needed him. Steve knew Alvin suspected he'd heard or seen what was happening that night.

When he got the first anonymous call in the middle of the night, warning him to keep his mouth shut and from a voice that sounded a lot like Lou, Steve was sure of his suspicions. Not only for his own safety and peace of mind, but for the sake of that little girl and God only knew how many other children, Steve went to the police who called in the FBI. It took several months to get enough evidence to pick up Lou and Alvin. They had been working through a Catholic adoption service with an adoption worker, Sara Martin, who had been intimately involved with Lou even before he had been dismissed from the priesthood. She also happened to be Father Alvin Martin's sister. Lou and Sara disappeared, escaping arrest. Alvin sang like a tenor in the church choir and was serving time for child trafficking. They had been bringing children in under the guise of having them adopted, then selling them to the highest bidder—families who, for one reason or another, had been deemed unsuitable to adopt.

After the trial ended and Steve continued to receive threats, including one narrowly missed bullet, the FBI determined he needed to be placed into witness protection and handed him off to the Department of Justice. Once they caught up with Lou and Sara, the coast would be clear for him to return to his former life.

So here he was—still a priest according to the Church—living in exile in the Northwest wilderness. A priest whose commitment could be seriously tested by the presence of Shannon Chase.

Chapter Five

Shannon stood at the sink washing vegetables for a salad while Jake grilled steaks on the small deck. She could see him through the window. For the first time since her ordeal began, she looked at him as a man—tall with dark hair that curled around his ears and over his shirt collar. He wore a faded denim shirt with the sleeves rolled up so that his tanned forearms were visible. His jeans hugged a nice backside and long, muscled legs. Most women would have been cautious or suspicious of a man like this living alone out here in the woods. But there was something about this man that put her at ease. Earlier it seemed he couldn't get enough distance from her. *Maybe women aren't his thing?*

He closed the lid on the grill and came inside carrying the bloodied plate that had held the steaks. "How do like your steak?"

"Rare. Well, medium perhaps. Not still walking."

He grinned. "Me, too. They should be ready in about ten minutes. The potatoes should be done then, too. I put them in the oven earlier."

When he moved closer to rinse the platter in the other side of the double-bowl sink, their elbows met. The brief warmth of him made her breath catch. He jerked his arm away and, in doing so, dropped the platter into the sink.

Shannon turned away. "I'll set the table." Her hand trembled as she lifted plates from the cabinet. Why was she so nervous all of a sudden? Or was she picking up his vibes? She set down the plates and collected the silverware, including steak knives. "Do you have steak sauce?"

"It's in the door of the fridge. I'll get it."

"No, I can get it."

They both turned and ended up chest to chest, although his chest was a bit higher than hers. For a moment, they stood, not breathing, just looking at one another. Then Jake took a step backwards. "Sorry."

"Sorry," she said at the same time. Shannon bit her lower lip as she felt the rush of heat to her face. "I'll get the steak sauce." She

30

welcomed the blast of cool air from the open refrigerator and took more time than needed to retrieve the bottle of A-1.

Jake returned to the grill, turning the steaks and then taking a long draw on the beer he'd carried outside earlier. She watched the way his Adam's apple bobbed as he chugged the drink. She determined that, no matter how Herb assessed the damages to her car, she would find a way to get of town within the next twenty-four hours. Or at least out of this house. She had about eight thousand dollars in the briefcase, money she hadn't planned to use. Tainted money. She just had to get it out of the car—something she should have done sooner. She could surely buy a clunker for a few thousand, one that would at least get her to Lynden.

"Steaks are done," Jake called as he came through the back door. He set the platter on the table and used an oven mitt to get the potatoes from the oven and drop one onto each of their plates.

They sat across from one another, staring at the food.

"Please, go ahead." Jake nodded toward the salad.

She filled a small bowl with salad and passed it to him.

Jake split his baked potato and dropped generous dollops of butter and sour cream onto each half. "So, Herb'll be out tomorrow to check your car. You may want to call your insurance company and see if they need to send someone out to view the damage, as well."

"I will." But she wouldn't. She couldn't. One phone call that attached her to Heather Carlson could set off a chain of events that would be catastrophic. She would simply have to consider the car a loss and move on. But how?

She toyed with her salad. "I was thinking. Do you know anyone in town who might have an apartment for rent? Cheap?"

His eyebrows lifted. "You thinking of staying here?"

She shrugged. "For the time being. I don't have to be in Lynden any certain time."

Jake chewed on a piece of steak and swallowed. "You know, I might know someone. There's an elderly couple that has a garage apartment. Mr. Swinson asked me a couple of weeks ago to come by and see what needed to be done to get it ready for a renter. I haven't had time yet to do that, so I don't know what condition it's in now."

"I don't need anything fancy. Just clean and safe. One bedroom is sufficient for me and Bailey."

He nodded. "We can check it out tomorrow. Mr. Swinson

used to be a handyman of sorts, so I can't imagine it's in a state of total disrepair. Arthritis had him sidelined the past year and he couldn't do the things he might have done to keep the place up."

She blew on a forkful of steaming potato. "I don't mind if it needs a little work. I can handle that. Thank you." Relief washed through her. She could just as easily settle here for a time as she could in Lynden. The bigger issue was going to be finding a job that wouldn't require identification. Shannon Chase had no identification. At least not current. Shannon Chase had died eleven years ago.

~ * ~

Governor Corinne Baker Hastings stood at a window in her library of the Governor's Mansion and watched dusk darken the waters of the Missouri River. At forty-six, she was beginning to show signs of age—lines at the corners of her eyes and around her mouth and a few grey hairs that she had quickly had her hairdresser cover up. The lines, she insisted, were the result of stress. Her state had recently been hit hard with several storms that produced tornadoes. It seemed they were always on the brink of a state of emergency. Much like her personal life.

She turned and stared at the photograph on her desk—a picture of herself and her husband, Mark, vacationing in Hawaii a couple of years earlier. They both looked happy, relaxed. Solid. Had he been cheating on her even then?

Corinne had married Mark Hastings three years after graduating from Columbia Law School at the University of Missouri. She worked then in one of the more prestigious law firms in St. Louis. Mark was an entrepreneur, always excited about some new opportunity, creating or investing in new business ventures. She found him to be intelligent, handsome, sexually creative, and exciting. They agreed on just about everything—politics, religion, and not having children. Both wanted a lifestyle without the responsibility of a family. He was enough for her, and vice versa.

When he came to her five months ago in this very room and confessed to an affair, she'd been stunned. But when he told her his mistress was pregnant and about to give birth to his child, Corinne felt as if he'd kicked her in the stomach. He didn't ask for a divorce but, rather, asked for money to make the whole mess and the woman in question go away. He wanted fifty thousand dollars.

After raging at him about his infidelity, knowing it was not the first time he'd strayed, Corinne told him she would have to think about it.

"Think about it?" he'd asked. "What's there to think about? If word of this gets out, it's your career on the line. Remember, I don't have one. I'm just your arm candy for political dinners."

"Arm candy? You can't be serious."

Mark flashed his easy grin, the one that had gotten her reeled in the first time. "Well, I'm not your secretary or your personal assistant. Hell, Corinne, I'm barely your husband. You haven't had time for me for the past three years. And with elections coming up, I doubt I'll see you for months. Unless, of course, you need an escort to some campaign dinner."

"You son-of-a-bitch. You've been leeching off of me and this office for the past three years and, now, you have the nerve to want me to pay off your mistress? I should just divorce you and let her have you."

He'd laughed at that. "Divorce me? That'll be the day. That would really put a wrinkle in the happily married couple image you like to throw out to the public."

She had stared at him long and hard, mainly because he was right. She had to maintain the image of a happily married couple until this next election was over and she was re-elected Governor of Missouri. "I want to meet her."

"Are you crazy?"

"If I'm going to pay her off for you, I think I should meet her."

He'd shaken his head. "No. She'll never agree to that."

"How do I know the money is for her, then? How do I know you won't take the money and run?"

"Oh, please. Fifty thousand dollars wouldn't get me very far. I'm not going anywhere."

"Fine. You can sleep in here, then." She strode from the library and down the hall to their bedroom, where she slammed and locked the door.

By the next morning, she had a plan. She and Mark would take the baby and raise it as their own. He owed her this much. He had cheated her out of a child by convincing her they didn't need a baby to complete their family. She had let him do it and now it was too late for her. Besides, adopting a poor baby whose mother couldn't care for it would win her favor with some of the pro-life groups in the state. Not to mention those affected by adoption.

When she presented the plan to Mark the next morning, he agreed. He talked to the woman whom he referred to as Heather, but reported back to Corinne that Heather wasn't so keen on the idea. The baby wasn't due for at least six weeks. He was sure he could get her to see the sense in giving him the baby. He assured her the child would be well cared for and that she would be compensated so that she could start a new life somewhere else.

Corinne called upon Phil Barclay, one of her personal body guards, to shadow Mark and find out more about the woman. Heather Carlson was seventeen years her junior, an attractive woman with shoulder-length chestnut brown hair. She worked as a bank manager in Jefferson City and lived in a modest apartment building just a few miles from the mansion. She was single, had a mother who lived in Jefferson City, no pets, and drove a more recent model Chevrolet. Corinne had looked at the photos her body guard, who had been sworn to secrecy, had taken. What did this woman offer Mark that she herself did not? The woman had no money, other than her paycheck. Sex with no strings attached. That was clearly the attraction for Mark. Well, that and her age.

It was risky to go outside the staff assigned to her to hire a private detective. She had to rely on the trustworthiness of Phil Barclay. Corinne continued to pressure Mark to get Heather to agree to an adoption. But the woman just wasn't listening to reason. The baby, a girl, was born two weeks early. Mark's feigned excitement about the infant made Corinne physically ill. She decided it was time to take matters into her own hands.

Late one May evening, she slipped out of the mansion and had Phil drive her to the woman's apartment. She sat outside for a long while, staring at the windows on the second floor, watching someone pace while soothing a baby. Her arms ached and a strange twinge tightened her uterus. Mark had stolen all of this from her. It was time for her to take it back.

Corinne hurried across the street, hoping she wouldn't be recognized. She entered the small outer lobby and found the buzzer for H. Carlson. When Heather's voice came through the speaker, asking who it was, she said, "Miss Carlson, this is Corinne Hastings. It's very important I talk with you. It's about Mark."

To her surprise, Heather buzzed her in. The apartment was small, but neat and clean. A stack of freshly laundered baby clothes had been folded on the coffee table in front of the sofa. Heather at least had the grace to be embarrassed as evidenced by the flare on her cheeks. She offered coffee or soda, which Corinne refused.

The baby's cry sounded through a monitor on the table, and Heather excused herself. Unable to resist, Corinne followed her to the bedroom and glimpsed the infant. She ached with the desire to hold the baby, to breathe in that sweet powdery scent most babies had, to feel that little body snuggle under her chin.

Corinne got to the point, stating she wanted to adopt the baby and raise her with Mark, the child's father. She re-stated the offer of fifty thousand dollars, ten thousand of which she tossed onto the sofa beside where Heather sat, feeding Amanda. She stared at Heather. "Mark told me you're reluctant to give us the baby. You do know as the father he could petition for partial custody. Maybe even full custody, given your current situation."

"My situation?"

"Single, alone, soon to be unemployed. I'll have my lawyers draw up the papers. I'll notify you when they're ready, probably a day or two, then I'll have the rest of the money." With that, she turned and walked out before Heather could argue or refuse.

But instead of showing up for a meeting with the lawyers, Heather had fled, taking the baby and the ten thousand dollars. Phil, who was supposed to be watching the woman, had painfully explained he had slipped away for a few hours to attend his niece's First Communion. If she wasn't afraid he would retaliate by leaking the story to the press, Corinne would have fired him on the spot.

Now what was she going to do? Maybe it was time to call in some favors and get a private investigator on the woman's trail. She didn't care about the money. She wanted that baby. And if she had to silence the mother to get it, so be it.

Chapter Six

"I'll take care of the dishes." Jake stood and carried their plates to the sink. "Sounds like Bailey is ready for her dinner now."

The baby lay in the makeshift cradle Jake had constructed and screwed up her reddened face.

"That's her diaper change cry," Shannon said.

"You can tell the difference?"

"You get to know the subtleties after a while. I'm going to take her upstairs and change her. Would you mind carrying the cradle up for me so I can get her to sleep soon?"

He wiped his hands on a dish towel. "Sure. Is it warm enough in that bedroom? Do you need a blanket for her?"

Shannon shook her head. "It's not good to cover a baby with a blanket. They can get it over their face or get tangled up in it and suffocate. She's fine."

"I have a trunk I can move in there to set this on so she's up off of the floor."

She was touched by his sensitivity to the baby's needs. She hadn't even thought about the possibility of a draft on the floor. "Thanks for thinking of that. But it's more stable on the floor. She's fine. Really."

Once she had the baby bathed and settled into the cradle, she returned to the kitchen to warm a bottle. Jake was outside cleaning off the grill. She stuck her head out the door. "It's a nice night."

"It is. I'm going to sit out here for a while. You're welcome to join me when you're finished."

"Thanks. I may do that. I could use the air."

She returned to the bedroom and fed the baby. Bailey sucked eagerly on the bottle, her eyelids gradually drooping until she was sound asleep. Shannon lifted her onto her shoulder and walked the room, rubbing circles on the tiny back until a burp sounded. She smiled and settled the sleeping baby back into the cradle.

The deck was dark except for a citronella candle that burned on the small round table between two Adirondack chairs. Jake occupied one chair, his long legs stretched so that his heels rested on the deck railing. She took the other chair. "It's beautiful here. So quiet."

"I had to get used to it."

She turned to look at him. "Did you live in the city before you came here?"

He nodded. "Phoenix."

"What brought you from the desert to the mountains?"

"I needed a change of scenery. What about you?"

She stared up at the dark sky and glittering stars. "Trying to make a new life for myself and Bailey."

"What about her father?"

"He's…uh…not in the picture."

Jake shook his head. "I'm sorry. It's not any of my business."

Silence lay between them dancing like the flickering candle flame.

Jake dropped his feet from the railing. "I'm going to have a beer. You want one?"

"Sure."

He stepped past her and returned with two cold bottles of Coors. "Did you want a glass?"

"No, the bottle's fine. My dad always used to say it tasted better right from the bottle."

"He's a wise man." Jake sat again and took a draw on the beer.

Shannon stared into the dark tangle of trees at the back of the property. Every so often, she imagined seeing the glow of eyes and a chill ran through her. Could someone have followed her here and would they be watching right now?

"Do you need a jacket?" Jake asked.

"No, why?"

"You were shivering."

"I'm fine." She sipped the beer and tried to distract herself from thinking about the 'what ifs.' "So, you're a carpenter. Did you build this cabin yourself?"

"Just the deck."

"It's nice." She was running out of ideas for conversation. He wasn't exactly talkative. Maybe he didn't want to talk and was just being polite when he invited her to join him out here. She picked up the half-empty bottle. "I'm kind of tired. I think I'll check my email, then turn in if you don't mind."

"Not at all. Have a good night."

"You, too."

She dumped the remainder of the beer into the sink and rinsed the bottle before placing it in the trash can labeled 'recycling.' At the computer, she opened Eve Adams' email to see if there was anything new. Only two spam emails trying to sell her penis enlargement products. She deleted those and went to the internet. She looked up the Jefferson City News Tribune and browsed for any articles mentioning the governor. She found one, a story of Governor Hastings and her husband, Mark, attending a benefit dinner to raise money for breast cancer research. She stared at the picture of Mark standing with an arm around his wife. Tears stung her eyes. How could she have been such a fool? How had she fallen for someone like him?

The back door swung shut and she heard Jake move about the kitchen. She hastily closed out of the internet and headed for the stairs. Then she remembered the briefcase. She'd have to come down for it later, after she was sure Jake was asleep.

~ * ~

Jake sat down at the computer. He was about to log into his email when a ding alerted him to a new message. He glanced down at the tool bar and saw a Gmail inbox. He clicked and opened the window. The email account belonged to Eve Adams. He stared at it for a moment and then turned to look at the stairs. What was going on? And who was the woman sleeping in his guest room?

Before his conscience could get the better of him, he opened and read the emails between Eve and babblingbrooke30. Nothing much there, just a few back and forths about missed get togethers and a family crisis. He re-read the messages. Nothing that piqued his curiosity. So maybe she used a different name for email purposes. Lots of people used other names on the internet. Who was he to question? He closed down the computer and headed to the stairs.

He brushed is teeth and crossed back to his bedroom, stripping down to his boxers. He settled into bed, then thought about opening the window to let in the cool night air. This time of year was his favorite, early summer when the days were warm and the nights still cool. After opening the window, he stretched and crawled back into bed. He always slept on the same side and the mattress was beginning to dip, like a boat that had taken on water. It was time to flip the mattress over. Or find someone to even it out.

Where had that thought come from? He didn't have to think too long and hard to find an answer. He lay in the dark, the cool night breeze wafting across his body, and he remembered his life before the life before this one. In high school, he'd been Steve Avery, top running back for the Leopards. He had girls falling at his feet, and he never missed an opportunity. He wasn't a stranger to women or to sex. It wasn't until his third year of college that he even considered the priesthood. The idea had come out of nowhere, but he couldn't shake it off. Long discussions with the Catholic chaplain on campus led him to a retreat that, in turn, led him to a weekend at a local seminary to explore life as a priest.

He'd been raised Catholic and had remained a faithful attendee at Sunday mass, even after a Saturday night of drinking and sex. After graduation, he made the decision to enter the seminary and study Theology. He struggled for a while to leave his earthly human desires behind him, until a visiting priest who was directing a retreat told him a priest could not divorce himself from his humanness, but rather had to find a way to channel those desires into a love for God and for God's people, to let that energy be used for good works.

He didn't believe that was possible, but as a priest he would have to put his desires—both worldly and sexual—aside and focus on ministry. After five years of study and preparation, Steve had been ordained into the priesthood. He was happy in his life as a priest and parishioners often commented on how much they appreciated the way he interacted with them, with their families. He took his role as priest seriously, believing his job was to serve, to teach, to help people find their way to God.

On occasion, a woman would attempt a relationship with him beyond the bounds of that of priest and parishioner. The first time it happened, he'd been shocked and confused, not sure how to handle the situation. He distanced himself from the woman and hated the look of hurt in her eyes every time he saw her. Only once had he been seriously tempted to break his vow of celibacy and that was with a young woman who came to him for counsel when she broke off an engagement. She was distraught at having caused her fiancé pain and felt guilty. In trying to offer her comfort, Father Steve must have given the wrong message because, then next thing he knew, she had sidled close to him on the sofa in his office and kissed him. That kiss dragged him back ten years as his body responded—much the way his body now responded when Shannon got too close.

Jake turned over and pounded the pillow into submission, then closed his eyes. She would be moving out in a day or two. If he had to work day and night on the Swinsons' apartment to make it livable, he'd do just that.

Sleep had just about claimed him when a sound outside brought him awake. He got up and listened again, hearing a car door, then shuffling. He pulled on his jeans and grabbed the baseball bat he kept in the corner in case of an intruder.

His bare feet made no sound as he descended the stairs and reached out to check the front door. Locked. He peered toward the kitchen where the nightlight over the stove cast a soft yellow glow. Tightening his grip on the bat, he move slowly through the living room and kitchen. The back door stood open. He paused and listened. More rustling sounds came from the driveway. Easing open the back door, he stepped outside into the darkness. A figure rummaged through the trunk of Shannon's car.

Just as Jake raced across the driveway in his bare feet and lifted the bat, Shannon jumped back from the car and shrieked. Jake checked his swing. "What are you doing out here? I could've killed you."

She breathed heavily, her eyes wide. "I was getting some things I need out of the car."

"You should have told me earlier. I could've carried this stuff inside for you. What do you need?"

Shannon pointed to a large suitcase. "That bag, and few little things. If you take that one, I can get the rest."

Jake lifted the bag from the trunk with ease. "Anything else?"

She picked up the briefcase and clutched it to her chest. "Just this."

He hoisted the suitcase and carried it into the cabin and straight up the stairs to her room.

"Thank you. I'm sorry I woke you," she said.

"I wasn't really asleep. Are you sure that's all you need?"

"That's it. Thanks again."

He nodded. "Good night."

"Is that bat your only form of protection?"

He lifted the Louisville Slugger. "I never cared for guns. I figure this and the element of surprise should do the job."

"You sure surprised me. I'll be sure to let you know in advance the next time I go outside."

"That would be a good idea." He stopped in the doorway. "Goodnight."

~ * ~

Shannon trembled as she closed the door and leaned back against it. That had been a close call. She couldn't imagine many burglars would wander out this far into the woods, but Jake had been prepared and quick to react. If a baseball bat could be considered preparation.

She set the briefcase on the bed and stared at it as if it might hold a live snake. She sat down beside it and laid her palm on top of the cool leather, only now realizing how close she had come to being bludgeoned to death by Jake. She recalled how he had looked in the moonlight, shirtless, his hair in disarray and eyes wild. She grinned as she thought of him as her protector—wielding a baseball bat. A shirtless superhero with panic in his eyes—those warm brown eyes. Shaking her head to throw that train of thought off track, she returned her attention to the briefcase, grateful for the combination locks.

She'd have had a hard time explaining herself if the case popped open and eight thousand dollars and a hand gun fell out.

Chapter Seven

"It could have been worse." Herb Hightower shoved his hands into the back pockets of his coveralls. "Aside from the front end, there doesn't appear to be other body or structural damage. I'll have to take it on a flatbed and put it up on the rack to be sure, though."

"Thanks. But I'm wondering if I could sell the car as is for parts, buy something that's running but cheap?" Shannon bit on her lip and squinted in the sunlight.

"You could, but you won't get what it's worth." He shifted his gaze from her to the cabin. "Where's Jake this morning?"

"He had a job in Seattle. So, how would I go about selling it?"

"You got the title?" he asked.

She hesitated. She had the title, but according to that piece of paper, the car was owned by Heather Carlson. "Actually, the car belongs to my mother. She gave it to me when I left and was supposed to have the title changed, but she hasn't gotten around to it."

His eyes narrowed. "Gonna be hard to sell it without the title, even as is. Maybe she could send it to you? I might be interested if you have the legal title."

Shannon forced a smile. "I'll see if she can do that, then I'll give you a call."

"You want me to send out a flatbed to take it into my shop?"

"Not yet. Let me get the title straightened away first. But, thanks, Herb."

"You're welcome. Jake knows how to contact me."

She waited until he backed his pickup from the drive then hurriedly emptied all of her worldly possessions from the trunk, carrying every bag and piece of luggage upstairs and stuffing them into the closet. Next she located the phone book and found an auto salvage service that promised 'Fair dollars for your junker.'

When the auto salvage truck backed up the driveway an hour later, Shannon breathed a sigh of relief. The driver, a man who

42

looked to be in his mid-twenties, wore ripped jeans, a worn tee shirt and battered leather boots. "That the car?"

She suddenly wished Jake was there. This guy gave her the creeps and, with Bailey sleeping in the house, she couldn't run for help. "Yes. I…um…decided it wasn't worth the repair. No insurance. You know how it is."

"Uh-huh." He walked around the car, bending down to check the undercarriage, then forced open the bent hood and peered inside. "You did a real number on this car, lady."

She attempted a smile. "You should see the tree."

"Got the paperwork?"

"See, that's a problem. The car belonged to my mother. She gave it to me before I left for this trip, but she hasn't had the title changed over. And she's…she's on a cruise right now, so I can't call her. But I really need to get this taken care of so I can get another car."

His eyes slid over her slowly, causing a chill to roll through her. "I can probably help you out. How much?"

"I don't know. What's the car worth in its present condition?"

"It's worth what you can get. I'll give you three grand."

"Three thousand? But…it's got to be worth more than that."

"Might be. But without the title…." He lifted his hands palms up and shrugged. "I'll give you three thousand. Cash." He dug into his pocket and removed a roll of bills.

He'd come prepared. Shannon knew this was not a legitimate sale, but she didn't have legitimate paperwork. The car was probably worth twice what he offered but, without options, she had only one decision to make. "I'll take it." She held out her hand and watched him count out the money, then stuffed it into her own pocket.

"You got everything out of there you need?" he asked as he prepared to load the car onto the flatbed carrier.

"Yes."

When he finished loading the vehicle, he nodded. "Have a good day."

"Wait. Do I get a receipt or something showing the sale?"

He flashed a grin bordering on a sneer. "Do I get a clean title?" He winked at her. "You have a good day."

She headed up the stairs, closing the bedroom door and sitting heavily on the bed. She peeled off the bills and counted them out twice. This gave her eleven thousand dollars. How would she find another car with no transportation into town? Then she remembered the computer and Craig's List. A place to start.

Bailey stirred and she picked her up. "Somebody needs a diaper change. Then maybe we'll go for a little walk. Would you like that, to go outside for a while?"

The baby grinned and waved her arms, tiny hands balled into fists.

Outside, a gentle breeze ruffled the baby's soft curls. Shannon walk the edge of the property near the line of pine trees, breathing in their scent. A glance upward revealed clear blue sky and slowly moving puffs of cloud. "This wouldn't be such a bad place to live, would it sweetie?"

The baby gurgled.

"I agree."

A sound in the brush made her jump and she turned. Branches stirred and the undergrowth rustled. *Probably a small animal. Or a deer. Or a bear.* She wasn't sure if bears roamed the area, but she wasn't going to take any chances. She headed back to the cabin. Perhaps she would show her appreciation for Jake's hospitality by making dinner this evening. She settled Bailey into her carrier and then searched the freezer and the pantry. With few choices, she settled on spaghetti and a salad, with garlic bread. If he had garlic. A small bottle of the powder sat behind larger spice bottles in the cupboard above the stove. It would do.

After setting out all the ingredients for dinner, she sat at the computer and logged into Craig's list, looking for cars available locally. She found nothing closer than Seattle. One caught her interest: *2001 Toyota Camry, 187k miles, but runs great, asking $800. Will need tires.* She printed out the ad and folded it into her hip pocket. Perhaps she could accompany Jake to Seattle the next day and arrange to see the car. When she called the owner, the man agreed to bring the car to her.

~ * ~

Jake came up the long drive and stopped, staring. Shannon's car was gone. He glanced toward the house and let out a deep breath when he saw Shannon sitting on the deck with the baby. And he wondered why he felt relieved to see her there. It was as if she'd always been there, belonged right there.

"Did Herb take the car in to his shop?" Jake asked as he

44

approached the deck.

"No. I found a buyer to take it as is. Just seemed more expedient, then I can get another car. I took the liberty of planning dinner. I hope you don't mind."

He stood staring up at her, sweat dampened his brows. He swiped a sleeved arm across his forehead. "I don't mind at all. I do need shower first."

"I won't start the pasta until you're finished showering, then."

As he ascended the deck stairs and moved past her she said, "Oh, I hope you don't mind. I have someone bringing a car by tomorrow for me to look at."

He stopped and whirled around. "You what? No, I don't want some stranger coming here."

Her face flushed and she did that annoying but sexy lip-biting thing. "I'm s-sorry. I should have asked first. I just thought.... I'll call them back. They're in Seattle. Maybe I can go with you tomorrow and meet up with them there."

Her embarrassment made him feel about ten inches tall. He'd over-reacted and he knew it. "I'm not working in Seattle tomorrow. Just let them bring the car here. I'll be around. I'm sorry I snapped at you."

"No, you're right. I was out of line to invite strangers to your house."

He wanted to rewind the scene back to where he was looking at her and thinking how she belonged on his deck, in his life. But he couldn't. "I'll shower and change. We can talk more about this over dinner."

In the shower, Jake let water pound over his head and down his face. He'd been here alone for so long now and was still always looking over his shoulder. He couldn't begin to explain to Shannon why he'd reacted so strongly to the idea of someone unknown bringing a car for her to look at. After all, she was a stranger and he'd taken her into his home. Maybe it would be best to just drive her over to Seattle to look at the car. Then he'd talk with the Swinsons about their apartment if Shannon had decided to stay in Snoqualmie. In a day or two, he could have her out of his cabin and he could resume life as it was before. That thought fell like a lead weight in his chest. Life as it was before was pretty damned lonely and boring.

When he walked into the kitchen, she was standing at the sink, draining pasta. In her carrier in the living room, Bailey built a whimper into a full-scale wail.

"One minute, Bailey. Just give me one minute," Shannon called.

"I'll get her if that's okay."

"Thank you."

Jake stood over the carrier and smiled down at the baby. When she became aware of him, she stopped crying abruptly and gazed up at him, wide-eyed. He bent down slowly and reached for her. She looked as though she wasn't sure if she should be okay or continue to cry. So she sniffled and stared at his face. And his heart melted. In another life, he'd have this—a wife and a child or children.

He settled the baby on his chest, her head tucked under his chin. Picking up the carrier, he headed into the kitchen. "She's fine. Just didn't want to be alone in there." He pulled out a chair and sat carefully, trying not to jostle the quiet baby who sucked on her fist.

"Do you want me to take her?"

"No. Finish what you're doing. We're fine."

He watched Shannon move efficiently around his kitchen, placing the pasta in a bowl and tossing it with sauce, then pouring the remainder of the sauce into a gravy boat. She set all of it on the table, pulled a tossed salad from the fridge, and then removed garlic bread from the oven.

"That smells great. I didn't think I had any sauce."

"You didn't, but you had tomato puree, paste, and diced tomatoes. I worked with it."

He grinned. "You do good work."

She bent down to take the baby off his chest. "I'll put her in the carrier so you can eat with two hands."

Her hair fell forward, grazing his cheek. He breathed in the scent of something fruity and sweet. He glanced down at her breasts, the cleavage visible as her tee-shirt fell forward. He found it hard to breathe, impossible to swallow. The slow, sweet torture ended as she straightened and lifted the baby with her, then lay Bailey in the carrier.

"Oh, I forgot ice for the water."

Jake's chair scraped as he stood. "I'll get it." Anything to get a little distance and cool down. He removed the ice container from the freezer and filled two glasses with cubes.

Shannon sat across from him at the table, waiting expectantly for his first taste. He filled his plate and twirled the angel hair pasta on his fork and stuffed it into his mouth, chewing slowly. "This is really good. You have to tell me how you made that sauce. I usually just open a can. I'm not even sure why I had those other ingredients on hand."

"I'll write it down. I'm glad you like it."

He set down his fork. "About what I said earlier. I'm sorry. I guess I've lived here alone for so long, I'm suspicious of strangers. Present company excluded, of course. I'm working at home tomorrow. Have the guy bring the car here if you want. And if you want a mechanic to look it over first, I'd bet Herb would be happy to do so. I can ask him."

"That's okay. I already rethought things. It's probably not a good idea to buy a car off Craig's list. If I'm going to settle here, at least for now, why do I need a car right away? I can have Herb find me something later on."

"So we need to visit the Swinsons then and see about that apartment?"

She nodded. "I'd appreciate it."

"I'll call them in the morning."

She watched him with a look of amusement as he emptied his plate and refilled it for a second helping.

He stopped with the fork half way to his mouth. "What?"

"I'm glad you're enjoying my cooking. I figured it was the least I could do."

"It's delicious."

Her perfectly white teeth shone behind an appreciative smile. "I couldn't find anything to make for dessert, though."

"Great. We can go to the Dairy Dream. It'll be my treat. They have homemade soft serve."

"Sounds good."

It wasn't until they pulled into the brightly-lit and crowded parking lot half an hour later that Jake thought this may have been a bad idea. It was a warm early summer night and the entire town of Snoqualmie was gathered here. He parked in a darkened corner of the lot.

Before he could suggest that he get their ice cream and bring it back to the truck, Shannon was out of her seat and removing the baby from the car seat. Already he could feel eyes on them, questioning this woman and child with him—the town hermit. A woman sporting a nasty bruise around her left eye.

As they crossed the parking lot, a loud roar and screech was followed by an eruption of screams and shouts as the crowd scattered. A motorcycle roared out of control through the scurrying bodies and directly toward them. Jake wrapped his arms around Shannon and the baby and pulled them out of the way just as the cycle sped past, kicking up gravel and dust. He shielded them with his body, backing them against the cement structure.

The cyclist gassed the bike and roared away.

"Are you okay?" Jake looked down at Shannon, his hand cupping the back of the baby's head.

Shannon trembled and swallowed. "Thanks to you."

A woman rushed over to them. "Jake, are you all okay?"

"We're fine Patsy. What was that about?"

"Don't know. Not sure if he lost control of the bike or did that on purpose. I called the police."

The police. The last thing Jake needed was his face plastered on the news and the police asking questions. "I didn't really see anything, Patsy. Just got out of the way like everyone else. My friend is pretty shaken up, so we're going to get the baby back home."

He turned Shannon around and moved her toward the truck as a siren sounded a few blocks away.

Chapter Eight

Jake was already up and in the kitchen the following morning when Shannon came downstairs. "Morning."

"Good morning."

"I talked with Mr. Swinson. He's expecting us around ten to look at the apartment."

"Okay, thanks." She waited until he was seated to approach the coffeemaker. In the last day, the kitchen seemed to have shrunk. Every room they were in together seemed more cramped.

She sat and wrapped her hands around the mug of steaming coffee. "Do you think that biker was trying to hurt someone last night?"

Jake stared at her, then glanced away. "I don't know. Probably just lost control of the bike."

She focused on her coffee. "You'll no doubt be glad to see us leave. We've done nothing but disrupt your life these past few days."

He almost smiled, the corners of his mouth quirking up just a little. "It hasn't been dull."

Shannon laughed. "That's a kind way to put it." She refilled her mug of coffee. "I'll be ready to leave before ten. Just need to shower and then bathe Bailey."

She wasn't totally convinced last night's event had been an accident. The driver had aimed straight toward them. If it hadn't been for Jake…. She shivered at the thought of moving into an apartment in town, alone with the baby. What if the biker came back? The briefcase lay on the floor in the far corner of the bedroom. Inside, her Smith & Wesson Bodyguard .38. She shuddered at the thought of having to use it, but she'd do whatever was necessary to protect Bailey.

~ * ~

Mr. Swinson looked a bit like an arthritic Santa, slightly bent, with gnarled fingers and sporting a long white beard and mustache. "Come on in. Helen's in the living room."

From her wheelchair, Helen Swinson offered a tremulous smile. Her head tilted a bit to one side and her body shook with the tremors of Parkinson's.

Jake made the introductions. "Shannon is looking for an apartment here in town and I thought about the one you have Abe."

"Sure, sure. But I think it might need a little work. Let me get the key for you. I can't climb those steps like I used to. Haven't been up there in about six months." He removed a key from a hook on the wall in the kitchen and handed it to Jake. "You go ahead and look around, see what you think."

The apartment entrance was above the garage at the top of a long, steep set of wooden steps on the side of the building. Jake went first, testing the steps. "These seem to be sturdy." He gave the railing a shake. "This, too."

At the top landing, he opened a screen door and inserted the key into the lock. The wooden door squealed open. He flipped on an overhead light and held the door for Shannon to enter.

She stepped inside and looked around. The apartment was small but with an open floor plan. A galley kitchen sat off to the right with the living and dining area occupying the rest of the open space.

Jake motioned her to a narrow hallway. "The bedroom and bathroom are back here. Watch your step on the loose carpet."

She looked down to see the strip holding down the carpet between the living room and the hall had lifted, making a tripping hazard.

"I can fix that easily enough," Jake said.

The bedroom was small, probably ten by ten. It held a twin sized bed, small night stand, and a narrow chest of drawers. It might accommodate a crib but not much else. The bathroom consisted of a shower stall, toilet and sink. No linen closet, but there was room for storage under the sink.

Jake walked around, inspecting the floors, flushing the toilet and turning on water faucets. Then he looked up at the ceiling and so did she. Numerous water spots had discolored the once-white paint.

"Looks like a new roof is in order, then some painting. I'll have to check those spots for mold and to see if the plaster needs replacing." He glanced around. "Other than airing out and a good cleaning, the place is in pretty good shape. Let's check out the furnishings."

She sat on the mattress that had been covered with an old sheet. It sagged a little, but she could make do. In the living room, blankets and sheets covered the few pieces of furniture—an old brocade sofa, a well-worn leather recliner, and a beautifully carved wooden rocker. "Oh, this is nice."

Jake ran his fingers over the intricate carving of the rocker's back. "It sure is. I'd bet Abe made this himself some time ago."

Shannon turned to the window, pushing back the curtain. A cloud of dust billowed and she sneezed. "Oh."

"Like I said, a good cleaning is in order. But what do you think? You'd be in walking distance of the grocery store and other shops in town."

She thought of living here behind the Swinson house. They wouldn't be much help if someone tried to break in, but her bigger worry was putting them in danger. She didn't plan to be here forever, just until she could get her bearings and find out what was happening in Jefferson City. Then she could move on. "I like it."

"Then let's go downstairs and talk business with Abe." Jake ushered her out the door with the baby and pulled it closed behind him.

They sat around the kitchen table. Abe offered them each a glass of lemonade. The drink was sweet as cough syrup and Shannon sipped to be polite. "Mr. Swinson, I'm interested in the apartment. Would I have to sign a lease?"

"Not if you call me Abe." His eyes twinkled and he grinned. "Jake, what's your assessment of the place?"

"Needs a roof. Otherwise, it looks pretty good. But until I check the areas that have leaked, I won't know about replacing plaster. The whole place needs to be painted."

"Uh-huh. What do you reckon that will cost?"

"The apartment isn't that big. The roof alone would probably cost about eight hundred for materials. I can do the work. If the ceilings have to be repaired, that'll be a little more. Paint, maybe one-fifty. I get a professional discount at Selby's Hardware."

"So were talkin' about maybe a thousand or so?"

Jake nodded. "Give or take."

Abe looked at Shannon. "Would four hundred a month work for you? That includes the utilities."

"Are you serious?"

"If that's too much…."

"No, not at all. I expected much more."

"You gonna be working?" Abe asked.

51

"I…uh…well, I need to find a job eventually. I just want to get settled in first."

Abe glanced into the living room where Helen sat in her chair watching a soap opera. "The thing is, I need to find someone to help out with Helen. We had a nurse coming in after the last hospitalization, but for now she doesn't need skilled care. Just needs a little help with bathing, that sort of thing." He held up his gnarled hands. "As you can see, I can't be all that helpful. I'm afraid she'll fall and I won't be able to catch her. I think she'd rather have a woman providing the care anyway."

"Are you offering me a job?"

"I was thinking along the lines of a barter, at least in part. You help out with Helen's care, sit with her now and then. In exchange, we provide the apartment."

"That's all?"

"Yup. And the utilities are included. Only things you'll have to pay for on your own are phone and internet. The phone's in my name, but you can change it over. Cable's already connected up there. There's a washer and dryer in the garage you can use."

She looked from the old man to Jake. "Is he serious?"

Jake smiled. "Sounds like it to me."

Shannon did some quick calculations. If she didn't have to pay rent or utilities or buy a car, the eleven thousand she had in the briefcase would carry her and Bailey a long way, as long as neither of them had a medical emergency. She couldn't risk using her health insurance card. And that was only good for another six months anyway.

"If Helen agrees, then it's a deal."

Abe's blue eyes sparkled with his smile. "Well, then, let's go talk to her. She can't talk back, but I know how to read her face."

She didn't know why, but his last comment went straight to her heart and brought tears to her eyes. Would she ever have someone in her life who knew her well enough to read her face if she couldn't communicate her thoughts? She hoped so.

~ * ~

Jake delivered Shannon and Bailey back to the cabin. "I have some things I need to do. I may be later getting back. Don't wait for me to have dinner."

"I'm sorry I'm taking up so much of your time. I'll be out of your hair soon."

"You're not in the way and my time is pretty much my own. It'll take three or four days at least to get that apartment ready."

"I can help."

He shook his head. "A construction site is no place for a baby, and you can't just leave her here."

She sighed. "That's true. Do you know anyone reliable who might babysit?"

"I don't. Look, it won't take me long to get the place ready for you. You can help by having dinner ready when I come in."

Grinning, she said, "Oh, that's how it is. The big man goes out and does all the hard work and the little lady keeps the home fires burning."

"No, that's not how it is," he chuckled. "I'd love to have an extra pair of hands to do some of the painting inside, but you can't have the baby around those paint fumes."

"I know. I'll just have to trust you, then."

"We'll go tomorrow to pick up paint. You can choose your colors." He headed back out the door. Her scent lingered in the truck and he opened both front windows before heading down the driveway.

He drove toward Seattle where he could get the best deal on the roofing materials he would need. After a brief stop for a burger and then unloading the truck at the Swinsons', Jake glanced at his watch. It was just past seven. He drove down 202 and pulled in at Rusty's. It was a favorite spot for most of the construction workers he occasionally worked with and he hoped to convince a few to give him a hand.

"Hey, Jake. What can I get you?" Angie, the bartender, flashed a big smile.

"Coors." He glanced around the dimly lit bar. "Any of the guys from Nickels Construction been in here tonight?"

The bartender set a beer in front of him. "A couple of guys are in the back room shooting pool."

"Thanks." Jake picked up the beer and slid off the bar stool. He found a small group of men gathered around the pool tables.

"Hey, Choirboy. Haven't seen you in a while," one of them said.

"Been working in Seattle on a job there." He greeted the other two men he recognized. "How's it been going? Keeping busy?"

"Nah. It's slow. Not much new construction."

"I'm looking for a couple of guys to help me with a job this week, maybe into the weekend. Putting a new roof on a garage apartment, about nine hundred square feet. There may be some interior ceiling repair."

"I could be interested. Let me get my brother-in-law. Hey, Don," the man called.

Another man walked over. "What's up, Rico?"

"This is a friend, Jake Garber. He needs a little help with a roof this week. Jake, this is my brother-in-law, Don. He just moved up here last week."

Don shook Jake's hand firmly. "Is this a paying job or one of those brotherhood things where we help each other out?"

Jake laughed. "It's a paying job, just not the best pay. It's coming out of my pocket."

"This out at your place?" Rico asked.

"No. I'm doing the job for friends. You know the Swinsons, older couple? Abe used to work in construction."

Rico nodded. "Yeah, I know him. Sounds like a job that might take two days, three at most, depending on the weather. I'm surprised you're hiring help."

"I need to get it done as soon as possible. It would take me at least five days alone. So, how much would it take?" He held his breath, knowing these guys could easily get twenty dollars an hour.

"Give us a minute," Rico said, ushering Don to the other side of the room.

They spoke briefly, then returned. "Okay, so we took into consideration that the Swinsons are a nice, old couple, that you're a good guy, and we have no other prospects the next few days. A hundred a piece per day worked," Rico said.

Jake did the calculations. "How about I hire you to help with the roof for that rate. I think I can handle the painting once the roof is done."

Rico extended a hand. "Deal. When do we start?"

"Tomorrow morning at seven a.m. You know where their place is?"

Nodding, Rico said, "I know it. We'll be there."

"Thanks."

"You up for a game?" Don asked, motioning toward the pool table.

"Not tonight. It's been a long day. I need to get home. See you tomorrow."

If the weather cooperated, the three of them could finish the roof in two days. He'd do the painting himself. If he could find a babysitter, Shannon could help and they'd finish in a day. He stopped by the bar. "Angie, you know of a reliable babysitter?"

Her eyebrows lifted almost to her hairline. "Something I need to know?"

"For a friend. I'm helping her get her place ready and we can't have the baby around the paint fumes."

"My mom keeps my sister's kids days when my sister works. I could ask her. How old?"

"Three months."

"Oh, she'll say yes. A little one like that's no trouble. They can't go anywhere. I'll ask her."

"Got a pen?" he asked. Then he scrawled his phone number on a napkin and handed it to her. "Give me a call. It'll probably be later in the week."

On the drive home, Jake found himself whistling. In three or four days, Shannon and Bailey would be settled into their own apartment and he'd have his privacy restored. He stopped mid-whistle and his heart sank. This was a good thing, right? Then why did he suddenly feel as if he'd planned a funeral?

Chapter Nine

Shannon paced nervously from the front door to the kitchen window. She kept hearing sounds outside she couldn't quite identify. Probably just the wind that had picked up a little, causing the trees to sway in an eerie moonlit dance behind the cabin. One she was sure she'd heard someone crunching up the gravel drive, but saw no one when she looked outside. Later, when she went upstairs to check on Bailey, she looked down over the garage and could have sworn the shadowed form of a man slipped along the wall to disappear into the darkness.

There was no mistaking the crunch of gravel and the sweep of headlights now. She breathed in relief when she recognized Jake's truck. Her earlier check of email had produced nothing from Brooke. She'd sent another cryptic message and now awaited a reply.

Jake opened the back door and called out, "It's just me."

She fought the urge to run to him, wrap her arms around him and let him make her feel safe. Instead she locked her fingers together behind her back and smiled. "There's leftover tuna casserole if you didn't eat."

"I had a burger early, so I might just do that. How was the rest of your day?"

She hesitated, then said, "Fine." No point in worrying him or having him think she was paranoid. Which she was. She watched as he filled a plate with the tuna casserole and popped it into the microwave.

He leaned back against the counter. "Your apartment should be ready by the end of the week. I got a couple of local guys who are going to help me with the roof. And, if you were serious about painting, I may have found a babysitter."

"Someone you know? Well?" she added.

"The mother of a friend. She keeps her grandkids during the day. She's supposed to call me." He must have read her face because he added, "You can meet her first and see what you think."

The microwave dinged and he removed the plate, retrieved a fork from the drawer and sat at the table.

"You want something to drink?" she asked. "I made iced tea. I'll get it for you." She filled a glass with ice and poured the tea, then set it beside him.

"Thanks. This is delicious."

She laughed. "Not much you can do to tuna noodle casserole." She sat opposite him. "Does anyone live nearby this place?"

"No. Why?"

"Just wondering."

He studied her for a moment. "Did something happen?"

She shook her head. "No. Just me imagining things. You know how it is, you're not used to the quiet so you hear every little sound and then you start to see things."

"What little sounds did you hear and what did you see?"

"Just the wind. And I thought I saw a shadow out by the garage a while ago."

"That's all?"

"I shouldn't have said anything."

He took a drink. "I'll take a look around." He gazed into her eyes. "Is there something else?"

"No. Nothing." She stood. "I'm going to check my email again, then head up to bed."

She opened her Gmail account and found two messages from Brooke. The first one read: *Hey, Eve. Things are quiet here, not much happening. Nothing new at the bakery, either, as far as I know. Mom sends her love. I do, too. Love, Babs*

Shannon translated—*Nothing new at the bakery* meant Brooke hadn't heard anything about Corinne Baker Hastings and Mark Hastings.

A second email sent just an hour later made her shake: *Mom just called. She had guests for dinner. Served her favorite dessert. Wish I'd been there. That stuff's like eating air. TTYL, Babs.*

She reread the message three times, trying to figure out Brooke's cryptics. Guests for dinner must mean someone stopped by her house. Favorite dessert—that was easy. Her mother made this Jell-O and fruit dessert with whipped topping. Shannon and Brooke always joked that it was like eating nothing. So she served them nothing—didn't say a word. Still it made Shannon tremble. Corinne had people pressuring her mother to find out where she was. She wondered how far they would go to get their information.

She typed a reply: *I know what you mean. Maybe your Mom should visit with you for a few days and feed you that stuff. Might be good for her to have someone else to cook for. If you two go out to dinner, set a place for me. It would be so good to talk with you both. Love, Eve.*

Re-reading her message, she could only hope Brooke would understand and follow through. She needed to get her mother out of the house so she wasn't alone. And she needed to talk to them on the phone. She hinted about dinner because she and Brooke often met for dinner at a sports bar, back before Bailey was born. If they went there, she could call the restaurant to speak with them.

It only took a few minutes for the reply to come through: *As a matter of fact, Mom and I are going out tomorrow after I get off work, then I'm hoping she'll stay with me for a few days. Wish you could be here. We'll set a place, just in case. Babs*

Shannon clicked off the email and on to the internet to look up the phone number of the restaurant in Jefferson City. She jotted it down.

She heard the back door swing shut. Jake was no doubt out scouting around the property, looking for footprints. Oh, God. What if someone was still out there? She raced to the back door and stood on the lighted deck. Finally, she spotted him, baseball bat in hand, creeping around the garage and out of her sight.

He shouted and something ran across the back yard. Shannon yelped.

"It's okay. Just a raccoon." Jake sauntered back up onto the deck. "There were two of them, but one ran the other way. They were sniffing around the trash. I keep meaning to put chicken wire around those trash cans." He sat on the top step, his breathing heavy.

He'd been startled, too, maybe expecting something more to jump out at him. Just then the roar of a motorcycle sounded from somewhere beyond the foot of the driveway. Shannon turned her head in the direction of the sound and shivered.

Jake was on his feet and rounding the cabin. The bike roared away, tires squealing. Shannon knew her mother wouldn't give Corinne Hastings' men any information because she didn't know where Shannon was. It was the only way to make sure her mother was safe. If they found her here, someone had followed her from Missouri. She could still run, get a car and head fa rther north, maybe even into Canada. Or she could stay here, live as Shannon Chase, and hope they'd get tired of searching and go away.

She looked at her reflection in the window. She needed to change her looks soon. Bailey's whimper came through the monitor on the kitchen table. Shannon went back inside and upstairs to tend to her daughter.

After changing the baby's diaper and before returning to the kitchen to warm a bottle, Shannon pulled the briefcase from the closet and popped it open. She lifted an old tee-shirt she'd placed in there and picked up the .38. It wasn't loaded and she briefly wondered if she should load it, be ready. The gun both terrified her and gave her reassurance. She hated having a gun anywhere near Bailey. But the thought that someone could come and take the baby from her, do God knew what to her in the process, pushed her past her feelings about guns.

"Shannon?"

She startled and dropped the weapon, turning to stare at him.

"What the hell is that?" He strode into the room, staring at the gleaming black pistol.

"It's a gun. Don't worry, it's not loaded." She shoved the gun back into the briefcase and snapped it closed before he could spot the cash. "It's for protection. Lots of women have guns now."

He locked his eyes with hers. "What aren't you telling me? Why did that motorcycle make you so jumpy, so much so that you came in to check your weapon?"

Bailey's hungry cry built into a wail.

Shannon stood and kicked the briefcase back into the closet. "I have to feed her."

"Okay, we can talk while you do that." He stood in the open doorway and made a sweeping gesture. "After you."

She picked up the baby and carried her down the stairs, quickly concocting a story he might believe.

~ * ~

While Shannon got the bottle ready, Jake took the baby and paced with her. What the hell was really going on here? He'd been suspicious also about the biker, but thought whoever it was might have been after him. Now he wasn't so sure.

"Can we go into the living room?" Shannon asked.

"Absolutely."

When she was seated in the recliner, he turned the baby over to her. He watched as she settled Bailey into the crook of her arm and the baby latched onto the nipple. Despite the tension, Shannon smiled down at Bailey's face.

He sat on the sofa and waited.

She looked up and her smile faded. "I can explain the gun. It's purely for protection. Think about it, I'm a single woman traveling alone with an infant. Anything could happen. Well, it did. I ran into a tree and destroyed the car."

"You don't know that the car was totaled. You were very eager to get rid of it."

"It just seemed easier. I…uh…let the insurance expire. I was short on cash after Bailey was born and I had to let something go."

That sounded plausible. "Why the rush to move to the middle of nowhere in the Northwest?"

She bit her lip and adjusted the baby in her arms. "Bailey's father. He's married and he didn't want me to give birth to her." Her face flushed and her eyes filled. "I c-couldn't do what he wanted. I just thought it would be good to move away somewhere to a small town and start over. That's all." She returned her gaze to the baby. "I can't imagine life without her."

Now he felt like shit for having made her cry. "I'm sorry. I shouldn't have pressed."

"It's okay. I at least owe you an explanation. When that biker drove toward us the other night and then I heard the motorcycle tonight, I thought he'd found me."

"Her father? Would he look for you?"

"He might. Probably not. He didn't want her in the first place and I'm not pushing him for child support."

Jake stared at the baby as her eyelids began to droop. She had released the nipple and a stream of formula dribbled down her chin. "How could a man walk away from something so beautiful?" He hadn't meant to say the words aloud and refused to meet her gaze. "If you see the guy hanging around again, let me know."

She nodded. "Thank you. I promise I won't load the gun while I'm here. If you want, we can lock it up until my place is ready."

"No, that's fine. Just don't shoot me if I come in late one evening. I'll be sure to announce myself ahead of time."

She grinned. "I'm going to put her to bed."

Jake watched her as she crossed the room and ascended the

stairs, noticing the sway of her hips as she walked away. His feelings about her were conflicted. On one hand, he wanted her to leave and let him resume life as usual. On the other hand, he wanted to call her back downstairs, wrap his arms around her and kiss her senseless. And no amount of prayer was going to make those feelings disappear.

He also wasn't completely convinced the cyclist wasn't after her. Or him. As much as he hated to do so, he'd have to make a call to his contact in the U.S. Marshal's office. He could only hope it wouldn't require another new identity, another move that would uproot him from Snoqualmie and rip him out of Shannon's life forever.

He chided himself for that last thought. He had to report the recent events with the biker. Just in case. He'd call tomorrow.

Chapter Ten

Rico and Don were both hard workers. They had the roof stripped down in no time and were hammering on new shingles. Jake took a break to go inside and examine the ceilings more closely. The stained areas were solid, just discolored. Kilz primer would prevent any mold and cover the spots. He looked around, deciding what colors he would use. But he'd promised to take Shannon to pick out the paint later.

"Hey, you guys okay without me for an hour or so?" he called up to Rico and Don.

"Sure. We're gonna take a lunch break," Rico called back.

Jake glanced up at the roof from a distance before climbing into his truck. They would be finished today if they worked into evening. He'd talk to the guys when he got back.

He was careful to announce his arrival when he returned to the cabin. No point getting himself shot. "I'm coming in and I'm unarmed."

"Very funny." Shannon stood in the kitchen wearing a pair of shorts that revealed long, shapely legs, and a v-necked tee shirt that revealed lots more. The bruise around her eye had faded to a pale yellow.

Jake tore his gaze away from that tee shirt. "I thought we could pick up the paint for the apartment."

"Oh." She looked down at herself. "I think I should change. It'll just take a minute. Can you keep an eye on Bailey? She's in the living room."

"Sure." He popped the top on a cold can of soda and strode into the room. Bailey lay on a blanket on the floor. She looked up at him and grinned as he approached. "Hey, pretty girl. How are you today?" He reached out to caress her soft cheek and she grabbed hold of his finger. "That's quite a grip you got there. I'll bet you have your mommy's determination."

"I hope so," Shannon said as she came back into the living room. "Determination can be a good thing."

"I agree." He sniffed, then asked, "You have a diaper handy?

She needs a change."

Shannon opened the diaper bag she'd brought down with her. "I'll do it."

But Jake held out a hand. "I've done this before and I don't mind."

"Really?"

"Diaper, wipes, lotion and powder, please."

She complied, then watched as he expertly cleaned and diapered the baby.

He grinned as he handed her the balled up dirty diaper. "You can dispose of this."

"Oh, thanks. I am duly impressed, though. How did you get diapering experience?"

"Nephew. Girls are easier, though. They don't take you by surprise."

Jake lifted the baby carefully and stood. Something ached in him. This felt so right. So natural for him. He argued that it was because he had been trapped in this limbo between lives for the past two years. Not really living, but more like going through the motions of living—someone else's life.

"Ready?" he asked.

"Let's go." She didn't insist on taking Bailey from him, but just picked up the diaper bag and carrier and headed for the truck.

The hardware store was the place to be. Apparently everyone in Snoqualmie was preparing to spruce up their houses, inside and out, now that summer was approaching. And all heads turned toward the couple walking in with a baby in a carrier between them. Jake felt the rush of heat up his neck. He nodded to those who spoke, but didn't offer to introduce Shannon, just steered her to the back of the store and the paint department.

He expected her to be indecisive, but she knew exactly what she wanted. She picked up a ring of paint samples. "I'd like white or off-white for the ceiling. It'll brighten up the place and make the rooms seem larger." She selected a soft yellow called lemon meringue for the kitchen. "Maybe I can find a border with small flowers to work with this. Oh, and look at this for the living and dining room. I'm thinking of this soft light beige or cream, but with an accent on that far wall in the living room, maybe a nice lighter turquoise? What do you think?"

"I think you know exactly what you want. I like those colors.

What about the bedroom and the bathroom?"

"The bathroom already has a lot of tile in blue and there's no sense ripping that out. We can use white in there, something water-resistant. I like this heather green for the bedroom."

"I can see that. And those colors all work with the carpeting. If you keep the carpet. I pulled up a loose corner. That apartment has beautiful hardwood floors. It wouldn't take much to rip out the carpeting and refinish them."

Her eyes widened and he saw in them the shade of turquoise she had talked about. "Really? I love hardwood floors. I can get a nice area rug for the living room for Bailey to crawl around on."

He calculated how much paint they would need in each of the colors, along with the Kilz primer. The clerk added everything up and Shannon pulled bills from her wallet.

Jake put a hand over hers. "Abe's paying for the paint. It's his repair job."

"But, he's already being so generous."

Jake asked that the material be added to his account. The clerk nodded, then came around the counter to help them carry everything to the truck.

Jake covered the paint cans with a tarp. "I have a little time. You want to get lunch? There's a café down the street."

"What about the paint? Will it be safe?"

"You're in Snoqualmie. It'll be fine right here."

"You mean you're willing to risk having the rest of the town ogle you while you walk around with a strange woman and baby?"

"Bailey's not so strange." He grinned. "I'm hungry. I'll take my chances." Jake felt better than he had in a long time, better in a way that felt whole. He felt…normal, even as he lightly pressed a hand to her back as they entered the café.

The waitress appeared at their booth with glasses of water. "Hi, Jake." She turned to Shannon and then glanced down at Bailey. "What a cute baby."

"Millie, this is a friend of mine, Shannon. She's relocating here to Snoqualmie. And that little cutie is Bailey," Jake said.

The waitress frowned. "You're relocating here? That hardly ever happens. Most people relocate out of Snoqualmie."

Shannon smiled. "I need a change of pace and this town seems perfect."

"Where you moving from?" the waitress asked.

"The Midwest."

"Oh?" When no further information followed, she said, "Well, welcome. The special today is a hot roast beef sandwich with fries. You want menus?"

"I'll have the special and iced tea, please," Shannon said.

"Same here," Jake said.

"Got it. Be right back with your drinks."

"So…." Shannon glanced around the café. "This is a nice place."

"It is."

They sat in silence while the conversations of other diners hummed around them.

Both jumped when Jake's cell phone rang. He stared at the number for a moment before answering. "Hello?"

"Jake, this is Angie. I talked to my mom and she'll be happy to babysit when you need her. Here's her phone number and address. Just give her a call ahead of time."

"Hold on." He motioned to Shannon. "Pen?"

She rummaged in her purse and handed him a ballpoint pen bearing some bank's logo. He jotted down the information on a paper napkin and thanked Angie. "I have the name and address of the babysitter."

"Someone you know?"

"I know her daughter pretty well. She cares for her grandkids most days. You can meet her first."

Millie returned and slid a plate in front of each of them. "You need a refill on your drinks?"

"Yes please," Shannon said. Then to Jake, she said, "When can we paint?"

"Depends on how much the guys and I get done with the roof today. If they're willing to work late, we'll keep at it as long as there's light. If we finish up tomorrow, I can start the primer in the afternoon. Then we can paint on Friday."

They ate in silence until a rumble of thunder sounded and Jake looked out the front window. Clouds began to build. "Uh-oh."

"What's wrong?"

"It's going to rain and we only have half a roof on the apartment. I have to get back there and help the guys fasten a tarp to cover the exposed roof. There's no time to take you and Bailey back to the cabin. You'll have to come with me. Are you finished?"

She popped a couple of fries into her mouth and then the last bite of her sandwich, nodding.

The sky darkened and wind whipped the trees. Jake was relieved to see Rico and Don on the roof, already tacking down the blue tarp. Abe Swinson stood on his back porch, watching. When Jake got out of the truck, Abe said, "It's looking like a storm's coming."

"I think you're right. I rushed back here to help the guys cover the roof and clean up." He helped Shannon down from the truck and removed Bailey in her carrier. Just as they reached the top of the steps, fat raindrops splattered on the wooden landing. He threw the door open and hurried inside with the baby.

"This storm came out of nowhere. It was gorgeous when we left the house." Shannon rubbed her moistened arms.

"Welcome to the Northwest. We've been lucky so far this week." He set down the carrier and hurried outside to help the other two men.

~ * ~

Shannon carefully removed the covers from the furniture, trying not to shake up too much dust. She ran her fingers along the brocade fabric of the sofa. It was worn and a little faded, but looked sturdy and comfy. Probably expensive in its day. She sat and was surprised by the life still in the cushions. Above, the sound of feet, male voices and hammering.

She turned on the TV and, sure enough, the cable was still connected. She was flipping through channels when Jake came in. He was soaking wet and his tee shirt clung to him, revealing a solid chest and well-defined abs. She forced her eyes away. The last thing she wanted was to be drawn to him, to any man, right now.

"Do you think there are any towels in the bathroom?" he asked.

"I'll check." She opened the cabinet beneath the sink to find a neatly folded stack of towels and grabbed two.

Jake stood at the kitchen sink wringing water from his tee-shirt. Shannon gasped at the sight of him, then cleared her throat, hoping he hadn't heard. "Here you go. They're old and a bit scratchy, but they look clean."

"Thanks." He rubbed a towel over his hair vigorously, then swiped his hair back with his fingers. "I hope this dries out soon." He draped the tee shirt over the sink. Then he looked down at his bare chest. "Sorry."

"Maybe we could pull up some of the carpet?"

He shook his head. "Not a good idea without protective masks. No telling what we'd be breathing in. And there's Bailey to consider."

"How long do you think this storm will last?"

"Could blow through in a few minutes. Hard to tell. As soon as there's a break, we'll head back to the cabin. At least the TV is working."

As if on cue, thunder boomed, lightning flashed—and the TV and lights went off.

Shannon jumped at the crash of thunder and backed into him. Bailey began to cry. Shannon picked her up from the carrier and held her close.

Jake dragged the rocking chair away from the window. "Here, sit down."

"She doesn't like storms, especially thunder." Shannon held the baby close, rocking and whispering in a soothing tone.

The storm continued to rage outside as the sky darkened. "We might be here a while." He pulled a chair away from the small dining table and sat.

"The sofa's more comfortable," Shannon said.

"My jeans are still damp. I don't want to get it wet. This is good."

The silence between them was interrupted only by the occasional clap of thunder.

"Tell me about Phoenix," Shannon said, her gaze focused on Bailey.

"Phoenix?"

She looked up at Jake. "You said you came here from Phoenix. I've never been to the Southwest. What's it like?"

"Hot. But it's a dry heat. Palm trees. Sand. Lots of retirees."

"Plenty of sunshine?"

"Uh…yeah." He went to the kitchen and pulled on his still-damp shirt. "You said you were from Pennsylvania, but you told the waitress you came from the Midwest."

She gave a nervous laugh. "Pennsylvania's sort of the Midwest, isn't it? That always confuses me."

"I think the Midwest begins with Ohio."

Drawing upon stories her mother told of her own childhood,

she launched into her lie. "Uniontown is a small town in the southwestern corner of Pennsylvania, near the mountains. My mother's parents had a farm there." All true, so far.

"College?"

"Yes. Then I worked in a bank. That's where I met Bailey's father." She glanced at her watch, remembering she was to call her mother and Brooke at the restaurant in Jefferson City in an hour. "I think the rain's letting up a little. Should we make a run for it?"

Jake looked to the window. "Let me go first and see if Abe has an umbrella I can borrow to keep the baby dry."

"Good thinking." Shannon placed Bailey back into the carrier. Bailey wasn't ready to be put down and fussed.

Jake returned with a large umbrella. "Want me to carry her? Those steps are steep and you have the diaper bag."

Once they were in the safety of the truck, Jake handed the umbrella back to Abe and climbed in. "This is going to set us back a bit on the roof. Let's hope it clears by morning." He started the truck and turned at the end of the driveway, heading for home.

Water lay in pools on the roads and Jake expertly maneuvered them through. By the time they reached the cabin, the rain had slowed to a fine drizzle. The temperatures had dropped and Shannon shivered while she waited for him to unlock the door.

"I think I'll build a fire, take the chill out of here." Jake began to stack kindling and split logs in the fireplace.

Shannon picked up the phone. "Do you mind if I make a phone call?"

"Not at all. Go ahead."

She carried the phone up the stairs and punched in the phone number of the restaurant. When the hostess answered, Shannon said, "My mother, Doris Carlson, is dining there this evening. It's very important that I reach her and she doesn't have a cell phone. Would you be able to check? She's with Brooke Jamison."

"I'll check. Please hold."

A moment later, Brooke came on the phone. "Your mom just went to the ladies' room. What's going on?"

Brooke already knew about Bailey's father and about Corinne Hastings' *offer* to adopt—or buy—the baby. "I had to get out of town. That woman's insane. She actually believes that adopting a baby will put her in better standing with voters in the coming election. She's hell bent on taking Amanda...er...Bailey from me. For the record, I'm using the name Shannon Chase and the baby is now Bailey. I can't risk Corinne pulling some stunt to try to prove I'm not fit as a mother and then have Mark swoop in to claim the baby as his."

"You're a wonderful mother. Where are you?"

"I'm in Washington State. A little town called Snoqualmie. Look, don't tell my mother that bit of info. It's better if she doesn't know too many facts."

"Okay. Here she comes. Talk to you again soon."

"Heather, oh honey, where are you?" Concern tightened her mother's voice.

She couldn't explain her new identity. Being called Heather felt foreign to her now. "I'm okay, Mom. So is Bai…the baby. We're in the Northwest. Mom, I want you to stay with Brooke for a while. She told me some men came to the house looking for me."

"They said they were from the bank, but I didn't buy that for a minute."

"Good. Now listen. Amanda's father has people looking for me. And they'll try to get you to tell them where I am. That's why I'm not being specific. You can honestly say you don't know. I'll communicate through email with Brooke and we'll arrange things like this for phone calls now and then. I just wanted you to know I'm safe. And…" Her throat tightened and she swallowed. "I love you."

"I love you, too, sweetheart. Give Amanda a kiss from her Grandma."

Shannon ended the call and set the phone down beside her on the bed. She'd held in her emotions for the past week and, now, having heard her mother's voice, the dam broke. Her shoulders shook as she sobbed.

She didn't hear Jake, but he was suddenly kneeling in front of her. "What's wrong? Did something happen?"

Needing to draw strength from someone, she slid forward and into his arms, holding on for dear life.

They knelt together on the floor, Jake's arms around her, his voice soothing, "It's okay. Whatever it is, it'll be okay."

She couldn't find words or her voice, just continued to cling to him and cry, letting out the fear, anger, and grief she'd been holding.

When she pulled away, she noticed the large, wet spot on his tee shirt. "I'm sorry. That was a clean shirt, wasn't it?"

He stared into her eyes. "I have lots of shirts. Want to talk about whatever happened?"

She reached to the nightstand and grabbed a wad of tissues, blotting her face and then blowing her nose. "I talked to my Mom. I...I miss her, that's all."

Then she looked down at the phone. He would know she was lying when he got the bill. The call wasn't placed to Uniontown, Pennsylvania. It would show a call to Jefferson City, Missouri. In the Midwest.

"I know what you need."

"You do?"

He stood and offered her a hand. "Come with me."

She followed him from the bedroom, still holding his hand until they reached the stairs. Then she walked behind him through to the kitchen.

Jake reached into the freezer and produced a half-gallon of ice cream. Next he took a bottle of chocolate syrup and other toppings from the fridge. "You need a sundae."

She sniffled. "Ice cream solves all problems."

"Can't hurt." He grabbed bowls from the cabinet and spoons from a drawer next to the sink. After scooping generous portions of French vanilla ice cream into the bowls, he motioned to the toppings. "Everything you need. Even crushed nuts." His face reddened as he looked up with a grin. "Let's not go there again."

She laughed and it felt good. Here, in this moment, with this man she barely knew, making ice cream sundaes, she was safe.

~ * ~

"I'm telling you, he's not here. The lead was a dead end." The biker sat in the last booth in the bar, a cell phone to his ear.

"That's not possible. My guy on the inside was sure Avery was relocated to that town. It's not that big. How hard could it be to find him?" Lou Crowley demanded.

"I checked out the guy. He looks nothing like this Father Avery and he's got a wife and baby. I'm telling you, it's not him."

"Shit. Don't leave that town until I get back to you. Where're you staying?"

"Some no-name motel—the Evergreen Motor Lodge— outside of town. How long do I have to hang here? This is one godforsaken place. No action, if you know what I mean."

"You'll *hang* there as long as I need you to. Did you show

that picture around?"

"I did. No one recognized him. They told me to check at the local Catholic church. The priest there says he never heard of a Father Avery and doesn't know this guy. Either he's not here or he has this whole town snowed."

"I'll talk with my source and then get back to you."

"What am I supposed to do in the meantime?"

"Go fishing. Make nice with the locals. Somebody is bound to eventually recognize Avery's photo. What have you been telling them about your reason for looking for him?"

"I said he's my long lost brother and I'm tryin' to find him to make amends. They're all real sympathetic to that story and say they hope I find him." He laughed. "Dumbasses."

"Sit tight. I'll call you tomorrow or the next day, once I talk to my man on the inside."

The biker snorted as he ended the call. "My man on the inside," he mimicked. "Who does Crowley think he is, Chief of the freakin' FBI?"

He'd trailed the guy in his truck today. But when the guy picked up his wife and kid for lunch and then rushed back to that roofing job he was doing, he figured it was a bust. Wrong man. If this Avery was still a priest, he wouldn't have a wife and kid. Would he?

Chapter Eleven

They spent the better part of an hour at Angie's mother's house while Shannon toured the premises and asked Dawn Kohler a thousand questions about her experience with children. Jake watched with some amusement as Dawn patiently answered each one. She had raised five kids and was the grandmother of seven. As far as he was concerned, that pretty much qualified her to babysit Bailey for a day.

"Okay, so you have Jake's cell number in case you need to reach me?" Shannon asked. "I packed two changes of clothing, more than enough diapers for the day, formula and two bottles, and her stuffed kitty that she likes." She dug deep into the diaper bag. "And there's a wind-up ballerina in here that fascinates her."

Dawn nodded. "Thank you. Seems you thought of everything. Do you think I could hold her for a minute while you're here?"

"Oh, of course." Shannon handed the baby over to the older woman.

Bailey stared up at Dawn's face in wonder, then reached for her long braid that hung over one shoulder. "You sure are a sweet baby," Dawn said. "I think we'll get along fine." She looked up at Shannon. "That is, if you're comfortable with me caring for her."

"Yes, I...um...." She glanced from Jake to Dawn. "You'd call me if anyone came here and wanted to see her?"

Dawn lifted her eyebrows. "Is that likely to happen?"

"Probably not. It's just.... I'm not sure Bailey's father won't try to find us. I left because it was a bad situation."

"No one gets this baby back from me except you. You have nothing to worry about," Dawn assured her.

"Satisfied?" Jake asked.

"I suppose so. I haven't been apart from her since she was born." Shannon bit on her lower lip.

Jake's gaze fixed on her mouth. He had the urge to lick his own lips. Instead he pressed them tightly together.

"I understand," Dawn said. "My daughters had a terrible time when they had to return to work and leave their little ones for the first time."

"I feel foolish."

"Not at all." Dawn patted her hand. "I'd be worried if it was too easy for you to hand her over."

"You have a beautiful home and you seem like a very nice woman. I'd appreciate it if you babysit Bailey while we're working on the apartment. Just for one or two days. How much do you charge?"

The woman gave a dismissive wave. "I'm already taking care of three of my grandkids. One more won't be any trouble. I'll be happy to help."

"Really?"

"Sure. Angie told me you're new to town. Consider it part of the Snoqualmie Welcome Wagon. Two days of free babysitting. More if you need it. That's what neighbors do."

"Thank you. I'll be back to pick her up at five or sooner." Shannon looked at Jake for confirmation. He nodded.

She snuggled the baby close, kissing her on the cheeks and saying goodbye before handing her back to Dawn.

Jake paused a moment once they were in the truck, then asked, "Are you all right?"

Shannon stared out the window, but nodded.

"No, you're not."

She sniffled. "I will be. Let's get to work."

He assigned her the task of covering the meager bedroom furnishings with a paint cloth while he stirred the paint. "We need to do the ceiling first so we don't drip on the walls. Why don't I do that while you work in the bathroom?"

"Sounds like a plan."

Jake climbed the ladder and set his bucket of paint on the fold-out shelf. Music blared from the living room. Oldies—not what he would have expected from Shannon. At thirty, even his definition of oldies fell somewhere in the sixties. She had to be a few years younger, unless this was music she listened to growing up, the way he had.

He'd finished half of the bedroom ceiling and was grooving to Smokey Robinson when a shriek and a loud "Dammit" sounded from the bathroom. He hustled down the ladder and across the hall.

Shannon stood with one foot on the lid of the toilet seat and the other buried above her ankle in gooey white latex paint. Her eyes were wide with surprise.

Jake stood in the doorway, unable to resist a laugh.

"This is not funny. If I make one move, I'll have paint all over the floor. Could you give me a hand here?"

He picked up the empty plastic waste basket from under the sink and set it down beside the paint. "Okay, I'm going to lift you up. Very carefully pull your foot up, toes pointed down, and step into the waste basket."

"My foot's too big."

"Not if it fits in the paint bucket."

"Okay." She sounded skeptical.

He placed his hands under her arms and lifted, surprised by the lightness of her body. "Raise your foot."

She did as directed and stepped down into the waste basket. But her foot wobbled and rolled. She lost all footing, falling into him, knocking him off balance. Jake tumbled backward trying to avoid hitting the shower and at the same time trying to cushion her fall. That landed him flat on his back with her spread eagle atop him.

He emitted a soft 'oof' as the wind was knocked out of him. She did the same. They lay there for a moment, each trying to catch a breath.

"Are you okay?" he asked.

"I think so. Are you?"

He was fine, but having her body plastered to his with nothing more between them than a scrap of cotton she called a tank top and a skimpy pair of shorts and his well-worn jeans and tee shirt was becoming painful. Especially because her thigh had wedged against his crotch and her effort to extricate herself was causing major chaos in his jeans. He hoped she interpreted his heavy breathing as a result of their fall.

"Stop moving for a minute," he ordered. "Use your hands to lift up so I can slide out from beneath you."

She pressed her palms on either side of him and pushed up. As she did, the neckline of the tank top dropped down, giving him full view of her breasts. He was no expert, but pretty sure hers were nearly perfect. He gulped.

In her attempts to push herself upright and slide away from him, her knee pressed into his already sensitive privates. "Ow."

"What? Oh, not again. I'm so sorry." She finally managed to

raise her body from his and land in a crouch near his feet. "I'm really sorry."

He didn't dare look down to see if his condition was obvious to her. He sat upright. Too fast. His forehead connected with hers as she leaned a bit forward to rise.

"Ouch," she cried.

He lay back down. "I knew I should have had Rico and Don help me with this, too."

She rubbed her forehead, grinning. "Would you rather have wiped out with Rico on top of you?"

"Uh...." He wasn't sure if she expected an answer to that question. Clearly, he would not prefer Rico. "Look, just remain still. I'm going to sit up, slide back, and get on my feet. Then it'll be your turn."

She remained crouched with her back to the wall until he was standing and offered her a hand. "I am so sorry. Did I hurt you?" Her gaze swept over his crotch and back to his face. The blush that colored her cheeks was not lost on him.

"I'll live, though I may never have children." The words were out of his mouth before he gave them a thought. *Of course you won't have children. You're a priest, for heaven's sake.* But that life seemed so far in the past, so removed from the man he'd become. Almost an afterthought. He extended a hand and helped her to her feet. "I hope you have other shoes."

"I do, but not here. I can work barefoot, I just need to get this shoe off and wipe off some of this paint."

He pulled another of the rough towels from beneath the sink. "Sit down and take off your shoe and drop it into the waste basket."

Once she'd done so, he knelt and wrapped the towel around her foot, rubbing to remove the excess wet paint. A memory flashed through his brain of the last Easter service over which he had presided and the foot washing ceremony. There had been much disagreement in the parish about including women in the foot washing. Jake—well, Father Steve—had stood up to the Parish Council and insisted that in the twenty-first century, women were equals.

"Jake?"

He looked up at her face then down to where his hands still cradled her foot. "That should do it." He dropped her foot. "I have some stuff at home to help remove this paint without burning your skin. You can use it before you shower tonight. Do you need more paint?"

She peered into the can. "I think I'm good. I just have this back corner behind the toilet to finish. I'll be more careful about where I put the can of paint, though, and where I step."

"I need a cold drink. You want one?" In truth, he needed a cold shower. He needed to run naked through a snow storm right now.

"No. I'll get something when I'm finished. How's the bedroom coming along?"

"The ceiling's almost finished. We'll take a lunch break before we start on the walls in there. Okay?"

"Can we check on Bailey then?"

He nodded. "Absolutely." He'd been thinking the same thing. Even though he trusted Dawn Kohler, he missed having Bailey around. It astonished him how quickly the baby had found a soft place in his heart. It worried him how quickly Shannon had found her place there, as well.

While he finished the ceiling, he struggled with his warring emotions. His sense of obligation to the Church because of his solemn promises stood diametrically opposed to his growing attraction to Shannon and his thoughts of having a family. When he had first learned about the child trafficking for adoptions and had gone to the authorities, he had been an "anonymous source." Once the Feds started to move in and brought charges, however, his cover was blown. His brother priests, well some of them, turned on him, accusing him of betraying the brotherhood they shared. He had been amazed at how they could ignore the fact that Father Alvin Martin had been involved in selling children. The Bishop had washed his hands of Father Avery, instead putting his energy into finding a way to spin the story and distance it and those involved from the Church. According to the Bishop, the former Father Crowley had been relieved of his priestly duties long before because of his "demonstrated inability to fully embrace the priestly life." Of Father Alvin Martin, the Bishop simply said that the priest had been "misguided" in his efforts to ultimately help the children involved. He had very little to say about the fortitude shown by Father Avery, simply saying he was young and inexperienced and should have come to his Bishop first for guidance.

His Church, the Church to which he had vowed his life, had

turned its back on him. He had no doubt that everyone from the Bishop down had breathed in relief when Father Avery disappeared for good. Lou Crowley and his female accomplice still eluded capture. Lou could be considered dangerous, if he had foreign contacts that would want Avery's head and would expect Lou to provide it. So far, the only international connection seemed to be Mexico. Even if Lou was captured, Jake might always be in hiding. He might never return to his former life and for now he wasn't free to embrace a new life. His reward for stepping in to save those kids and probably hundreds more—a life sentence in limbo. And he'd do it again. The frightened face of that little girl being escorted by Lou still haunted him.

Chapter Twelve

Corinne Hastings glared across her desk at the man seated there. "You went to her mother's house? What is wrong with you?"

"But you said to find out where she is."

"Yes, as in follow a trail. By now, I'm sure she's aware of your visit and she'll be more careful than ever. She knows someone is looking for her. And did her mother tell you anything?"

The man shifted uncomfortably. "Well, no. We told her we were from the bank and that we wanted to know where to send her severance pay."

She had turned toward the window, but now whirled at him. "We?"

"Yeah, I took one of my off-duty partners along. He's been working with me."

"You're an idiot," she shouted.

"I'm sorry you think so, because I followed dear Mom to dinner the other night. She was picked up by another woman, younger. I ran the plates on the car. It belongs to one Brooke Jamison who just happens to be a former co-worker of Ms. Carlson. Soon after they arrived at the restaurant, Ms. Jamison got a phone call and then gave the phone to Mrs. Carlson. Mom was in tears, I'm guessing because she was talking to her missing daughter."

Corinne rounded the desk and leaned on the edge, glaring down at him. "And?"

"And I checked the restaurant's phone records. The call came from an unlisted number in Snoqualmie, Washington."

"Unlisted, huh? Any way to find out whose number that is and the address?"

He pulled his cell phone from his pocket and flipped it open. "Best way I know—call." He pulled a small notepad from his inside jacket pocket and opened it, then punched numbers into the cell phone before handing it to the Governor.

Corinne lifted the phone to her ear, listening to it ring. Then voicemail came on, *Please leave a message. I'll call back as soon as*

I can. "Son-of-a-bitch." She snapped the phone shut and tossed it to him. "I want that number. And I want you to find out to whom it is registered and the address."

"Yes, Madame Governor."

"And watch your mouth. You forget who I am—and who you are."

He jotted the phone number and ripped the paper from his notebook. "You remind me all the time." He stood and headed for the door.

"You have a stake in this too. Don't forget that, little brother."

Anthony Baker, stared at her. "Can I ask you something, Corinne? Why in the hell do you want Mark's bastard in the first place?"

"Forcing him to raise that child will be a constant reminder of how he betrayed me. He thought he could screw around on me with that little bitch and walk away without taking any responsibility when she ended up pregnant. Well, the joke will be on him. I have to give the girl credit for one thing—she didn't bow to his insistence she terminate the pregnancy. Hell, she probably voted for me in the last election based upon my pro-life platform."

"Has it occurred to you that you will also be raising that child?"

She pressed her lips together and glowered at him. "Don't be ridiculous. I'll hire a nanny."

Anthony snorted. "Perfect. Another young thing working at the mansion for Mark to screw. Why don't you just cut him loose? He's never been faithful. He doesn't love you and I can't imagine you love him."

"Love?" She shook her head. "Do people marry for love? I married Mark Hastings to get exactly what I've gotten. Benefit from a legacy of the Hastings family name. I see one more term as Governor of Missouri, then I'll run for the Senate. Or maybe even bypass that step and go straight after the White House. By then this country will be ready for a female president, don't you think?"

"If you say it's so, Corinne, it's so. You have a photo of that girl?"

She opened a locked drawer in her desk and produced a photograph she'd snapped with her phone during her late-night visit to Heather Carlson's apartment.

Anthony stared at the photo. "Mark has good taste." He shoved the picture into his jacket pocket. "I'll be out of town for a few days."

"Where are you going?"

He shrugged. "The great Northwest."

~ * ~

After checking in on Bailey and finding her completely happy and smiling in a baby swing Dawn had on hand, she and Jake headed to the cabin. She needed another pair of shoes and lunch.

"I'll make sandwiches while you get your shoes," Jake said.

"Just be a minute." Upstairs she first went into the bathroom. While standing at the sink to wash her hands, she stared at her image, wondering how she'd look as a blond with a short, spiky cut.

She opted for a pair of flip-flops figuring another painting accident wouldn't do much damage. She recalled how Jake's body had felt beneath hers—strong, solid, and if she wasn't mistaken, turned on. She hadn't meant to rub herself all over him, but getting off of him in such a tight space made avoiding that impossible. When she left Jefferson City, she had vowed that it would be just her and her daughter, at least for a year. Maybe longer. She clearly had poor taste when it came to getting involved with men. Her boyfriend before she got involved with Mark had taken her for a couple of thousand dollars, a loan he promised he'd repay. His repayment had been to take off without so much as a "see ya'." She had convinced herself that was the reason she had responded Mark. She knew who he was, that he was married when he cajoled her into having drinks with him. His unavailability and his mature good looks made him more appealing. They'd only been together a few months when her conscience got the best of her and she broke things off. Then she discovered she was pregnant.

Replaying the scene in her head when she'd told him about the baby still made her physically ill. His grim expression and insistence that she "take care of it," followed by a tirade that she was the one who was irresponsible and he was not going to leave his wife for her. "You do remember who I'm married to, don't you?" he has asked.

She had almost laughed out loud at the question, wanting to retort, "Like you remembered you were married?" But she'd seen Mark Hastings' anger a few times, and she had no interest in bringing his wrath down on her when they were alone in her apartment. She was firm, though, about keeping the baby and assuring Mark he didn't have to do anything.

He called her a few times during the pregnancy under the guise of making sure she was okay. His last call came a few weeks before the baby was born when he told her his wife had found out about the affair and the baby and had suggested they arrange a private adoption. When she reacted with horror at the idea, Mark swore at her and told her if she knew what was good for her, she'd reconsider.

Now, here she was, using the identity of a dead college classmate and hiding out in a stranger's cabin in the Northwest. She felt she knew Jake better in just a week's time than she'd ever known Mark. Or maybe she wanted to believe that. Jake was everything Mark was not—gentle, caring, hard working, and a man of integrity. She caught him at times staring at her, his eyes warm, but he never made a move on her. She gave herself a mental shake. Getting involved with Jake would be a huge mistake, at least right now. She sighed and headed back to the kitchen.

"Turkey sandwiches and chips okay?" Jake asked.

"Sounds great. I'm ravenous. I haven't worked that hard in a long time."

"What kind of work did you do?" He set a glass of iced tea beside her.

"I was a bank manager." She took a sip of tea, then asked, "Can we stop by a store before we come back here later? I need to pick up a few things." *Like scissors and hair dye.*

"No problem."

They ate quickly and, while she rinsed their plates, Jake dropped some apples, cheese and chips into a bag, along with two cans of soda. "Afternoon snack," he said.

The day was beautiful, in the low 70s and with a gentle breeze. They had left the windows open and left the fans Jake had hauled over there running. The work they had done was just about dry.

Jake set up the paint for the bedroom walls. "We'll use rollers. Remember to roll some of the paint off the roller so it doesn't run. And don't roll all the way to the top. I'll go around and do that last." He glanced down at her flip-slops. "You're going to work all day in those?"

She stared down. "Probably not a good idea. I'll work

barefoot." She kicked of the rubber footwear and shoved them aside. Jake filled two pans with paint and handed her a roller, then took his paint to the opposite wall. She didn't have the heart to tell him she had painted plenty of rooms and knew exactly what to do.

"We need music." She retrieved the radio from the kitchen and plugged it into a hall socket just outside the bedroom door. This time she found a light rock station. She was shaking her butt to the music when she turned to add paint to her brush and saw Jake staring at her. Their eyes met briefly, then he turned away and resumed painting. It was her turn to watch the way the muscles in his arms and back rolled along with the strokes of the roller. How in the hell had this man stayed unattached? She'd been with him in close quarters for a week and couldn't identify a single flaw. He was perfect. Too perfect.

Chapter Thirteen

That night after they'd had pizza because both were too tired to cook or to eat out, Shannon put Bailey to bed. Jake heard the shower kick on a second time, but only for a few minutes. He finished checking email and then turned on the TV to relax.

When Shannon padded back down the stairs and sat on the sofa, he didn't look her way. "Bailey asleep?"

"Yes. She's a little fussy. I think she's teething."

"Already?" With that he looked over at her. He blinked and looked again. "What happened to your hair?"

"I cut it and lightened it."

He wasn't sure what to say. "It's…uh…different."

"It looks like I was run over by a lawnmower. But I wanted to try something new."

"No, it's nice. Very blond. Is there a name for that style?"

She laughed. "It's called I cut my own hair and I'm not ambidextrous. I may have left the hair color on too long, too." She got up. "I'm going to get something to drink. Do you need anything?"

"No, thanks."

The phone rang and he crossed the room to answer it. "Hello."

"May I speak with Heather, please?"

"Who?"

"Heather Carlson."

"I'm sorry. You have a wrong number."

Shannon came into the room as he hung up. "Who was that?"

"Some guy looking for a Heather something."

The soda can slipped from her hand and landed with a thud, spraying soda over his legs. He bent to pick it up, then looked at her face. "Are you okay?"

"D-Did he identify himself?"

"No. It was a wrong number." Then he asked, "Wasn't it?"

She closed her eyes and drew in a deep breath. "Jake…. We should sit down."

"Okay." He set the foaming soda can on a section of newspaper on the coffee table. "You look like you've seen a ghost."

"I am the ghost."

He furrowed his eyebrows. "What are you talking about?"

She sat back and closed her eyes again. When she opened them, she steadied her gaze on his face. "I'm not who you think I am."

"I don't really know who you are."

"My name is not Shannon Chase. It's Heather Carlson. And Bailey's name is Amanda."

"Why the aliases?"

"Someone wants to take Amanda from me. I have to protect her."

"From whom?" He thought of what he'd done to protect innocent children and what it had cost him. "If someone is threatening you, the police could help."

She shook her head. "No, they can't. The woman who wants to take her from me is in a very powerful position."

"Kidnapping is illegal regardless of one's position."

She sighed. "You don't understand. Her father is Mark Hastings, husband of Governor Corinne Baker Hastings of Missouri. Corinne wants the baby."

It took a moment for all of what she was telling him to sink in. "Why?"

"How do I know? To get even with me, or with Mark. They don't have children. All I know is, she will stop at nothing to take Amanda away from me. My only choice was to change our identities and disappear."

"Okay. So, who is Shannon Chase?"

She stood and began to pace. "Shannon was a friend of mine in college. Sadly, she was killed in a car accident at the beginning of our sophomore year. When I realized I had to get out of town fast, I needed a different name. So I took Shannon's name."

"And Bailey?"

"I saw an ad on the side of a bus for Bailey's Irish Crème."

He couldn't keep from grinning. "I'm sorry. This isn't funny."

"That part is, kind of." She forced a smile. "The rest is an ugly mess." She told him the whole story. "And I don't know how they would have found me here, but...."

84

"But?"

"I called my mother the other night while she was at a restaurant. I set it up via email with a friend. They must have been following my mom and somehow traced the call from the restaurant phone records." She sat down again. "How could I be so stupid?" She looked up again, wild-eyed. "I have to get a car. I have to get us out of here."

"Wait. Slow down." Jake got out of the recliner and sat beside her. "You look different. You have a new name. And the only phone number they have is mine. You'll be in your own apartment soon. That phone is in Abe's name, so leave it at that. I'm certainly not going to tell them where you are. Let's wait and see if anyone shows up here first."

"You don't understand. They want Bailey."

"I do understand. I also know that you can't run forever. At some point, you have to stop." He reached out to squeeze her shoulder for reassurance. But when he did, she leaned forward and fell into this arms, crying softly on his chest. So he tightened his hold.

"I've never been so sc-scared." Her body shuddered. "I know I was stupid and irresponsible. But I won't let them take my daughter."

"Neither will I." Jake wrapped her with both arms and pressed his lips to the top of her head. "I promise."

Long after Shannon went to bed, Jake sat in the light of the television. He wondered if the person who had called was Mark Hastings or someone paid to track down Heather and Amanda. If someone did come after them, how was he going to protect them? With his Louisville Slugger? As much as he hated the idea, he would have to buy a gun. Which would require a background check. He'd been told his identity as Jake Garber was rock solid, so that shouldn't be a problem. But he'd never tested it out before, had always kept a low profile. He didn't want to take Shannon along for his gun purchase, didn't want her to even know once he'd bought one. He'd leave her at the apartment tomorrow and run an errand. She and Bailey would be safe enough there.

Then he thought about the guy on the motorcycle who tried to run them down. The second thing on his list was to find out if that guy was still hanging around town.

~ * ~

85

Shannon lay in bed, unable to sleep. The chirping of crickets and the occasional screech of a night bird sounded from outside. A gentle breeze ruffled the curtains and swept across her legs. She shivered, but not from a chill. They had found her. Now she worried more about her mother. Both Mark and Corinne had to know that the one thing that would bring her back to Jefferson City would be her mother. Before coming to bed, she'd emailed Brooke: *Hey, Babs. Had a call tonight from an old friend. Said he ran into you and Mom at dinner. Hope all is well. Love, Eve.* She could only hope Brooke would put the pieces together and figure out they'd been followed.

Bailey began to whimper and Shannon got up to lift her from the cradle. She was going to have to buy a crib. "Shhh, sweetie. It's okay." She stuck her finger in the baby's mouth and Bailey clamped down on it, gnawing with her gums. "My big girl's getting her very first tooth already." She was also going to have to find a pediatrician soon. The doctor would want the name of her former pediatrician to request records. Thank goodness she had her copies of Bailey's medical records and had been able to make new copies with the slight change of name.

The baby was inconsolable. Thinking it was near time for her to eat and that might help her sleep, Shannon carried her down to the kitchen to prepare a bottle. The television was on, but Jake was nowhere in sight. She managed to juggle the baby with one arm while mixing the formula with the other hand. She'd never been much of a multi-tasker until she had Bailey. Now she could soothe a crying baby, mix formula, and make a sandwich all at the same time.

When she noticed that the back door was open, she looked out to see Jake sitting on the deck. The night air was too cool for Bailey and Shannon really did not want more conversation right now. She carried the baby back upstairs to feed her.

As Bailey drifted into sleep, Shannon eased the nipple from her mouth and set the bottle aside. She lay the infant in the cradle Jake had made. In the stillness, she heard him talking to someone and moved closer to her open window.

He paced below, his cell phone to his ear. "I'm sorry, but what else could I do. She and the baby had nowhere to go." Pause. "I know it's a problem. But if you want my cooperation, you're going to have to help." He paused. "I can't go into all the details right now, you're going to have to trust me. I can't do what needs to be done. You're going to have to take care of it for me. The sooner the better." Pause. "Fine. Meet us at her new place." He rattled off the address, then said, "I'll see you tomorrow."

Shannon froze. Who was he talking to about her? Her stomach twisted as she thought of all the possible scenarios, settling on one—that Jake Garber saw an opportunity and took it, calling Mark Hastings to turn her in for God only knew how much money. Her whole body shook as she went to the closet, removed her Bodyguard .38 from the briefcase and gently placed it in the drawer of the nightstand beside her bed.

She packed a bag with all their essentials, along with the briefcase. Then she waited for Jake to come up to his room. After half an hour, she tiptoed down the hall. Through the closed door, she could hear him snoring.

First she carried her bag, the diaper bag, and the briefcase down the stairs and set them by the back door. Then she returned for Bailey. She slipped the gun into her jeans at the small of her back, the way she'd always seen it done on TV. Her eyes stung as she lifted the baby from the cradle Jake had made. What an idiot she'd been to trust him. He'd sold her out. Well, she didn't know what he had planned for tomorrow, and she wasn't waiting around to find out. All she had to do was find the keys to his truck.

The keys were right where she thought they would be, hanging on the wall rack behind the door. She slipped the truck key from its hook and then carried the bags outside. As she returned for Bailey, the baby stretched and screwed up her face. "No, no, no. Not now. Shhh." She managed to get all of their things into the truck and the baby in her car seat before the outdoor lights blazed and Jake appeared on the deck.

"What are you doing?"

"Don't come near me." She felt behind her for the gun and raised it with a shaking hand. "Don't make me shoot."

He stopped, his eyes wide and hands raised. "Please don't point that gun at me. I'm not going to hurt you."

She backed up against the truck, taking the stance she'd learned in her one firearms lesson, legs spread to shoulder width, feet planted firmly, both hands on the weapon to keep it steady. But it wasn't working. She only shook harder.

"You don't have to run. I have a plan."

"I heard you talking. I know all about your plan."

He put his hands down and took one step.

She squeezed and the gunshot echoed in the silence.

Chapter Fourteen

The bang resounded through Jake's head and instinct told him to drop to the ground.

Shannon yelped and lowered the gun. "Jake?"

"Are you crazy?" Jake shouted. "Put that gun down."

She dropped the gun and rush to him. "Are you hurt? Oh, my God, I never shot anyone before." Tears streaked her face. "Are you bleeding anywhere?" Her hands shook and she ran them over his chest.

He pushed her hands away. "I'm fine. You're a lousy shot, thank God." He stood and brushed the dirt off his pajama bottoms. "Why did you try to shoot me?"

"I heard you earlier, talking on the phone."

"Okay."

"You said I was a problem you couldn't fix, that whoever you were talking with would have to take care of it."

"Yes, I called a friend who I thought could help with your situation. It was late and I figured I'd tell you in the morning. He's coming here tomorrow."

"A friend. Would his name be Mark Hastings?" she shouted.

Jake was grateful he had no neighbors, no one to report a gunshot followed by a woman shouting. From the truck, Bailey began to cry. "No, it isn't. But it's chilly out here. Bring the baby back inside and I'll explain."

She closed the door to the truck and her hand tightened again on the gun she'd picked up. "You can explain right here."

"This friend of mine can help with things like a new identity. From what you told me, all you have is a different name and, now, a new hairstyle and color. That's not going to help you much. You need identification, papers to show that you exist as Shannon Chase and that your daughter is Bailey Chase."

"You weren't talking to someone in Missouri?"

"No. I was talking to someone in Seattle in the U.S. Marshal's office. Now will you put the gun down and come back inside?"

She leaned against the truck and studied him for a moment. "I swear if you're lying to me, the next time I shoot at you, I won't miss."

"Deal." He took a tentative step toward her. "Let me help you get your stuff. You take the baby. And for God's sake, put that gun away, preferably unloaded, before you hurt one of us."

"I put the safety on." She shoved the gun down into the diaper bag and hoisted it onto her shoulder before lifting Bailey from her car seat.

Jake removed her overnight bag and briefcase from the truck, followed her back inside and dropped them onto the floor. Hands on hips, he stood for a moment, staring at her. "Is she okay?"

Shannon patted the baby's back, pressing her lips to her forehead. "She's warm. I think she has a fever, no doubt because of the teething."

Worried, he crossed and felt Bailey's forehead. "She does have a fever. Are you sure that's all it is."

"I think so. She's eating okay, so I'm not too worried."

"We should take her to a doctor tomorrow, first thing."

"*We* aren't taking her anywhere until you tell me what's going on."

He pulled out a chair. "Sit down. Look, I know this guy who's in law enforcement. He's in a position to help people with new identities."

"You mean like the witness protection program?"

He hesitated, knowing he could not tell her too much about himself. "Something like that. If someone is on your trail, you need to become someone else. And while the haircut and dye job are a start, having a solid identity built for you will give you added security."

She narrowed her eyes at him. "How do you know this guy?"

"He's an old friend. He can be trusted, but you'll have to be cooperative. Might be best to not let him see that gun or tell him you have it."

"What time will he be here?" she asked wearily.

"Around nine. He's meeting us at your apartment. I thought that would be safer, given the phone call earlier tonight. You might want to try to get some sleep." He frowned. "Did you really think I was going to turn you in?"

"I'm sorry. I don't know who I can trust right now. And, face it, I really don't know much about you."

He stood. "We'll save that conversation for another day. You take Bailey. I'll bring the rest of your things upstairs." Then he held out his hand. "Keys."

She pulled the truck keys from her pocket and tossed them to him. "You going to sleep with those under your pillow?"

He grinned. "For tonight."

~ * ~

The marshal introduced himself as Caleb Wilson. He was tall, broad-shouldered, with jet black hair and matching dark eyes. And he must have been at lease six foot five. An imposing presence, especially to Shannon.

She and Caleb sat on either end of the sofa. Jake took the wooden rocker. It dwarfed beneath him.

"You're telling me you think the governor of Missouri is out to harm you and take your child?" Caleb asked.

Shannon glanced to Jake who nodded for her to respond. "I have every reason to believe that." She recounted her story and he listened. "Jake can tell you about the phone call we got last night."

"We?" Caleb turned his gaze onto Jake who shifted in the chair.

"A call came to my place, a man asking to speak with Heather Carlson. I didn't know Shannon's whole story at the time and told him he had a wrong number. But he was clearly looking for her at my place."

Shannon told Caleb about the conversation with her mother at the Jefferson City restaurant. "That's the only possible way they could have tracked me here."

Caleb pressed his lips together and frowned. "How do you know the call came from Mr. Hastings?"

"I don't. But if it wasn't Mark, then it's someone Corinne…Governor Hastings has sent to find me."

He turned to Jake. "And you want me to wave my magic wand and turn Heather into Shannon Chase?" Focusing back on Shannon, he said, "And who, may I ask, is Shannon Chase?"

She explained about her college friend who had died at the age of nineteen.

"So I'm just supposed to steal her identity and give it to you?"

Jake leaned forward. "The girl's been dead at least ten years.

How hard can that be?"

Caleb stood and began to pace. "How hard can that be? Do you have any idea what goes into creating a new identity for someone?" He blew out a breath. "Okay. Tell me everything you know about the Shannon Chase whose identity you've been using. If she has a clean record, I may be able to get the documentation you'll need to assume her identity. I'll need a copy of the baby's birth certificate. Of course, this all depends on *your* background check."

"I've never had so much as a parking ticket," she said. "I'll tell you anything you need to know."

He nodded. "How can I contact you, Ms. Chase?"

"I…uh…." She looked at the phone—an ancient beige corded model sitting on a lamp table. "I don't know the phone number here."

Jake stood. "I'll get the number from Abe. Be right back."

Once Jake was gone, Shannon said to Caleb, "I'm sorry about this. I'm sorry I got Jake mixed up in this. Maybe it would be better if I moved on, went somewhere else."

Caleb shook his head. "Eventually, you're going to need documentation to prove who you are. Whether that's for work, a place to live…hell, you can't even get a damned credit card or open a bank account." He removed a cell phone from his pocket. "I need your photograph." He glanced around. "Stand against that wall." He motioned toward a blank wall to serve as background and snapped a few photos. Then he took one of Bailey.

Jake came through the door and handed a slip of paper to Caleb. He punched the numbers into his phone and the phone on the table rang. "You might need this." He handed the paper to Shannon. "I'll see what I can do, Ms. Chase. It might take a few days."

"Thank you. Should I have a phone number for you?"

"No, you shouldn't. Jake, can you walk me to my car?"

When both men were gone, Shannon leaned back and let a out a breath she hadn't realized she'd been holding. She had so many questions about Caleb and how Jake knew him, but she had a sense Jake was not going to answer them all.

Jake clambered up the steps and into the apartment. "Feeling any better?"

"Some. Thank you. So, now what?"

"Now you lay low until we see if someone shows up looking for you." He tilted his head. "Though I doubt he'll recognize you now.'

She fluffed her spiky hair with her fingers. "Good disguise, huh?"

"Did you ever wear glasses?"

"No, why?"

"We'll stop at the pharmacy. They sell non-prescription reading glasses. Then we'll gather up your stuff and get you moved in here."

"Tonight?"

"You'll be safer here than at my place. I have one errand to run. Will you be okay for about an hour?"

"I guess so."

"Good. I'll be back soon. If you need anything in the meantime, let Abe know." He paused at the door. "By the way, what kind of gun is that you have?"

"It's a Smith & Wesson .38. It's called the Bodyguard. Why?"

"No reason. I'll be back soon."

She listened to his footsteps on the stairs and his truck pull from the drive. She made sure to lock the door behind him. A soft breeze came through the windows and the paint odor had significantly evaporated overnight. Shannon lifted Bailey from the carrier and gave her a tour of their new home. She would spend the night here alone with her baby. While some maniac was coming to find her.

~ * ~

Caleb was pissed. Jake knew it. But he also knew he had the upper hand in this. If they wanted him to stay in hiding and be prepared to testify once they captured Lou Crowley and Sara Martin, Caleb was going to have to work with him here. Since Jake came into the program, Caleb had been nothing but respectful and fair. He'd become a friend, for as much as having minimal contact with someone can forge a friendship. Jake hated putting him in this position, but it was the only way he could protect Shannon and Bailey.

A gun shop in Issaquah would serve his purpose. He'd always believed in the importance of gun laws. Today he wished there were an exception. He had to wait five days to pick up his gun. His gun. The words rolled around in his brain like some invading foreign object.

93

Before driving back to the apartment, Jake decided to ride around a bit, get his head together. It had been hard enough to become Jake Garber and assume a new life. Now he was involved with a woman and assuming responsibility for her protection, ready to take a stand. He was just about to shove aside the feelings Shannon roused in him when something caught his eye in a motel parking lot. A gleaming black and silver motorcycle. Jake pulled his truck to the side of the road. One bike looked pretty much the same as the next to him. But this one looked particularly familiar and he could image the helmeted rider roaring toward him and Shannon a few nights earlier.

He turned into the lot and cruised past the bike, noting the license plate. That didn't tell him much—it bore a Washington State plate. But it could be a rental. Who would rent a motorcycle instead of a car? Someone who wanted to make a really fast get-away? He parked at the far end of the lot and waited, watching the bike. Half an hour had passed before a man clad in jeans, a black leather jacket and carrying a helmet approached the cycle. He was dark-complected with a couple days beard growth and a gleaming bald head. Dark in every possible way. Jake didn't recognize him, until he put on the helmet, lowered a visor and started up the bike. Jake decided to follow.

The cyclist roared toward town, then slowed as he navigated the main street. At the intersection on the west side of town, the biker turned right, up Mountain Pine Road. Jake's road. They were the only two vehicles on the road now, and Jake eased off the gas, creating more distance. The bike slowed as it approached Jake's driveway, then pulled over, the rider cutting the engine.

Jake sped up a little, driving by without looking to his right. He pulled off at turnaround a few hundred feet past the curve and got out. He could walk back to his place, but then what. He opened a tool box in the back of the truck and removed a tire iron, his fist clenching around the cold metal.

Chapter Fifteen

Twigs snapped under him and his feet slid on blankets of pine needles. Jake worked his way through the woods until he came to the tree line behind his cabin. It was about a twenty yard dash to reach his garage workshop. He waited and watched until he saw the man round the corner of the cabin and climb the steps to the deck. Jake had locked up better than usual that morning, in light of the phone call. The only way in would be to break in. The guy tried the window and then the door, cupping his hands and pressing his face to the glass to peer inside.

When the man crossed the driveway and moved toward the garage, Jake tensed. He couldn't remember locking that door. He heard the rattling of the door and muttered swearing. So he had locked up. He tightened his grip on the tire iron. He felt like a coward crouching in the bushes while some scum who had tried to run him down now tried to break into his house. Playing it safe had always been his choice. He couched it in the name of being a peaceful man, a priest. Well, look where that had gotten him. It was time to make a change. And he'd start with this guy.

Jake made a mad dash from the trees to the back of the garage. He leaned against the wall, panting to catch his breath. Sweat beaded his upper lip and dripped down the sides of his face. His chest burned and his arm was nearly numb from holding the tire iron. Through a narrow window, he could see through the garage to the guy standing by the door. Then the man moved, presumably to round the building. Jake moved, too, to the corner. He raised his arm and waited, holding his breath.

The man stepped into the open and Jake swung down feeling the sickening thud and the reverberation of the contact all the way up his arm. The man lay at his feet, a gash on the side of his head bleeding profusely. Jake stood there, stunned, unsure of what to do next. The guy was huge, probably close to three hundred pounds. Moving him was not an option. Jake went into the workshop and found a large coil of rope. He grabbed a pair of clippers and, as a last thought, a clean rag to stop the bleeding. After securing the man's hands and feet and propping him up against the building, he pressed the rag to the wound. It was soon oozing with blood. Jake patted him down, locating a gun holstered inside his jacket and a knife in a sheath on his right leg. He was grateful he watched police dramas on TV. Otherwise, he'd have never known where to look.

The guy was breathing but still unconscious. Jake ran to the house to get a towel and bandages. How would he explain a stranger bleeding to death while bound behind his garage? By the time he returned, the guy was coming around and moaning.

While Jake tried to stem the flow of blood and bandage the wound, the guy opened his eyes. He stared groggily at Jake for a moment then his body jerked until he realized he was bound. "What are you doin'?"

Jake sat back on his haunches. "Shouldn't I be asking you that question? What are you doing here? You tried to run me down the other night at the Dairy Dream and now you're sneaking around my house."

The guy closed his eyes and his head dropped back against the garage. "I was lookin' for someone. You're not him, though."

"Him? Who are you looking for?"

The man's eyes glinted in the sunlight. "You know Steve Avery? Or maybe you know him as *Father* Steve Avery?"

Jake's breath caught. This guy wasn't after Shannon. He was the target. "Never heard of him. What did he do?"

"He's wanted back east for child trafficking. I'm an undercover Federal Agent."

"Really? You have identification then?"

"No. Like I said, I'm workin' undercover."

Jake grimaced. "This is your lucky day. I happen to be good friends with the Feds." Jake stood and pulled his cell phone from the front pocket of his jeans. "Don't go anywhere. By the way, you have a name?"

The man glared at him and kicked wildly, trying to free his feet. Jake's Boy Scout training from years ago still paid off. Those ropes weren't coming loose any time soon. Jake walked back toward the house, keeping the guy in is view. He punched in a series of numbers and waited.

"Jake, I don't have anything for you yet," Caleb said.

"Unfortunately, I have something for you." He gave Caleb an accounting of what had happened.

"Oh, for chrissakes. Where is he now?"

"He's tied up behind my garage. He has a pretty nasty gash on his head. I bandaged it, but I think he needs stitches."

"You hit him over the head, then fixed him up?" Caleb chuckled. "You're a piece of work, you know that? Let me get a clean-up crew together. I should be able to pull a few guys from the Seattle office. I'll call you when they get close and give you their names and descriptions. You don't say a word to them. You just point them to your prowler. They'll take it from there. They'll take the bike, too."

"What will they do with him?"

"Find out who he is, for starters, and who he works for. Clean up the area after they take him—hose it down or dig up the ground, get rid of any evidence like blood. And do not tell anyone about this, even your girlfriend."

Jake felt heat sweep up his neck. "She's not my...."

But it was too late to explain. The line was dead. Jake walked back to the man. "Your ride will be here shortly. I'm sorry I had to hit you so hard."

"You coulda killed me, man. You know, you look a little bit like the guy."

"Yeah? Well, I'm not the guy."

"No, really. Check it out, man." He nodded down toward his chest. "There's a picture in my inside pocket."

Jake reached down warily, keeping his eyes on the man's face, and tugged a photo and a cell phone from an inside pocket. He tossed the cell phone aside with the gun and knife, then stared at the photograph. He must have been about twenty-four when this was taken, just recently out of the seminary. The photo held a sincerity and innocence Jake could no longer relate to. It was like looking at the face of a total stranger. What he had told this man earlier was true—he didn't know Steve Avery at all.

After a quick run to the house for water, Jake returned and sat a few feet away from the guy. He'd offered him water and poured from the bottle into the guy's mouth. He was not about to untie his hands.

"So, that girl you were with? That your wife and your kid?"

"No."

"Too bad. She's hot, if you know what I mean."

Jake wanted to punch the guy for talking about Shannon that

way. "It's probably best if you don't talk."

"Ooh. She's not puttin' out, huh? Won't give you a second look, am I right?"

Jake sat in silence, staring at the woods along the property's edge.

"I bet she'd be a wild one, too. You can always tell. Those nice long legs wrappin' around you. Diggin' her heels in and beggin' for more."

Jake leaped to his feet and bent over the man, grabbing the front of his jacket. "Just shut up!"

The man brought his head forward with full force, hitting Jake in the nose and sending him sprawling. Jake felt blood gush over his mouth. The man rolled and got to his knees, trying to get onto his feet, but his ankles where still tightly bound. He dropped again and reached for his gun. Jake was on him, jamming a knee hard on his wrist, his other knee on the man's chest. When in the hell were those guys from Seattle going to get there? He knew it would take them at least another half hour.

"Stop. You're gonna dislocate my shoulder." The man's face contorted with pain.

Jake picked up the knife and held it to his throat. "Don't make me do this."

The man stilled, his eyes wide. "You couldn't let me bleed to death. I know you won't cut my throat."

"I've recently done a lot of things I never thought I would do. If you force me to, I'll add this to my list." Even as he said it, Jake's hand trembled and the blade scraped the outer layer of skin, leaving a narrow red line.

He picked up the gun that was almost within the man's reach and then scuttled backwards. "Don't make another move." He sat with the gun trained on the man's chest. The afternoon sun was straight overhead and perspiration poured down both their faces. Jake wiped a hand across his face to remove the stinging sweat from his eyes. Blood still trickled from his nose and it thumped like hell. He reached for his bottle of water and took a long drink.

The guy nodded to him. "I'm thirsty, too."

"Too bad. You had your chance." A flash of guilt hit Jake. *When I was thirsty, you gave me a drink.* Two things had compelled him to become a priest—the desire to provide service and comfort to those in need and his Irish Catholic grandmother. And, now, here he sat outside a remote mountain cabin holding a gun on another human being who had asked for a drink of water. It took every ounce of strength to sit there and refuse the man, even though he knew the risks.

He glanced at his watch. Shannon must be frantic by now, either wondering what happened to him or thinking he'd simply abandoned her once he got her into the apartment. His phone rang and he saw it was Caleb.

"Three agents are headed your way—Tillman, tall, black, thin; Costello, caucasian, medium height, balding, average build; and a woman, Borghatti, small with dark hair and attitude. They should be there in fifteen." With that, Caleb was gone again.

Less than fifteen minutes passed before Jake heard a vehicle crunch up the gravel drive. Two men in business suits looking every bit like upper echelon law enforcement got out. The woman was dressed in leathers and carried a helmet. The two men approached while the woman, presumably Borghatti, stayed behind, surveying the area.

One of them reached for his gun, calling out, "Drop the weapon."

Jake complied and showed his hands.

Tillman flashed a badge as he approached. "We'll take care of things now. Might be best if you go inside," he said to Jake.

"Why?"

The officer didn't respond, just stared at him and then shifted his gaze toward the house, giving another slight nod. Borghatti strode toward them. "He got the bike keys?"

Jake motioned toward the man on the ground. "Maybe in his pockets."

He watched as Borghatti knelt, placed one knee across the man's chest and one very near his crotch, then dug into his pocket for the keys.

The man had the audacity—or stupidity—to grin up and her. "A little deeper, baby, you'll strike gold." She shifted her knee and dug it into his crotch. He howled with pain before gurgling and turned his head to puke.

"Deep enough?" She stood, holding up the keys, and looked at Tillman. "He's all yours."

Jake felt lightheaded himself, recalling the pain of Shannon's foot making contact with his privates. He almost felt sorry for the guy. "Okay, so I guess I'll go inside and get cleaned up."

Tillman nodded, then he and the other man hauled the biker to his feet. From the foot of the driveway, the motorcycle roared to life, then squealed away.

Jake headed straight for the bathroom, ripping off his bloodied shirt. His nose was red and swollen, and just a little out of line. Sad. In his moments of vanity, he'd always thought his straight nose was his best facial feature. Now his eyes would have to do the job. He cleaned himself up hastily and placed an ineffective bandage across the bump, wincing at the pain that radiated from his touch. He was going to have to stop at the clinic. But, first, he needed to get back to Shannon.

Chapter Sixteen

Shannon paced by the window, soothing an unhappy Bailey when Jake's truck pulled back into the drive. He'd been gone for almost three hours. She unlocked the door and swung it open as his feet pounded up the stairs. Then she gasped. "Jake, what happened to you?"

"I stumbled on something." He sat down heavily on one of the dining chairs.

"Your nose looks broken."

"It is. I had to go back to the cabin to change. Sorry I didn't call."

She leaned closer, examining his face. "Did you get that looked at?"

"Not yet. There's a medical clinic on the other side of town. I wanted to come back for you first." He handed her a brown paper bag. "These are for you."

Opening the bag, she found a plain pair of glasses with tortoiseshell frames. She slid them on and looked around. "How do I look?"

"Like a punk librarian." He grinned, then winced. "Between your hair and the glasses, no one would recognize you as your former self."

"Thanks." She hoisted up the diaper bag. "You need to get medical attention right now."

"I'm not all that eager to have someone manipulate this back into position." But he stood and went ahead of her down the steps. "I don't think we can move your stuff over here tonight. Is tomorrow morning okay?"

A wave of relief washed through her. "Tomorrow is fine. Abe isn't expecting me to help with Helen before Monday, said I'd need a few days to get settled. He managed to get up here while you were gone and really liked the paint job. He told me to let him know if I need anything else, within reason, and he'll provide it. He such a nice man."

"You'll need a crib. I have a job next week, but I was going

101

to make one."

"Oh, no. Dawn told me her oldest daughter has one. I made an offer and she accepted. I just need your help getting it here."

Jake held the truck door open while she fastened Bailey into her car seat. "Not a problem."

The clinic was crowded and Jake insisted she sit down with Bailey while he stood to fill out forms. Shannon rummaged through the diaper bag—formula, bottles, teething ring, everything else under the sun but what she needed right now. A diaper. "Jake, I have to run out and get diapers. I saw a convenience store just down the street."

"I'll go with you. This could take hours."

"No. I don't want you to lose your turn. I'll be fine."

A woman sitting across from her and two chairs down had a baby about Bailey's age in a carrier. "Excuse me, I couldn't help overhearing. I have extra diapers." She handed two to Shannon.

"Oh, thank you. She does not like being wet, but who can blame her?"

"You're welcome. She's adorable. How old?"

"Three and half months. Yours?"

"He's four months. He's been running a fever and I'm sure it's teeth, but my husband insisted I bring him in. Lucas is our first and my husband is overly-protective. I shouldn't complain. Is she her daddy's girl?" The woman smiled and glanced up at Jake.

"She...uh...."

Jake ran and palm softly over Bailey's head. "She sure is. My one and only."

To avoid the conversation going any farther, Shannon excused herself to change the baby. What was he thinking? She fastened the clean diaper into place and ran her fingers lightly over Bailey's tummy, an action that elicited a smile. *Daddy's girl.* She would never be her Daddy's girl—not if Shannon could help it.

When she returned to the waiting room, the woman was gone.

Jake must have read her expression. "I'm sorry. I thought it was easier than an explanation."

He made a good point. "It's fine."

A nurse opened a door to the exam area and called, "Mr. Garber."

Jake stood and hesitated. "Wish me luck."

She grinned. "You don't know pain until you've given birth.

I think you'll survive." She asked the receptionist if she would fill a bottle two thirds of the way with tap water. The water in the cooler would be too cold. Then she scooped in the formula and shook it before offering it to Bailey.

Jake emerged twenty minutes later from the exam area with white tape over the bridge of his nose and very watery eyes. He paid his bill in cash and then came to her.

"Was it bad?" she asked.

"Bad enough." But the words came out as 'bat eduff'. "Let's get out of here. I'm famished."

They picked up take-out from the one Chinese restaurant in town and headed back to the cabin. After dinner, Jake said he had some work to do in the garage. Shannon sat at the computer to check email. Only one unopened message from Brooke. *Eve, I have some vacation time, so Mom and I are going out of town, back home. Will let you know once we arrive. Hope we can chat. You take care. Love, Babs*

Shannon read between the lines and the words. Brooke was taking her mother back to Pennsylvania. That would be fine as long as no one followed them. She would have to wait for the next email for a clue as to where to call them. She couldn't use Jake's phone. That number had been compromised. But the number at her apartment was listed to Abe Swinson, and she had no intention of changing it. She would pay Abe for the costs of the phone and all calls. She made a note for herself to call about internet service at the apartment.

She went to the Governor's website for the State of Missouri, not sure what she expected to find. Corinne Hastings would hardly put her picture up on the website with a big 'Wanted' above it. There she saw photos from the Governor's Ball to raise money for the children's hospital in St. Louis. Pictures of Mark standing next to Corinne, smiling as if he was actually happy, sickened her. She examined his face closely, looking for some part of him in their daughter. Bailey had his mouth, but her eye color and face shape were all Shannon. Thank God for that.

She went to the kitchen for a drink. Standing at the window, she saw Jake digging around the back of the garage. Odd place to plant flowers, she thought. She was on the sofa and flipping channels on the TV when Jake came inside.

"Anything worth watching?" he asked.

"I was looking for a movie, something to take my mind off all that's happened." She looked up. "How's your nose?"

"Better since I took the pain meds the doctor gave me." He dropped into the recliner and put his feet up.

"Is there something you like to watch?" she asked.

"Not especially. You pick."

She browsed the online TV guide. "Ooh, I love this movie."

"What is it?"

"Nights in Rodanthe. Richard Gere and Diane Lane. It's based on a book by Nicholas Sparks."

"Oh. Is that what they call a chick flick?"

"It's Richard Gere."

Shannon found herself caught up in the romantic tension between the characters in the movie. It wasn't until Jake stretched and sat up that she remembered he was there. "I'll be right back," he said.

By the time he returned, the movie had reached its end and Shannon sat sniffling and dabbing her eyes.

"What happened?"

"They fell in love, but didn't end up together."

"I thought you'd seen this before. Didn't you know how it ended?"

"Yes, but I keep hoping for a happier ending."

"Why couldn't they be together?"

"He was on his way to South America to make amends with his son. She's married, but she isn't happy." She blew her nose. "That's what Mark told me, you know. That he hadn't been happy for a long time. That's got to be the oldest line ever. I know it was wrong but, somehow, that made it okay."

"You were in love with him?"

She nodded. "I thought I was. I was bouncing back from a broken engagement. That's no excuse, but an explanation."

He sat down beside her. "I sort of know what that's like, thinking you're doing the right thing and then, wham, it hits you that it was all wrong."

"You do?" She turned her face to gaze at him. "You were in love and it fell apart?"

"You might say that."

Without warning, it hit her—sadness, anger, grief, loneliness—all at once. She hunched her shoulders and wept.

Jake patted her back at first, then put his arm around her to soothe her. She leaned into him, enjoying the warmth and strength of him. His palm moved along her arm and he whispered soothing words to her.

Shannon heaved a deep, shuddering breath and wiped her eyes. She lifted her face to his. The draw was magnetic. Her lips touched his and she was sure she felt a spark. She pressed closer, the kiss deepening. He didn't move into the kiss, but didn't move away. She felt his arms tighten and heat build between them.

She parted her lips and welcomed his exploring tongue. Her breasts strained against his chest.

Easing her down onto the sofa, he moved over her, his body covering hers. His mouth teased her earlobe before leaving a hot trail down her neck. His hand slid beneath her tank top, searing her skin. She slipped her hands beneath his shirt, feeling the firmness and heat of his back.

The evidence of his arousal pressed against her thigh and she moved her leg slightly, causing him to groan.

Then he stopped abruptly and rolled off her, getting his feet under him. "Oh, God. Shannon, I'm so sorry. I don't know what...."

"Jake, it's okay." She sat up, breathing hard.

He turned away from her, dragging his fingers through his hair. "No, it's not okay." He grabbed his keys. "I'm going out for a bit. Lock up behind me and don't answer the phone."

Shannon watched as he strode to the truck and then sped down the driveway like someone was chasing him. She wrapped her arms around herself, feeling the absence of his embrace. She locked the doors and went upstairs, though she knew she wouldn't sleep. Tomorrow she would be out of here. She and Jake would have some distance and maybe eventually he'd tell her why their being together was so wrong.

What had possessed her to initiate that kiss? What must he be thinking of her now? She literally slammed into his life a little over a week ago, a single mother with a baby born out of an affair with a married man. And now she was putting moves on him. He was clearly into it, too. She touched her thigh. Clearly. So what was the problem?

Chapter Seventeen

Jake pulled into the parking lot at Rusty's and sat with the truck idling. He was still trying to catch his breath. If he had any doubts of a mutual attraction between himself and Shannon, that kiss had dispelled them. He hadn't seen that coming, but he also hadn't done anything to stop it. Confusion roiled in his head. His heart still pounded and he needed to sit for another minute.

The parking lot was full, meaning a lot of the guys he had worked with one time or another were likely inside. Maybe a beer or two and a few games of pool would clear his mind. He made his way to the bar.

"What happened to you?" Angie asked.

"I tripped over something."

She slid a Coors in front of him. "I can't believe you drink that stuff. You ever gonna try something different?" she asked.

The question caught him off guard. He'd just tried something different. "Not tonight. Thanks, Angie."

"We don't usually see you here this time of night. Couldn't sleep?"

"Nope." He sipped the beer.

"My Mom's enjoying that baby girl she's minding for your friend."

He grinned. "Bailey. Yeah, she's a cutie."

"And her momma don't look so bad either. What's the story between you two?"

"There's no story. She's a friend. She had car trouble on her way north. Now she's decided to stay here in Snoqualmie for a while."

Angie's eyes twinkled in the overhead lights of the bar. "How good a friend?"

Jake drained his beer and slid off the stool. "Not that kind of friend."

She picked up his empty glass and swiped a rag along the bar. "Too bad."

Jake found Rico and few other construction workers in the

106

back room shooting pool.

"Choirboy, what's with the nose?" Rico asked.

"I ran into something hard."

One of the other guys shouted, "Yeah, I had that happen once, too. It was her husband's fist."

Jake ignored the comment.

"You wanna shoot a game?" Rico asked.

"Yeah, thanks."

By the time Jake checked his watch, it was past one a.m. He placed the pool stick back in the rack. "Time for me to head out. Thanks, guys."

He gave Angie a wave on his way to the door. As he approached the cabin, he saw that every light in the place was on. He sped up, his heart racing as he pulled the truck to a stop and hurried inside.

"Shannon? Hello." He searched the downstairs with no results. He took the steps two at a time to the second floor. "Shannon?"

Her bedroom door opened and she stepped out into the hallway, gun aimed at the floor. "Oh, thank God. Someone was here. A car pulled up in the driveway and just sat there."

"You should have called me." He pulled her close for a moment, then released her and took a step back. "Are you okay?"

"I didn't know where to reach you. I didn't have your cell number. I turned on all the lights and the TV and then locked myself and Bailey in our room."

"What did the car look like?"

"I don't know. It was dark. Whoever it was parked out of range of the outside lights. It looked like a bigger car, black or dark blue. The driver never got out, just sat there for about fifteen minutes, then left."

"How long ago?"

"Half an hour or more."

"I'm really sorry. I should have stayed here." If the biker was after him, then who had come here earlier? Someone to finish what the biker started, or someone looking for Heather Carlson a/k/a Shannon Chase?

"Let's go downstairs so we don't waken Bailey," he said.

In the kitchen, he poured her a glass of wine. "Sip this. It'll help you relax."

She accepted the glass and set it in front of her.

"The car pulled in at the bottom of the drive, sat running, and then pulled out again?" he asked.

She nodded.

"Might have been someone who got lost. They pulled into my driveway to check directions or reset their GPS."

"That makes sense. I'm so on edge, I see someone after me at every turn."

He understood that feeling. "There weren't any calls, were there?"

"No."

He could see her anxiety level dropping as they talked and she drank the wine. "So let's not assume the worst."

"You're right." She finished the wine and stood. "I'm so sorry for crashing into your life and disrupting it this way. You've been more than generous to us."

"I did what any decent human being would do. That's all."

"There aren't that many decent human beings around, though." She bent next to his chair and kissed his cheek. "You're a good man, Jake Garber."

He sat for a while, confused. A good man? A good liar was more like it. It seemed as if his two worlds had collided when Shannon and Bailey crashed into his life. He'd responded to their needs the way he believed a priest should respond. And they'd both found a place in his heart, making him question his priestly vocation. After what he'd done in the past twenty-four hours, how could he call himself a priest?

Weariness overtook him. He walked around turning off lights before ascending the stairs. He had to believe things would work out the way they were intended to. But he hadn't convinced himself the car in the driveway was a coincidence. He doubted he'd convinced Shannon.

~ * ~

Shannon was wakened a few hours later by Bailey, demanding to be changed and fed. Her body felt weighted as she tried to get out of bed. Jake was already in the kitchen brewing coffee. He looked as bad as she felt.

"Good morning," she mumbled.

"Morning."

"What time do you want to leave for the apartment? I'm sure

108

you have work to do, so I can be ready any time." She strapped Bailey into her carrier and prepared a bottle.

"I'll be ready when you are." He poured a cup of coffee and sat at the table, smiling at the baby who smiled right back at him.

"I'll shower, then bring my things downstairs."

"I'm going out to the garage. Give me a shout." He picked up his coffee and strode out the door.

She watched him go, then settled in the living room to feed the baby. She made a mental list of all she still needed—pick up the crib, fill the refrigerator and pantry, arrange for internet service. Until Caleb got back to them with documents, she couldn't even set up a bank account. The thoughts of carrying around eleven thousand dollars in a briefcase made her understandably nervous. But it would all work out. She had to tend to one thing at a time.

By noon, she had her belongings in the apartment, had a good supply of groceries, and Jake had gone to fetch the crib from Dawn Kohler. Abe called up to her from the driveway.

"Oh, hi, Mr. Swinson."

"Can you come down for a minute?"

"Sure. Let me get Bailey." She picked up the baby and slipped into her shoes.

"I want to show you something." He opened the garage door to reveal a very old Buick the size of a small boat. "She doesn't look like much, but she runs."

"That's good."

"I'm not allowed to drive anymore. Cataracts and arthritis in my hands." He held up a gnarled hand. "I've kept the registration and insurance up to date. So I want you to feel free to use the car."

"Me? Oh, but…."

"It would be a big help if you did our grocery shopping. We've been having things delivered and they charge a fortune."

"Well, of course. I'll be happy to."

"And you use it for yourself. Young woman like you, you need to get away now and then, go shopping."

"That's very generous. I'll let you know any time I'm taking the car out."

He shrugged. "Okay. You want to come in and see Helen for a minute? I know she'd like to see the baby."

"I'd love to." She followed him inside.

Helen sat in the middle of the living room in her wheelchair, tilted slightly to one side, a cloth draped on her shoulder and chest to catch the stream of drool. It was sad, Shannon thought, to end up like that.

"Helen, look who's come to see you? Remember Shannon and Bailey?"

Helen rolled her eyes up to look at them and a semblance of a smile tugged at one side of her mouth.

Shannon knelt in front of the woman, balancing Bailey on her knee. "How are you today?

Helen grunted a response.

"I'll be coming to help you out starting on Monday. Bailey will be here, too."

Though Helen couldn't respond, Shannon saw the change in her eyes, a twinkle that said she was happy about this.

She stood and turned to Abe. "What time should I come down on Monday?"

"I give her breakfast at eight, so any time after eight-thirty is fine. She'll need a shower. I can show you how to get her out of the chair and into the shower chair. She has some strength still in her legs and she'll help. You won't have to be here all day. We'll work out the schedule."

"Sound great."

"If anything happens up there and you need help, you just call." He produced a three by five card with a number scrawled on it. "That's our phone number down here. If you was my granddaughter, I'd hope someone was looking out for you."

"Thank you." Her throat ached and tears threatened. She hadn't known her grandparents, but Abe's concern made her think of her mom. She wondered if or when she'd see her again.

"Well, I won't keep you. You probably have lots to do to get settled in. I'm glad you're with us."

"I am, too, Abe." She stopped and waved. "Bye, Helen. We'll see you on Monday."

When Jake returned with the crib, the two of them unloaded it from the truck. Jake stood and stared and the long, narrow steps. "If I take the bottom end, I can support most of the weight. You take the top and just make sure it clears the steps and the railings. Okay?"

"Sure. No problem."

He hesitated. "Should I wear body armor? I mean, you've shot at me and nearly turned me into a eunuch. This task could either

110

go very right or terribly wrong." He grinned.

"I swear I'll try not to hurt you."

They made a slow climb up the stairs with Shannon tugging on the crib and steering it between the building and stair railing. When they got to the top, she set her end down on the landing. "Now what?"

Jake still bore the weight of his end. "Now we take it inside," he grunted.

"Yeah, um…how do we turn it to take it inside? Is it even going to fit through the door?"

He braced the crib against his shoulder and peered around it. "Okay, we'll have to lift it above the rail and angle it."

Shannon looked at the height of the railing. "I don't know."

Under his constant instruction she managed to raise her end high enough for him to lift the crib and swing it above the railing. It barely fit through the door, but was finally in the apartment.

Jake set his end down and stretched, rubbing his lower back. "How can a little baby need a bed that heavy?"

Shannon ran her hands over the crib painted white and decorated with flowers and teddy bears. "This is beautiful."

"I'll get the mattress. It's still in the truck." He plodded back down the stairs and returned. "Dawn says you might want to wipe it down with disinfectant. It's been in her garage."

"I will. Can we take it back to the bedroom?"

"Of course. That'll be easy. It's on wheels and here are the locks." He demonstrated how to lock the wheels so the crib wouldn't move.

Steering the crib into the bedroom without scraping paint as they turned proved another challenge. Soon it was in place against the wall across from the foot of Shannon's bed. The room shrunk considerably with the added furniture, but it would be cozy.

Jake looked around. "So, this is it. You're all set."

"This is it. I can't thank you enough. I'll have you over for dinner some evening to thank you."

Things were suddenly awkward between them.

"That's not necessary. I mean, to thank me. Dinner, now I won't turn that down." He returned to the living room and she followed.

Jake bent over the carrier and grinned at Bailey. "I'm going to miss you, that's for sure."

Shannon swallowed the lump in her throat. "You can come by any time to visit." Then she asked, "Have you heard anything from your friend Caleb?"

"Not yet. He said it might take a week. He's good for his word. If he calls me, I'll let you know. If he calls you, I'd like to know, too."

She nodded.

Jake walked to the door and stood with his hand on the doorknob. "So, I guess I'll see you?"

"I hope so." She took a hesitant step forward and hugged him. "Thank you for everything. You were our Godsend."

Chapter Eighteen

Jake drove back to the cabin. He had gotten behind on a few carpentry projects that would soon be due and needed to make up for lost time. Shannon's parting words kept pinging around in his brain like a pinball, "You were our Godsend." Was that all it had been? God finding a way to use him out here in the middle of nowhere? Or was it the other way around? That Shannon was sent to show him his true path, to give him the clarity he needed to choose his future.

If that was the case, it hadn't worked. He was more confused now than ever. He got out of the truck and stood for a moment, staring at the cabin. It was empty. And it would be empty when he went inside at the end of the day. He wished to hell they'd just capture Lou Crowley and Sara Martin, find out about their possible international trafficking connections, and let Jake go back to New York and testify. It was time to end this. Maybe Caleb's men had been able to get something out of the biker.

Jake unlocked the garage door and stepped inside, turning on the lights and the fans. He looked at the three specialty pieces he needed to finish, chose an ornate headboard a newly-married couple had ordered, and set to work. It felt good to focus on the intricacies of the carving and keep all other thoughts at bay.

Three hours later, Jake stopped for a much-needed break. He went into the cabin and was assaulted with the softest hint of Shannon's shampoo. He popped the tab on a can of soda before realizing it was her diet soda, not his Coke. She'd only been here for a little more than a week. How could she still be everywhere?

He checked the phone to see if Caleb had called the house instead of his cell. But he knew better. Caleb only called his cell. In the living room, he found the little pink stuffed lamb that Bailey liked to cuddle with. She was going to want it. Perhaps he should take it to her, make sure they were okay.

But he stopped himself. He needed to back off, give her time to get settled on her own. She needed more than he could offer. Hell, for all he knew, once they caught up with Crowley and Jake was called back to testify, he might be put back into the program under

113

yet another identity. If not, he'd be returning to his life as Father Steve Avery.

He chugged the soda and crushed the can with his hand, tossing it into the recycling bag. He pulled the door shut behind him and returned to the garage. He needed to work with power tools, maybe drill something.

~ * ~

Shannon rearranged the kitchen cabinets while the tech set up internet service. Since she didn't have a valid ID, she'd arrange with Abe to get the service added onto the phone with the understanding she'd pay the bill. He was more than happy to do so. She was anxious to get online and check email. She glanced at the phone every five minutes, willing it to ring, expecting Jake to call to see how things were going. He didn't.

The technician tapped keys on her laptop. "There you go. You're connected. I've jotted down your web key in case anything happens and you have to log on again. You might want to change it to something you'll remember."

"Thank you. Do I owe you anything?"

He shook his head. "The charges will be added to your next phone bill. You have a good day."

The minute he was out the door, Shannon logged into her Gmail account. A new message from Brooke popped up: *Hi, Eve. Mom and I will arrive tomorrow. We're staying at your second favorite motel. Having a good trip so far. Will talk to you soon? Love, Babs*

Shannon hated that her mother and her best friend got dragged in her mess. But Brooke never took all of her vacation time and her mother was probably enjoying the trip. The clue was too easy—her second favorite motel. Holiday Inn. She preferred the Sheraton when she traveled, which wasn't that often, but Holiday Inn was always her next choice. She looked up motels in Uniontown, Pennsylvania and found the listing for one Holiday Inn, jotting down the phone number.

When the phone rang, she startled. She stared at it or a moment before answering as if it might bite her. "H-Hello?"

"This is Jake's friend, Caleb. I'm sending someone with the items you requested. I'll call once I know they've been delivered, in case you have any questions."

"Caleb? Hello?" But the line was dead.

Twenty minutes later, footsteps sounded on the stairs and someone knocked on the door. Shannon peered between the blinds. A young man peered back and held up an envelope. Shannon opened the door and unlatched the screen.

"Delivery for Ms. Chase," he said.

"That's me." She accepted the envelope. "Thank you."

"Have a nice day." He turned and hurried back down the stairs.

Shannon locked the doors again and sat at the small dinette table, ripping open the manila envelope. She was astounded at what was inside—birth certificates for herself and the baby as Shannon and Bailey Chase, a social security card, a Washington State driver's license, a diploma showing she'd graduated from high school in Akron, Ohio and a liberal arts degree from the University of Akron. Birth records showed that Bailey Chase was born at Akron General Medical Center—father 'unknown.' Shannon winced at that one.

She sat back and stared at the table, the papers that made her a legal person. Everything except passports. She could open a bank account, eventually get another job. More importantly, she could apply for health insurance for Bailey. The one thing she'd have trouble doing was to leave the country.

She went to the phone and called Jake's cell.

"Hi, Abe," he answered.

"It's me," she said. "The phone's still in Abe's name. Your friend, Caleb, is a miracle worker. I just got my identity delivered in a manila envelope. Everything Bailey and I need."

"Great. I knew he'd come through for you."

"Yes, well…." She paused. "I just wanted to thank you."

"You're welcome. Oh, Bailey's stuffed lamb is here. I'll try to drop it by sometime this week."

"I could pick it up. Would you believe Abe gave me keys to his car so I can use it?"

"Good, because he shouldn't be driving."

This new awkward tension between them was almost worse than the previous sexual tension when they were together.

"Everything's okay with the apartment?"

"It's great." She paused. "I won't keep you. I'm sure you have work to catch up. I'll call you about dinner soon. I need to see what my schedule will be with Helen."

"I look forward to it."

"Okay, then. Bye."

"Goodbye, Shannon."

His goodbye sounded much more formal and definite than hers. Maybe Jake had done all he intended for her and now she was truly on her own. And maybe that was for the best. But the thought squeezed at her heart. She liked Jake. She could fall in love with him, but that could not happen.

The phone jangled, startling her. "Hello?"

"I trust the papers are all in order?"

"Yes. Oh, God, yes. Thank you so much."

"There is one thing. Do not leave the country. Don't even try to obtain a passport. It was fortunate you happened to take the name of someone who died without a police record and without leaving much of a trail. This is a temporary fix until your situation is resolved and you can return to your former identity."

"I understand." There went her plans to run to Canada if necessary. "Thank you, again."

"No problem. Good luck, Ms. Chase."

Luck. Her luck did seem to be turning in her favor. Maybe she'd get through her first night alone in the apartment and tomorrow morning would be a new day, the start of a new life.

Chapter Nineteen

Anthony Baker navigated the crowd at Sea-Tac searching for the car rental counters. He could cheerfully strangle his brother-in-law. He knew from the beginning of his sister's marriage to Mark Hastings that the guy couldn't keep it in his pants. Anthony had tried to tell her, but she wouldn't listen. And now he had to clean up Mark's latest mess.

It pissed him off. He was nothing more than a janitor. Corinne had always been the golden child. He'd always been the screw up. From the time he was born, he'd been considered a mistake. Corinne was fifteen years his senior and had been the only child until her sophomore year of high school. Then he was born—unexpected and, he always felt, unwanted. His parents' unhappy accident. No matter how hard he tried to get attention, to prove himself worthy of being a Baker, his efforts gained him nothing. At least not until he tried a different approach—and that gained him a police record and short stint in Juvenile Detention.

Corinne relied on him to do the dirty work, fearing she couldn't trust anyone on her own security staff. He should have driven from Jefferson City. That way, he could have brought his own supplies. He wasn't used to walking around unarmed. How much trouble could a one-hundred-ten pound girl present? He'd try to reason with her and, if that didn't work, he'd have to resort to Plan B. Or perhaps Plan B would be his best course of action in the first place.

He signed for the rental and picked up his bag. Once inside the car, he programmed the GPS with the address he'd tracked from the phone call. This should only take a day, maybe two.

After a stop for lunch, Anthony drove into Snoqualmie. He located a B&B on the edge of town and secured a room. Then he went for a walk. Time to scope out the community. He found a quaint town with boutiques, cafés, and Native American craft stores lining the streets. People nodded or smiled a welcome as he walked by. The sidewalks were surprisingly crowded. Tourists. Better for him. Unlikely he would be remembered.

He'd wait until dark to check out the house where Heather Carlson was supposedly staying. He wondered about the guy who'd answered the phone the few times he called. It sure hadn't taken her long to move on from Mark. Maybe they were two of a kind. He wondered how the new guy felt about taking on another guy's kid. If things went according to plan, the kid wouldn't be an issue much longer.

He ducked into a café for coffee. A smiling waitress approached. She set down a glass of water and handed him a menu. "May I get you something else to drink?"

He glanced at her name tag. "Thanks, Millie. I'll have coffee."

"Just coffee? We have homemade pie. Today's specials are blackberry and peach."

"Homemade? Did you make them?" He flashed a grin.

Millie flushed a little. "No. That's why they're special. Naomi, the owner, is a master with pies."

"Then I should have a slice. Peach. With ice cream."

She picked up the menu. "It'll be just a minute."

Anthony browsed the other patrons. At mid-afternoon, the place wasn't too busy. A few families at tables on the other side of the café, a group of men at the counter enjoying Naomi's special pies, and one guy sitting by himself in a booth.

Millie returned with a steaming mug of coffee and huge slice of warm peach pie melting a scoop of vanilla ice cream on its top. "Here you go. Enjoy."

"I know I will." He dug his fork into the pie. She hadn't lied. It was great. When she returned to warm his coffee, Anthony pulled a photo from his jacket. "Millie, did you ever see this woman around town?"

She took the photo of Heather Carlson and studied it. "She looks familiar, but…." She glanced toward the guy sitting alone, then carried the photo to him. "Hey, Jake. Check this out. Looks a lot like your friend, Shannon."

Jake and Shannon. Bingo.

Jake looked at the photo, then shook his head. "Nah, it's not Shannon. Look at the eyes—all wrong. And that's not her nose, either. Does look a little like her." He handed the photo back and returned to this lunch.

Millie handed the picture back to Anthony. "I thought I knew her, but seems I'm mistaken."

Anthony tucked the photograph back into his pocket. "No problem. My brother's daughter. Took off after a family dispute. You know how that happens. Last we heard she was in this area, along with my grand-niece. Cute little thing."

Her eyebrows furrowed. "A baby, huh? I hope you find them. You want anything else?"

"No, just the check." He pulled a five dollar bill from his wallet. "And this is for you."

Anthony watched as Jake left the café. Now he had a face to go with the name of the guy on the phone. The guy who would eventually lead him to Heather. This was his lucky day. He smiled. Maybe he'd spend a few hours at the casino later.

~ * ~

Jake sat in his truck and watched the café door through his side mirror, waiting for the man to leave. It only took two minutes. The guy was about his height, a little heavier, with short brown hair, probably in his late twenties. He looked like half the guys you'd pass on the street. He wore jeans, a golf shirt and a sports jacket. And he was looking for Shannon. Or, rather, for Heather. Fortunately, she hadn't spent that much time in town, so few people would recognize her.

Life had been much simpler when he was only looking over his shoulder for someone out to get him. Now he'd been thrust into the position of protecting Shannon and Bailey. He couldn't call Caleb for one more thing. If his life continued to attract so much chaos, they'd move him and assign a new identity. He couldn't go to the local police because all he had on this guy was that he was a stranger in town. Hell, if they arrested all the strangers that came to Snoqualmie, the business district would fold.

He needed to warn Shannon. He waited until the guy had walked a few blocks in the opposite direction, then pulled his truck away from the curb.

Shannon was seated on the top step with Bailey in the carrier behind her on the landing. She smiled when she saw Jake. Then her smile faded. "Something's wrong."

He reached the step below her and sat. "There's a guy showing your picture around town."

"Who is he?"

"I don't now. About my height, a few more pounds on him,

dark brown hair, about thirty, give or take. Nothing remarkable. Sound familiar?"

"Yeah, like a hundred other guys. Did you talk with him?"

He shook his head. "No. He was asking Millie at the café. She brought the photo over to me, but I convinced her it wasn't you, just someone who looks like you. I don't think that guy's leaving any time soon, though."

She stood. "I have to get out of here." Tears filled her eyes.

Jake stood and reached for her hand. "Wait. Give it a day or two. You don't look at all like that photograph and no one in town will recognize you in the picture."

"I can't be sure of that." She picked up the carrier and opened the door.

Jake followed her inside. "If someone tracked you because of that phone call to your mother, they tracked it to my place. You should be safe here. Just don't go walking the streets of town for a few days. If you need anything, call me."

She lifted Bailey from the carrier and the baby spied Jake and grinned. Jake reached for her. "Hey, how's my girl?"

Bailey sputtered and snuggled her face under his chin.

"I can't live like this, always waiting for the other shoe to drop, for someone to break down the door and take her from me." Shannon sank down on the sofa.

Bailey whimpered and Jake sat down beside Shannon so the baby could see her. "Are you going to run forever, always watching to see if they're behind you?"

She glared at him. "What do expect me to do? Just hand her over to Mark and his wife? That woman is a modern-day walking version of Cruella de Ville. Even if I'd been inclined toward placing Bailey for adoption, I couldn't imagine someone like that raising her."

"I'm not suggesting you hand her over. I'm only suggesting that you take a stand."

"Mark is her biological father. He could have me dragged back to Missouri and file for partial custody. He could even try to get full custody."

"Okay, so let's come up with a better plan. You think about it while I change this one's diaper. Are her things all in the bedroom?"

Shannon nodded and let out heavy breath.

Jake changed the baby and placed her in her crib. "Your

mommy and I need to talk. Okay?" He turned on the mobile that hung over the crib.

Returning to the living room, he found Shannon standing at the window, arms crossed over her chest. He walked to her and put a reassuring hand on her shoulder. "I'll do everything I can to help you."

She turned to face him. "Why?"

"Why? Because… Because it's the right thing to do. Because I care."

She stared into his eyes as if searching for the truth. He hoped she saw it there. She took a step forward, leaning against him, her cheek on his chest. Slowly her arms went around him and she held on. Her body began to shake as tears fell. "I've never been so scared."

He drew her close, the top of her head grazing his chin. "I know."

"My best friend got my mother out of town for the week. I arranged a call to them today. It's so hard. I could hear the fear in my mom's voice. I convinced her to stay with my aunt for a while. I know she's only doing it because it'll make me feel better."

Jake gave her a hug, then released her. "Surely they'll give up on this before long. Wouldn't you think the Governor's main interest is in having her husband's love child out of the picture?"

"You'd think so, but not if I know Corinne Hastings. She wants revenge. She wants to win at any cost and that means I have to lose. And the only thing I have to lose is Bailey." She walked away, once again folding her arms in front of her as if for protection. "That man asking about me works for Corinne."

"Give him a day or two. He won't find Heather Carlson here and he'll move on."

She nodded. "I hope you're right." She went to the kitchen and opened the oven. "I made lasagna. I want to take some down to Abe and Helen. They eat early. Do you mind staying for minute with Bailey?"

He sniffed the aroma coming from the pan. "I wouldn't even mind staying for dinner."

"And you're welcome to. I just need to let this cool a bit before I cut it. Are you hungry now?"

"No, I had a late lunch."

She glanced at the wall clock. "Bailey will be ready for her dinner soon. I'll have to get a highchair in a week or so. She's almost ready for cereal and baby food." She prepared a bottle of the formula and set it aside. Just as she began to cut the lasagna, Bailey could be heard fussing in the bedroom. Shannon went to get her.

"I guess I'll feed you before I feed Abe and Helen."

"I could feed her," Jake said.

"Oh. If you don't mind."

He reached for the baby. "Will you have dinner with me, Mademoiselle?" He picked up the bottle and sat in the rocker. Bailey stared up at him for a moment, then sucked vigorously on her bottle. One hand rested on her tummy, the fingers of the other wrapped around Jake's little finger. He started to feel all warm and fuzzy inside. He smiled up at Shannon. "I think it's safe for you to go."

She grinned. "The way to that girl's heart is through her stomach."

"Yeah? What's the way to your heart?" At the look on her face, he wished he could erase that last question. But it just hung there between them.

"I like food, too." She wrapped the plate of lasagna and then bagged brownies from another platter. "I'll be right back."

Chapter Twenty

Jake looked around at the feminine touches Shannon had added to the apartment—a few ruffled toss pillows on the sofa, flowers on the dinette table, varying colored scatter rugs on the newly polished hardwood floors. It felt homey and comfortable. How had she accomplished that in such little time—turned this place into a home?

He lifted Bailey onto his shoulder and patted her back. She rewarded him with a resounding burp. "Nice one." He laid her on his thighs so she could lookup at him. Her feet kicked at his stomach and she gave him a wet grin. The tiniest nub of a tooth showed on her gums. "Look at you growing teeth. You'll be demanding steak in no time."

Shannon came in the door, laughing. "And you'll buy it for her. Otherwise she'll have to be content with chicken."

"How are Abe and Helen?"

"Good. Abe was happy to not have to cook dinner. I think my job description just might be expanded." She went into the kitchen and grabbed two brownies, then came back to where he sat. "Appetizer?"

"Isn't that dessert?"

She blushed, something that endeared her even more to him. "I don't have cheese and crackers."

He took the brownie and bit into it, careful not to drop crumbs on the baby in his lap. "Delicious."

"Thanks." She sat on the sofa. "I always add a little extra chocolate fudge sauce." She gazed at the baby. "She's very content there."

"If she falls asleep, I may be spending the night in this chair."

"Do you mind if I check my email?" she asked, nodding to the laptop on a folding TV tray beside him. "But don't get up. She's been fussy lately. It's good to see her quiet." She opened her email and squatted down beside the rocker. "Nothing new."

"Do you have a photo of Mark Hastings, so I'd know him to see him if he came around?"

She shook her head. "I don't. Oh, wait." She pulled up a website for the Governor of Missouri then clicked on one of the links. Photographs popped up of the people dressed in formal attire. Shannon pointed to a photo of the Governor and a tall, handsome man standing beside her, smiling. "That's Mark. And this…" She pointed. "…is the great Governor Corinne Baker Hastings at a fundraising ball for Children's Hospital in St. Louis. If people only knew the truth." She clicked in the upper corner and the web page disappeared.

Bailey gurgled and kicked and he bent to smile down at her. When Shannon turned her head to look at the baby, their faces were just inches apart. She blinked, her eyes the deepest shade of turquoise he'd ever seen. His heart stuttered.

He wasn't sure if he moved closer, if she did, or it was both of them but, before their lips could meet, Bailey let out a wail that startled them both.

Shannon pulled back so abruptly she lost her balance and landed on her backside at his feet.

Jake laughed. Then lifting the baby onto his shoulder, he stood and offered Shannon a hand. That blush returned to her face and gave him a warm feeling as he hauled her to her feet.

"She's needs a nap. I'll be right back." Shannon took the baby and hurried down the hall.

He should leave. He should just make an excuse and leave right now.

"Ready for dinner?" Shannon returned and moved smoothly around the small kitchen, setting a bowl of tossed salad on the table along with two bottles of dressing. "We can begin with salad while the lasagna and garlic bread warm a bit. I'm sorry I don't have a bottle of wine."

"Whatever you have is fine." He sat at the small table.

"Iced tea or water."

"Tea, please." He unfolded the paper napkin and laid it in his lap.

Dinner was pleasant, though quiet, with both of them lacking for small talk. He noticed the way she tensed when a motorcycle passed and again when a truck backfired. She was more on edge than ever now that she knew someone had come looking for her. And he understood that feeling. "Are you going to be okay tonight?" he asked.

"I have to be, I suppose. It unnerves me to know they're here."

She said it as if an alien force had landed to invade. "You want me to stay tonight? The sofa looks comfortable enough."

Her relief was evident as her body relaxed and she exhaled. "Yes, please. I was trying to find a way to ask you, but you've already done so much."

"Not a problem." He picked up their empty plates, but she took them from him. "I'll do the dishes."

"Okay, but…." He glanced toward the platter of brownies. "Is there dessert?"

"Sure. Want coffee? I can make decaf." She carried the dishes to the sink.

"I'll make the coffee while you rinse those plates. How's that?"

The kitchen proved too small for two people, especially if those two people were struggling to keep some space between them. Every time he turned around, she was running smack into him. Finally, he took the plates from her hands, turned her around and guided her to the sofa. "Sit. I'll serve the dessert and coffee, or one of us is going to get hurt. And past experience tells me it'll be me."

She laughed. "I can see why you'd think that. I'm not armed—at the moment."

He loved hearing her laugh. At least he'd been able to take her mind off things for a little while.

They had dessert and watched an old episode of Law and Order. Shannon stood and stretched. "I'm going to turn in. I'll get you a sheet, blanket and pillow." She went to the bedroom and returned with bedding and a towel and washcloth. "Do you need anything else?"

"No. This is fine. Thanks."

"I'll be getting up in a few hours to feed Bailey. I'll try to be quiet."

"Don't worry. I sleep like the dead." Then he laughed. "That's probably not comforting since I'm here to make you feel more secure."

"If someone tries to get in here tonight, I assure you, you'll wake up. Goodnight."

"Goodnight."

He waited until she'd finished in the bathroom and closed her

125

bedroom door. He kicked off his shoes and socks and spread the sheet and blanket on the sofa. When he laid down and settled on the pillow she'd given him, he realized it must have been from her bed. It bore her scent and was going to drive him crazy. He closed his eyes and willed himself to sleep.

~ * ~

Shannon tiptoed into the kitchen, hoping Bailey didn't waken Jake. She prepared the bottle then eyed the rocking chair on the other side of the sofa. It was the best place to sit to feed Bailey. She retrieved Bailey from her crib and crept to the rocker. Only a dim nightlight burned above the sink and cast soft shadows around the room. Shannon eased into the rocker. She watched Jake sleeping. He had removed his shirt and was barefoot, sleeping in his jeans. His hair was tousled and he snored softly. He was beautiful and heat in her chest burned, traveling downward. She squirmed and shifted the baby in her arm, focusing on Bailey.

As the baby fed, Shannon watched her face, the subtle changes she was beginning to notice. She kissed Bailey's forehead and, when she looked up, saw Jake watching her.

"I'm sorry if I woke you," she whispered.

"You didn't." He continued to stare. "What time is it?"

"Four-thirty. It'll be daylight soon. She's about finished." A moment later the baby spit out the nipple. Shannon stood and passed Jake, stopping to set the bottle on the counter. Once Bailey was back in her crib, Shannon returned to the kitchen to rinse the bottle. But she found Jake standing at the sink, doing that very thing. He rinsed the bottle and nipple under steaming water and set them aside to air dry.

She couldn't help revisiting their brief exploration a few nights earlier. The heat that made her squirm earlier now built into a current. He dried his hands and turned toward her. After a glance, his eyes darkened. She walked to him and snaked her arms around him.

He remained still for a moment, then pulled her close, his hands on her hips. His mouth crushed down on hers, stealing her breath. He backed her toward the sofa.

Shannon stroked his back and tilted her head back to give him better access to her throat. His mouth seared her flesh. She reached down and gripped the hem of her tank top, pulling it over her head.

Jake gave her breasts an appreciative gaze before lowering

his mouth to taste first one and then the other. Shannon gasped as his tongue swept over each nipple. His hands massaged her bottom, pulling her against him so that she felt his desire. She fumbled with the button and zipper of his jeans, slipping her hand inside to stroke him.

Jake groaned at her touch. She grasped the waistbands of his jeans and boxers and pulled them down, then wriggled out of her own pajama bottoms. They stood there in the dim light, naked, breathing raggedly.

"Jake."

He must have heard the invitation in her utterance, because he stepped forward, pressing his body to hers, and kissed her deeply. Her body responded as if struck by lightning, every nerve ending thrumming wildly. His tongue danced with hers and she moaned, feeling his arousal against her sensitive apex.

She backed to the sofa and pulled him down on top of her. She was afraid to say a word for fear it would snap them both out of this spell. Jake lowered his face to her breast, then slowly kissed his way down her belly. Her hips lifted of their own accord, her fingers tangled in his hair.

When his mouth once again covered hers, she shifted position and opened herself to him. She was almost there, cresting the wave, when Jake's body arched and he collapsed on top of her.

Between heavy breaths, he said, "I'm sorry. It's…uh…been a long time."

"It happens. It's okay." She shifted and spooned back against him. "Just hold me."

Jake wrapped his arms around her. "That pretty much sucked for you, huh?"

"You have a lot to learn about women. Intimacy for us is about more than an orgasm, though that's nice, too. There's always next time." This time had been spontaneous. Would there be a next time? She wondered what he thought of her so easily opening herself to him in more ways than one.

He held her close, the rhythm of their breath matching.

"Jake, I know it might not seem like it, but I really don't sleep with every man I meet. I was with Mark for two months and, once I knew I was pregnant and told him, he didn't come near me again." She turned in his arms to face him. "I don't want you to think I just jump into the sack with everybody."

127

He gazed into her eyes, his arms holding her against him. She could feel his heartbeat. "You don't have to explain yourself to me." He pressed his lips to hers in a sweet, soft kiss.

This time he took his time exploring her body—every single inch of her body. This time her pleasure seemed to be his only goal and the man was focused. When she arched against him for the second time and dug her heels into his back, Jake let go as well. They lay together for a moment, panting, then laughing.

She wakened as the first light of morning shone outside the window. Jake lay behind her, pressed against the sofa back. His arm held her tightly against him. She needed to pee, but didn't want to wake him. Perhaps she could slip back into his embrace, if she could first get out of it. She pried his arm loose and lifted it, sliding to the floor and locating her pajamas.

She looked in on Bailey who was sleeping soundly, then used the bathroom. When she returned to the living room, however, she found Jake standing and zipping up his jeans. He tugged his shirt over his head, then sat to pull on his socks and shoes.

He looked at her with a mixture of wonder and embarrassment. "Good morning."

"Morning. I'm sorry I woke you. It's still early."

"That's okay. I'm working in Seattle today. I need to get an early start."

Confused by his abrupt and hurried preparation for departure, she asked, "Do you want breakfast or coffee?"

"No, thanks. I'll pick something up."

It seemed like he couldn't get of there fast enough. Had she misread what happened between them last night?

"Jake?"

He gazed at her. "I shouldn't have let that happen."

"I could have stopped it, too."

"I'm afraid I've given you the wrong impression. I can't…. I'm not…." He closed his eyes and drew in a breath. "I have to go. I'll call you later." With that, he strode out the door and pounded down the steps. His truck engine roared to life and the truck squealed out of the driveway.

The spell was sufficiently broken. She stared at the rumpled sheet and blanket, then sat down and cried. She felt stupid and cheap and used, and so very lonely.

Chapter Twenty-One

Jake drove home like a maniac, nearly wiping out on the same tree that had brought Shannon to him. He stripped on his way to the shower. No amount of soap and water could wash away the guilt, remorse and embarrassment he felt. He had no right to use Shannon in this way, to let her think they could have a future. He was no better than the men who had come to him for confession years earlier, telling of their sins of the flesh and promising God they'd never do it again. Until the next time.

She had felt so good in his arms, her skin against his skin, her eyes closed as she moved beneath him, taking him into her. And then, like a horny sixteen year old, he'd misfired. She was so damned understanding it made him want to cry. But that next time. My God, that second time.

Now he felt sick. He couldn't imagine where to go from here. Would Shannon expect this new intimacy in their relationship to continue? Jake admittedly didn't know much about women. But he knew that moving from a friendship—a very brief friendship—to an intense physical relationship meant something. If he were honest, he'd admit it meant something to him. Something he wasn't free to act on. Even though he already had. How in the hell would he ever explain this to her? Show up at her door dressed in clerics and say, "There's something I should have told you?" What if he just never called, didn't see her again? He'd be no better than the other men in her life who had used her and hurt her. And he wanted to be better than that. He wanted Shannon and Bailey in his life.

He dried off, wrapped the towel around his waist and returned to the bedroom. His cell phone lay on the dresser. He picked it up and punched in Caleb's number. His call went to voicemail. "Caleb, it's Jake. We need to talk as soon as possible."

There, he'd initiated a conversation. He would tell Caleb he'd give whatever additional testimony was needed to nail the coffin shut on Lou Crowley and Sara Martin, once they caught up with them. Jake would let them videotape, give him a lie detector test to prove the truth of his testimony, do whatever they wanted. But he had to end this charade now. He had to get himself free.

After getting dressed and grabbing a quick breakfast, he loaded the carved pieces into his truck to be delivered to two customers in Seattle. By the time he returned home this evening, he'd hopefully figure out what to say to Shannon. He'd promised to call, and he would to that.

~ * ~

Lou Crowley shoved a stack of clean shirts into a suitcase. "You want something done, you just have to do it yourself."

"I don't like this, Lou. It's not safe to go back." Sara chewed on her thumbnail.

"You don't need to worry about it. You're not going. Besides, I'm not going back, I'm going to Washington State." He zipped the bag closed. "Bruno found Avery and now Bruno's in the wind. He's not answering calls. But I know where to find Avery now, and it's time to end this."

"It's already ended if we just leave things alone. Please don't go," Sara pleaded.

"The Feds won't stop looking for us, you know that." Lou laughed. "Don't you find it ironic that they moved Avery to Washington State, practically our back yard? It's like they want me to find him."

"He's already told them about our involvement with Alvin and the kids, and I'm sure Alvin's given them an earful, too. Lou, we've been here for almost two years. I like it here. No one knows who we are. We have good friends. Why risk all of that?"

He whirled on her. "You don't get it, do you? This is about one thing only—revenge. Avery was a pain in my ass from the start. The shining star of our graduating class at the seminary. Father Perfect."

She stared at him. "Tell me again why you became a priest in the first place?"

"We've been through this. What better cover? At least it was until people started screaming rape and every priest was suspect. But not Father Avery. Everyone loved him. If he'd just looked the other way, followed the code and kept his mouth shut."

"When will you be back?"

"Don't know. It'll take as long as it takes." He picked up his bag and grinned at her. "Wish me luck." He leaned in to kiss her, but she pulled away. He sighed. "I'll call."

"Wait. I'm going with you." Sara pulled a suitcase from the closet and laid it open on the bed.

"You couldn't have decided this sooner?"

Crowley punched the address Bruno had given him into his GPS. It would be a twelve hour drive, give or take. He drove out of Logan, Utah and headed west. If they drove straight through, they'd reach Snoqualmie around midnight. He'd locate the house, make sure this Jake Garber was Steve Avery, then make sure he was dead for good.

Sara fussed with her seat belt. "How long is the drive?"

"Twelve hours."

"Where will we stop for the night?"

"We won't. With two of us to drive, there'll be no problem driving straight through."

Sara played with her iPhone. "We go through Boise."

"Yeah, so?"

"There are things to do in Boise. I've never been there. Oh, look, there's a Casablanca-style café. I loved that movie. Can we stop there?"

Lou slid a glance toward here. "This isn't a freakin' vacation."

She blanched at his tone. "We're goin' there anyway. I don't see the big deal."

Her finger slid across the screen of the phone. "Okay, so when you're finished with business, can we drive over to Seattle and see the Space Needle?"

Lou made a hard right into the parking lot of a Dunkin' Donuts and slammed on the brakes. "You didn't want to come. I was fine with that. Then you decide to come along. I was fine with that. But hear this—" He turned in the seat and leaned toward her. "This is not a vacation. This is not a trip to see the tourist sights. I'm here to kill a man," he shouted.

Sara flinched and cowered. "Okay. I'm sorry. I just thought…."

"Well, don't think." Lou shifted into drive and peeled from the lot, narrowly missing a minivan. The driver laid on the horn and flipped him a one-fingered salute.

Lou stuck his arm out the window and returned the signal. "Asshole."

He thought about his life, growing up in Trenton, with a

drunk for a mother and a dead-beat con man for a father. The only place he'd felt safe as a kid was at the church. He was an altar boy. Not an angel, by any means. But the priest, Father Corrigan, believed in him, thought he had potential. That priest probably kept Lou out of Juvie. His own decision to pursue the priesthood had a double motive. On one hand, he thought just maybe his having Father Corrigan come into his life at a difficult time was a sign of where he was heading. On the other hand, he saw how loved and trusted the priest was. What a great cover. He was, after all, his father's son.

Then he met Steve Avery. Father Squeaky Clean, all high ideals and piety. No matter what Lou did, he could never measure up, never have all the right answers. He got drummed out of the priesthood after some money went missing and Lou had been to the casino for a long weekend. He didn't get it. Other priests got away with much worse, just a got a slap on the hand and changed to a new parish. But Lou, no, there was no mercy for Lou.

Alvin Martin saw some redeeming qualities in Lou. The dumbass actually thought he was helping Lou to help poor orphan kids connect with good homes. Sara was a good actress, he'd give her that. She'd convinced Alvin everything was above board, at least until he was in too deep to do anything about it.

Just Lou's dumb luck that Father Perfect was assigned to Alvin's parish. And he screwed up everything. Lou's fingers tightened around the steering wheel, imagining it was Steve Avery's neck. He sure the hell hoped Bruno got things right before he fell off the earth, that this Jake Garber was Steve Avery incognito.

Everybody thought Avery was dead. Lou would just make that a reality.

They'd driven in silence for over two hours before Sara said, "Lou, I have to pee. Can we stop?"

He shook his head. Not only did they not need to take forever to get to Snoqualmie, wherever the hell that was, they didn't need to make a lot of stops and risk finding their pictures posted on some damned bulletin board. Sara had gotten far too comfortable with their anonymous life in Utah. But they were still wanted by the Feds.

He exited off of 86 at Twin Falls and found a fast food joint. "We might as well have lunch."

"What do you think happened to Bruno?" Sara asked before popping a fry into her mouth.

"Hell if I know. He wasn't too happy about being stuck in that town. He may have just given up and ridden off."

"What if he got caught?"

"If he has any sense at all, he'll keep his trap shut."

"What if Steve killed him?"

Lou snorted. "Father Do-Right? Are you kidding?" He crumpled the wrappers from his burger and fries. "Hurry up. We need to get back on the road. I'm gonna hit the men's room." While washing this hands, Lou looked at himself in the mirror. He'd watched the court proceedings against Alvin on TV. The Bishop had testified and had called Lou "soulless." As far as Lou was concerned, religion was built on the premise of the existence of both good and evil. Without evil, how would one recognize good? He was just playing a role, fulfilling his calling. Hadn't Judas been just as important as Peter in that regard?

When they got back into the car, Sara turned on the radio and flipped through the channels—over and over and over.

"Pick one or turn it off," Lou ordered.

She turned it off and faced him. "What is wrong with you? All you've done is snipe at me since we left Logan. Before we left, even."

"I'm sorry, okay. Gimme a break." He paused. "Tell you what. Since we're so close by, when I finish the job, we'll go see that Space Needle."

Sara smiled. "Thanks. Maybe we can take the long way home."

Lou shook his head. Maybe Steve Avery wasn't the only thing he needed to get rid of. They were going through the money fast now. He needed a new resource, or he needed to reduce his spending. He'd thought about moving up to Canada, but it was hard to take up residence there. Mexico, now that would be a new market for him. He already had connections there.

It was close to one a.m. when Lou drove into Snoqualmie. He pulled into the parking lot of a closed grocery store and checked the address Bruno had given him. Looked like he was only about three miles from the Garber place. He'd check out the location tonight, then find a place to crash.

A light misty rain had begun to fall, just enough to make the wipers necessary. "Turn right in thirty feet," the robotic voice told him. "Drive four fifths of one mile. Your destination is on the left in thirty feet."

Lou slowed when he saw the sign indicating a sharp curve. Just beyond the curve, he saw the mailbox: J. Garber. He'd arouse too much suspicion if he pulled into the drive at this hour. He kept moving until he found a place to turn around. On his return trip, he discovered a pull-off just around the curve. Perfect for his morning observation.

Sara snorted and coughed, then wakened. "Are we there yet?" She sat up and blinked. "Where the hell are we?"

"The middle of nowhere. Garber's place is just behind us around that curve. Let's find a room."

The desk clerk at the small motel on the edge of town was not all that happy to be called to the desk. He yawned and buzzed the outer door open.

"You got a room?" Lou asked.

"Single, double, or king?"

"King."

"Smoking or non?"

"Non." Lou presented his ID and a credit card. He'd purchased the fake ID for five hundred bucks. Good investment.

The clerk ran the credit card, copied his ID, and slid a registration form across the counter for his signature. "That'll be one twenty-nine a night."

"Jesus, who do you think you are? Conrad freakin' Hilton?"

"No, sir. It's peak tourist season. How many nights?"

"Two." He filled in the form indicating two adults and signed the charge slip.

"You're in 206 around the back. Have a good night."

Lou took the small cardboard folder containing two key cards. He drove to the back of the building, removed their bags from the trunk, and followed Sara up the steps.

Inside the room, he sniffed. "I should just bring Avery's body here. The room already smells like something died in it."

"Turn on the AC. That'll help," Sara said.

He was getting really sick and tired of her attitude, her optimism.

While Sara unpacked, Lou went to take a shower. His muscles were in knots after more than twelve hours of driving. When he came back to the bedroom, Sara was already snoring softly. He opened his bag and removed his gun, checking it for readiness for morning. Lifting the weapon, he aimed it toward Sara. "Pow," he said softly and smiled.

Chapter Twenty-Two

Shannon sat in the rocker with one knee drawn up to her chest and her chin resting on her knee. She was grateful that Abe hadn't said a word about Jake's truck being parked outside her place all night. She felt on the verge of tears ever since Jake's hasty departure a few hours earlier, and the slightest thing just might cause the dam to break. After helping Helen get washed and dressed and feeding her breakfast, Shannon returned to her apartment. She wouldn't be needed again until lunch.

Now she sat and rocked, staring at the sofa and remembering the feel of Jake's arms around her. The feel of his body skin-to-skin with hers. A warm hum rolled through her. She barely knew this man and, yet, felt like she belonged with him. Things had heated up so fast between them. She knew she shouldn't trust that, but she wanted to. She wanted to trust Jake.

She stretched her legs and then stood. Maybe it was time to relax and act like she belonged in this town. She was tired of running and hiding. Even Jake told her she looked nothing like the photo of the former Heather Carlson. As soon as Bailey was awake, she'd take Abe up on his offer and take the car for a spin around town. Maybe they'd stop at the café for lunch. She remembered seeing a second hand shop in town. Perhaps she could find a stroller and a playpen there for the baby.

Bailey woke in a good mood and smiled as Shannon strapped her into the car seat. Shannon climbed into the driver's seat, moved the seat forward, then looked in the rear view mirror. The car seemed to fill the entire garage. She'd never driven anything this big. She eased off the brake at the same time she stepped on the gas. The car leaped backward. She hit the brake again, then slowly backed out of the garage, checking both side mirrors to make sure they remained intact.

She stopped once she was clear of the garage and pressed the remote to close the door. Abe stood on his back porch watching her with an expression that was a mixture of amusement and concern. She smiled and waved. It didn't take long for her to get a feel for handling the larger vehicle. Parallel parking would not be on her agenda today.

After parking in a lot behind Yesterday's Treasures, she removed Bailey from her car seat and headed into the store. Twenty minutes later, she left pushing Bailey in a stroller and guiding one of the employees to the car to put a folding playpen in the trunk. She left the car parked there and cruised the main street, browsing shop windows.

The café was busy, but she managed to find a small table for two and pulled the stroller up beside her.

Millie came toward her with a menu in hand. "She is such a sweet baby. Can I get you something to drink?"

"Iced tea, please." She grinned, realizing the waitress didn't recognize her as Jake's brunette friend.

When the waitress returned, she set down the tea and pulled an order pad from her pocket. "What can I getcha?"

Shannon ordered a grilled chicken salad. It felt good to do something normal. Seated by the window, she watched people stroll by while she ate. She felt as if she'd been set free from some invisible prison.

When Millie returned with her check, she studied Shannon for a moment. "Do I know you?"

Shannon shook her head. "They say everyone has a double somewhere."

"I guess that's it. I love your hair, by the way. I've often thought of having mine cut short."

"Thanks. The salad was delicious, by the way." She handed Millie cash that included a healthy tip—recompense for her little white lie.

Outside, the sun shone brightly and the temperatures had risen into the upper seventies. Shannon donned her sunglasses and took her time strolling to the parking lot. On her way to the car, she glanced down at Bailey and ran smack into some guy with a camera. They were the only two on the sidewalk and the contact made her immediately suspicious. He apologized, she told him she was fine and kept moving so he couldn't get a good look at her. She hated feeling suspicious of everyone.

She had one more stop to make for groceries, then she'd head home. Abe had told her not to worry about lunch, that he'd take care of it. She wanted to make something special for dinner and share it with the couple. When she reached the turn for the apartment, though, she kept driving. She needed to see Jake. He'd never brought Bailey's stuffed lamb to her. She could use that as an excuse, but she had to see him, to gauge his reaction at seeing her. It would only take a few minutes.

~ * ~

Jake couldn't get Shannon off his mind as he drove back from Seattle. He'd been such a coward that morning. The only way he could've gotten out of her apartment faster would have been to jump out the window and onto his truck. He needed to apologize and explain himself. That was the catch, though. There were things he could not explain. That was a rule of the program and also something about him that, if she knew, could put her at risk.

He was surprised to realize the guilt he felt had more to do with Shannon and less to do with the fact that he'd broken a major promise he had made to God and to the Church. Distance had not made his heart grow fonder for his priestly vocation. If anything, he'd slipped far too easily into a new life that took him away from that vocation.

And then there was Shannon. Making love to her last night had been surreal. Their first time, he'd felt like a teenager. Unfortunately, he'd responded like one, too. Embarrassment still heated his face. He was pretty sure he'd redeemed himself the second time, though. Sex was pretty much like riding a bicycle, once he got past his nervousness. She was beautiful and had felt so good in his arms. It was the first thing that had felt right to him in a long time.

There was no way of knowing when he could be completely honest with her, offer her the kind of life she deserved. How was he ever going to look her in the eye again? Everything had been fine. They were friends, he was helping her out. He wanted to kick himself for letting things go too far. Now he'd ruined it.

When he saw the old Buick parked in his driveway, he recognized the car as Abe's. He'd barely stopped the truck and shut off the engine before jumping out. Something must have happened to Shannon. The he heard Bailey's cooing and looked up to find Shannon and the baby sitting on the deck.

"Hey," he said as he approached.

"Hey."

Jake climbed the steps and stood for a moment, grinning at

Bailey in her little yellow dress and matching sun bonnet. "She looks cute. New dress?"

"We went shopping."

He sat on the chair next to hers. "So, out and about in town today, huh?"

"Yeah. You know Millie at the café didn't even recognize me with this cut and color."

"You do look different."

She grinned. "In a good way, I hope."

"A good way."

They sat in silence for a moment.

"Jake, I…" Shannon began.

"I was going to…" he said. He nodded. "You go first."

She glanced down at her hands clasped together in her lap. "I wanted to stop by to get Bailey's stuffed lamb. She misses it."

"Oh. Sure. I'll get it." He strode to the back door, unlocked it and retrieved the stuffed animal from the living room. Handing it to Shannon, he said, "I'm sorry. I meant to bring it to her."

"Thanks. What were you going to say?"

"Nothing. Look, do you want to come in and have something to drink?"

"Uh…maybe for a minute."

He picked up the baby's carrier and held the door for Shannon to go ahead of him. As she passed, her arm brushed against him and her scent wafted around him. He felt intoxicated, the way he'd felt with her last night. But for her sake, he had to back off, let her go.

~ * ~

Anthony Baker, dressed in khakis and a blue shirt with the sleeves rolled up and a camera hanging around his neck did his best to look like a typical tourist. He glanced at any woman carrying a baby or pushing a stroller. She had to be here somewhere.

There weren't that many people out on the streets. He browsed shop windows, staring inside to scan the customers. He'd driven out of town to the house he'd tracked the call to, but no one was around. This town wasn't that big. Heather had to be here somewhere or someone had to have seen her. But so far, no luck.

What the hell? He'd had a good night at the casino and his sister was paying all of his expenses. He might as well take his time and relax a bit. The redhead he'd met at the casino bar said she'd be there again tonight. If he played his cards right…. Anthony laughed at the pun. He could get lucky all the way around.

He leaned close to look through the window of a book store and, when he turned around, bumped into a cute blond. "Sorry."

"I'm fine." She lowered her head and kept walking.

He looked after her as she continued down the sidewalk pushing a baby stroller. She crossed the street and walked to an older model Buick with Washington plates. Heather drove a newer Chevy. He turned and headed back toward his motel. He probably should report in, give Corinne something to nibble on so she didn't cut off his expense account and call him home.

"Hey, Sis."

"Hold just a moment."

He could hear her issuing orders to someone and then heard a door close. "Do you have good news for me?"

"There's not much to this town. It won't take me long to find her and the kid."

"You need to wrap this up fast. Are you sure she's there?"

"As sure as I can be. I'm watching the house she made those calls from. I'll have her in a day, two tops."

"Do not screw this up. I want them both back here so we can settle this. Once she knows just how serious I am about getting that baby, I think she'll see the wisdom of making a deal. If she resists, handle it."

"Tell me something. What does Mark think about your plan?"

"I don't give a damn what he thinks. He'll do exactly as I say or I'll expose him for the cheating bastard he is. Besides, I think it's only justice that he spend the rest of his life with this child right in his face. Don't you?"

His sister's coldhearted response made him shiver. If she wasn't family and held the purse strings, he'd walk away right now, find a nice place near the beach, maybe Miami, and watch the girls play beach volleyball. "I'm sure you'll see he gets what he deserves."

"You find that girl and her baby, bring them back here. Now! I have to go. I have a meeting with my pro-life constituency."

Anthony stared at the phone before ending the call. *Pro-life, my ass.* He wondered if Mark knew Corinne's past, the abortion she had right after high school. And what would happen if her "constituents" found out? There was a definite advantage to having all the inside dirt on Governor Corinne Baker Hastings.

He glanced at his watch. He could stake out the house for a couple of hours and, if nothing materialized, he'd head to the casino for a little fun.

On his first cruise past the cabin, he saw both a truck and a car in the driveway. The damned mountain road provided no place to pull over and park. He needed to keep the car out of sight anyway. A half-mile down the road, he came to a sign for a scenic overlook. He pulled in and started his walk back toward the cabin. He found a larger tree that could hide him and still allow for a clear view of the vehicles and the cabin. He recognized the Buick. Probably another wild goose chase, but he'd wait and watch for a bit.

Twenty minutes later, the woman came out of the house carrying the baby carrier. She placed the baby and carrier in the car, then turned toward the man standing on the deck. He couldn't tell what they were saying, but it was clear she wasn't happy with him. She got into the car and slammed the door. The same chick he'd bumped into in town.

The guy just stood on the deck, dragging a hand through his hair. Poor schmuck. He didn't have a clue what to do. Anthony had to chuckle. Then the guy raced toward the car waving his hand, and the car stopped.

It took Anthony a moment to realize his car was nearly half a mile away and he'd need it to follow her. He jogged to the overlook and was just ready to pull out when the Buick cruised by. The woman was sure taking her time, not driving like someone who'd been angry a minute ago. He followed her back into town. She turned off the main street and, two blocks later, pulled into a drive. The car slowly disappeared into a garage and the door closed. He parked on the street at the side of the house and watched. The blond emerged from the garage, carrying the baby and a couple of shopping bags up the stairs on the side of the apartment.

This had to be Heather. Yeah, she'd changed her hair. But she'd been at that cabin where he'd traced the phone calls to and she has a baby about the right age. He'd just have to hang around for a few more days, watch her and see what he could find out. Satisfied that he'd found his prize and she wasn't going anywhere, he pulled away from the curb and headed to the casino.

Chapter Twenty-Three

Shannon was furious as she pulled from the driveway and headed down Mountain Pine Road. With Bailey in her car seat in the back, she reminded herself to take it slow. What had she been thinking when she slept with Jake? *Idiot.* She of all people should have known better. And now he had the nerve to tell her he thought they needed to slow things down. Sure, now that he'd gotten what he wanted. She swiped at a tear that spilled down her cheek.

She'd made a fool of herself running to him to check the temperature of their relationship. Relationship? Well, that was clearly a joke, and the joke was on her. Jake didn't want a relationship. He'd said, "I let things happen too fast, and I'm sorry. You need more than I can give."

How did he know what she needed? Then when he suggested they keep some distance from one another for a while, she'd gone off on him. So much hit her at once—rejection, feeling used, and the fear of having no one in her corner. No one to even call if she needed help. He seemed stunned by her reaction. Well, what did he expect?

Parking in the driveway, she first carried Bailey upstairs and settled her in the playpen she'd bought at the second-hand store. Then she ran down the stairs to unload the groceries. She couldn't help but look over her shoulder, down the driveway and out to the street. Not another car in sight.

Upstairs she put away the groceries and set about making rosemary chicken for dinner. She found herself staring at the phone periodically, sure it would ring. Certain Jake would call to apologize. When the meal was ready, she prepared plates for Abe and Helen.

She gathered up Bailey and delivered the dinner.

"You don't have to cook for us," Abe said.

"I know, but it's just as easy to cook for three as for one. Besides, I appreciate the use of the car." She set the plates on the table. "Where's Helen?"

"She wanted to take a nap a while ago. I should get her up."

"I'll get her. You can pour your drinks." She shifted Bailey in her arms and went to the bedroom where Helen slept. She bent down and gently touched the old woman's shoulder, calling her name. "Helen, it's time for supper."

Helen blinked her eyes and then, upon spying Bailey, broke into a crooked smile.

Shannon helped Helen to sit up and brought her wheelchair close the bed. She lay Bailey on the bed long enough to help Helen maneuver into her chair. After a bathroom stop, Helen was seated at the table where Abe had already cut up her chicken breast into bite-sized pieces.

"Gooo," Helen said—her version of good.

"It's rosemary chicken. I hope you like it. I'm going upstairs and feed Bailey. I'll be back in a bit to clean up and help you get ready for bed."

"Thanks," Abe said. "This is delicious."

Shannon grinned. "I'm glad you like it. I'll be back soon."

Her phone was ringing as she reached the top of the stairs, but stopped as she opened the door. With no answering machine attached to the vintage phone, she had no idea who had called. Only two people she knew had the number, other than Abe—Dawn, who had babysat with Bailey, and Jake. Then there was Caleb, but she doubted she'd ever hear from him again. He'd done what he could for her.

She fed Bailey and readied her for bed before warming her own dinner. Sitting alone at the dining table, she pushed chicken and rice around her plate. The sun was beginning to set and shadows of swaying tree branches danced across the windows. She wished she could call Brooke or call her mother. An almost unbearable weight sat in her chest. This was no way to live, always worrying, always looking back to see what or who might be behind you. Maybe she should just go home and face Mark and Corinne Hastings. Why was she on the run like a criminal? She hadn't done anything wrong except get involved with Mark, a married man. That was wrong, she knew, but not something that should have sent her into exile. Mark had made it clear he wanted nothing to do with parenting the child they'd created. She accepted that and her role as a single mother. And all was well until Corinne Hastings showed up at her door.

~ * ~

Jake sat on the deck with his heels resting on the rail. He watched the sun set and the sky darken. He felt as if he'd skipped a major section of the directions on how to do a relationship with a woman—if there was a manual. He replayed his time with Shannon from the moment he was wakened by the blare of the car horn. Her vulnerability shook something loose in him. Inviting her and Bailey to stay with him just seemed the right thing to do. What unsettled him was how quickly he found himself drawn to both of them, seeing himself as a part of their lives, a family. When he responded to what he believed was his call to the priesthood, he was so sure, so certain. But the longing he felt at that time was nothing like what he felt with Shannon and Bailey.

He had run headlong into an intimate relationship with her, heedless of his commitments and the fact that he could be pulled back into his former life at a moment's notice. She had been hurt and angry when she left, and that was his fault. He felt sick, disgusted with himself. He couldn't expect her to understand. He only hoped he'd have the chance to explain.

Anger burned in his chest. What kind of sick joke had God played on him? Was this encounter a test, or was he being given an option, a second chance to be happy? He wasn't sure he remembered how to pray for guidance. For the last two years, his reliance had been upon himself and, occasionally, upon Caleb. It was time to put his faith to the test.

Jake went inside, locked the door behind him, and prepared to do battle.

~ * ~

"What do you think he's doing in there?" Sara asked.

"How do I know?" Lou scanned the area around the house through his binoculars.

"You sure he's still in there?"

Lou lowered the binoculars. "He's in there. His truck is still sitting where he parked it. One way in and one way out."

"It's almost noon. I'm getting hungry," she whined.

"Then hike back to the car and get something. I'm not leavin' this spot and chance him slippin' away." Lou raised the binoculars with one hand and, with the other swatted at a fly that buzzed around his sweat-soaked shirt collar.

"Fine. I'll do just that. And I'm not walking back here. I'll wait for you in the car." Sara stomped down the winding road without looking back.

"Take a flyin' leap while you're at it," Lou muttered.

By four o'clock, he'd had it. He was out of water, hadn't

eaten lunch, and the flies were making a picnic out of him. He needed dinner and a shower, then he could drive back out here and keep watch later. Clearly Avery wasn't planning to go anywhere.

When he reached the overlook, he saw the other car parked a few spaces away. Sara stood by the stone wall, chatting with another couple. He slowed his pace, trying to look casual. "Ready to go?"

She waved him over. "In a minute. Come here, meet Tom and Deb. They're from Canada."

He groaned inwardly, but forced a smile. "Hi, folks. Visiting the area, eh?"

"Yeah. Beautiful spot. What's the name of the town down there?" Tom asked, pointing to the village below.

"Snoqualmie."

"That where you folks are staying?"

Before he could respond, Sara piped up with, "Yes, there's a small motel on the edge of town. Nothing fancy, but it's comfortable. They probably have vacancies. You could follow us."

Deb smiled. "Oh, that would be great. Maybe you two could join us for dinner in a bit?"

"We have plans. Sorry." Lou grasped Sara's arm and turned her toward the car. "But, thanks anyway."

He glanced in the rear view mirror and the Nissan behind them. "What the hell are you thinking?" he growled at Sara.

"What? They pulled in to the overlook and started a conversation. Was I supposed to be rude and ignore them?"

"Yes. That would have been a plan. We don't know who they are or what they're doin' here. You can't trust people who just show up like that. They could be Feds. I suppose you told them your name?"

"Of course. I told them I'm Sue Nicholas. That's the name I've been using." She shook her head. "Feds. You know your problem, Lou? Your imagination runs away with you. The Feds have Avery tucked away nice and safe, so they think. I doubt they have babysitters watching him." Sara straightened her blouse under the seatbelt and stared out the side window. "I don't see why we can't have dinner before we trek back up that mountain."

"Before *I* trek up the mountain. You're not coming with me tonight. I'm gonna make a move and try to catch Avery while he's asleep."

"You're going into his house? Lou, that's a bad idea. What if he has a gun?'

"Father Peace-and-Love? Are you kidding?"

"Then maybe I could have dinner with Tom and Deb?"

"Fine, whatever. Just keep your mouth shut about who we are, where we live, and why we're here."

"I know. I know. Jeez, you think I'm an idiot."

He slid a sideways glance, but didn't speak. When he pulled into the motel parking lot, the Nissan stopped at the entry. Tom got out and waved before going into the lobby. Deb walked to their car. "Are you sure you can't join us for dinner? We don't really know the area very well."

"Depends on what you want. The diner in town closes at seven. There's a bar that serves decent food a little ways out of town. Rusty's. I have business to take care of, but Sue will go with you, if you don't mind."

Deb smiled—a little too broadly he thought. "Great. Meet us here in about fifteen minutes?"

Sara nodded.

Lou drove around the back of the motel and parked in front of their room. "I'm gonna take a quick shower and I'll grab a sandwich at the fast food place before I go back up to Avery's."

"Let me use the bathroom first. I want to freshen up before dinner." Sara grabbed her toiletries bag and closed the bathroom door.

Lou took the opportunity to check his gun, make sure it was loaded. Though he planned to only need one shot. Without Avery's testimony, the Feds would never be able to pin anything on Lou. Well, there was the matter of Father Alvin, but that problem was being taken care of from the inside. The only thing that would stand between Lou and a truly fresh start was primping in the bathroom.

Sara came out of the bathroom. "Should I pack our stuff and be ready to go?"

He stared at her hard. "You should be ready to go." She'd been an asset to him when he had the business up and running. She was good at finding adoptive families for the kids he brought into the country. But the business was effectively shut down when Avery blew the whistle. Sara was more of a liability now, and lately she'd been talking about marriage and kids before it was too late. He hated to tell her, but it was way too late.

Chapter Twenty-Four

Damn, it was dark. Lou could barely see six feet in front of him. He'd found a pull-off a little closer to Avery's cabin. His feet crunched across pine needles, the slick soles of his dress shoes sliding as he attempted to climb a small grade. He stood in the cover of trees and scoped out the area around the house. No lights, no movement. The truck still sat where it had earlier. He slapped at a mosquito that hummed around his ear. "I hate nature."

Using his cell phone for light, he made his way through the trees and to the edge of the clearing. Still no sound or movement. Confident he wouldn't be seen or heard, he closed the phone and made his way across the lawn toward the house. He ascended the steps onto the deck at the side of the cabin and peered through the window, then moved to the door and tried the knob. Locked. Hell, why couldn't one thing be easy?

In the back of the cabin, he found a window that slid open. But getting his six foot two frame through it would be difficult. Now is when he needed Sara to slip inside and open the door. He was about to try the front windows when something cold and metallic pressed into his neck. He froze.

"Don't make a move, Crowley. Both hands up against the wall."

"What the hell?"

"Do it."

Lou stretched his arms, palms flat against the cabin. A second man frisked him, removing the gun from its shoulder holster.

"Louis Crowley, you are under arrest. I'm U.S. Marshal Caleb Wilson." He was read his rights and escorted back around the cabin as two vehicles pulled into the drive, lights glaring.

Sara sat in the back of one of the vehicles, her face stained with tears and running mascara. Tom and Deb sat in the front seat, now with U.S. Marshal IDs clipped to their collars.

"I swear I didn't tell them, Lou. I didn't say a word." Sara cried and choked.

"Shut up. Just shut the hell up."

The marshal shoved him into the vehicle roughly, letting his head slam on the doorframe. "Oh, I'm sorry. Be careful there."

Caleb Wilson leaned in and spoke with Tom, "Get them to the airport. I'll follow with our witness."

~ * ~

Jake heard commotion in his driveway and saw the glare of headlights. He'd never gone to pick up the gun after applying for a permit, so he reached for his ever-faithful Louisville Slugger.

He met Caleb Wilson at his back door. "Caleb? What's going on?"

Caleb pointed to the vehicles. "We got Crowley and his girlfriend. He was trying to get into your place, presumably to kill you."

Jake whooshed out a deep breath. "So it's over."

"Not quite. You'll need to testify. Pack some things."

"Now?"

"Right now. We're heading to the airport. We have a plane waiting to transport us to New York."

"I can't just leave right now. Can't I fly out there in a day or two? Surely they're not ready for a trial tomorrow."

"No, but I can't let you out of my sight until the trial is over. We have a place set up for you in New York. As far as we're concerned, you're still Jake Garber until it's time for court."

"I need to make a phone call."

"The girlfriend?"

"I have to at least let her know I'm leaving town. I won't tell her anything more. You can stand right here and listen."

"Jake…."

But Jake had already dialed. "Shannon, it's Jake. I can't explain, but I'm leaving town for a while. I don't know how long. But I will be back. I promise. If you need anything, talk to Angie at Rusty's. She's a good friend and she'll be a friend to you, too." He paused. "I can't say any more right now. I've got to go. I… I love you."

He stared at the phone, then looked at Caleb. "I'll be ready in ten minutes." He shoved clothing into a suitcase, then reached into the back of the closet for a dark garment bag. He laid the bag on the bed and unzipped it. Inside lay a pair of black pants, black clerical shirt, and jacket. He reached into the pocket of the jacket and removed the white tab that slid into the clerical collar. He wasn't even sure this suit fit him any longer, in more ways than one. But he would be expected to appear in court as Father Steven Avery. He zipped the bag and retrieved his black shoes, tucking them into the suitcase.

He carried the bags downstairs and met Caleb again in the kitchen. "Ready."

On the way to the airport, Caleb said, "We got word yesterday that Alvin Martin was murdered in prison."

Jake closed his eyes. Alvin deserved prison for his part in the child trafficking ring, but he didn't deserve to die. "I'm sorry to hear that."

"Crowley was tying up all the loose ends. You were the last one."

"Thanks for watching my back," Jake said.

The five hour flight in the private jet seemed much longer. All he could think of was the tremor in Shannon's voice when she asked if he was coming back. He couldn't say when, but he knew beyond any doubt he would be back. His first order of business in New York was to meet with the Bishop and set in motion his dispensation from the solemn promises he had made as a priest. The last few days had given him the clarity he needed. The God he wasn't sure was listening had answered his prayer.

~ * ~

The Bishop sat behind his desk, looking much older than he had two years earlier. The investigation had taken its toll on him as well. "I can't say I'm surprised by your request, Steven, but I would like to know why now?"

The name still seemed foreign to Jake. He'd become a different person in the past two years. "I've had time to examine my reasons for becoming a priest. I find that what I thought to be a calling may have been in error."

The Bishop lifted his eyebrows. "You're telling me God made a mistake?"

"No. I'm saying I made the mistake. Though I'm not exactly sure it was a mistake. It was right at the time, but now...."

"What about now?" The Bishop leaned forward. "What has changed?"

Jake's mouth went dry. "I'm not the person I was two years ago."

"You do remember that a man who promises himself to the

priesthood is considered, in the eyes of the Church, to be a priest forever."

Perspiration dampened his collar. This wasn't as simple as he had hoped. The Bishop wasn't making it difficult, but being honest. "Yes, I know. I'm telling you that I cannot fulfill those promises and I'm asking to be released of my commitment to do so."

The Bishop sat back in his chair and stared hard at him. "Are you having doubts about returning to active priestly duty because you're not sure how your brother priests will treat you after the trial is over?"

"It has nothing to do with that. There's... I've met someone. A woman."

"Ah. I see. And this woman knows you're a priest?"

Jake shook his head. "I haven't told her. I couldn't tell her anything because of being in the program." Jake stood and paced. "I'm trying to do the right thing here, but I realize no matter what I choose, I let someone down." He turned and faced the Bishop. "I won't let her down. I ask that you get my papers ready to sign and release me from my commitment to the Diocese."

Jake walked out of the Bishop's office and nodded to the Marshal who was assigned to stay with him until after the trial. As they strode toward the waiting car, he reached up and tugged the white tab from his collar, shoving it into his jacket pocket. He'd only spent twenty-four hours locked in his cabin, wrestling with himself and with God before Caleb showed up to capture Lou Crowley. But in that time, he knew what he was to do, and he knew God was fine with it. He didn't much care if the Bishop approved or not.

Chapter Twenty-Five

Shannon emerged from the Swinsons' to see a woman standing at the top of the steps at her door. "May I help you?"

"There you are. It's me, Angie. Dawn's daughter?" She came down the steps. "I just stopped by to see how you and Bailey are getting along?"

"We're okay. Why?" She caught the tone of suspicion in her voice too late.

"Jake called to say he'd be away for a while. He asked if I'd stop by."

"You can tell him we're fine and he no longer has to worry about us." She stepped past Angie and headed toward the door. Then realizing she'd been rude and none of this was Angie's fault, she stopped and turned. "You want to come in? I made iced tea and there's chocolate cake."

Angie grinned. "Chocolate cake? I'm right behind you."

With Bailey in the playpen, Shannon set two glasses out for tea and then cut slices of the rich chocolate cake. "Here you go. Do you want sugar for the tea?"

"I think there's enough sugar in the cake. This will be fine, thanks."

Once Shannon sat down, Angie cast a steady gaze at her. "Jake's a good guy. He wasn't checking up on you. You're new to town and he wanted you to have someone you can call if you need anything."

"You and Jake are good friends, then?" she asked.

"Friends, yes. Nothing more, if that's what you're wondering."

Shannon felt heat spread into her face. "I'm sorry. That's none of my business."

Angie tasted the cake and closed her eyes, moaning softly. "Oh, this is good. Did you make this from scratch?"

"My mother's recipe."

"I'd give her a blue ribbon for this one." She took a sip of tea. "What are you doing Saturday night?"

151

"Me? Uh, nothing special. I'll be here with Bailey."

"Good. I'm going to Seattle with two friends for dinner and a movie. I get one Saturday a month off from Rusty's. Come with us."

Shannon glanced toward Bailey. "I can't."

"Sure you can. My mom's the designated babysitter. I already asked if she could handle one more and she said yes. She thinks your daughter is adorable, which she is. Come on. It's our monthly girls' night out. We'll be home by eleven."

"Did Jake put you up to this?"

"No. I thought of it all by myself. It'll be fun. And Bailey will be fine. She already knows my mom."

Shannon considered the invitation. If she was going to live in this town, she needed to start making friends. And if Angie was a friend of Jake's, she must be okay. "Thank you, I'd love to come along."

Angie scraped the last of the icing from her plate then set down her fork. "Fantastic. I'll pick you up around four and we'll stop by my mom's to drop off the baby."

"I can meet you at Dawn's. I have Abe's car for my use."

"Okay. See you then. And thanks for the cake."

Shannon reached into the cabinet for aluminum foil. "Wait, take a piece with you. Otherwise I'll eat all this by myself."

Angie grinned. "Can't have that."

Shannon watched the woman get into her SUV and pull from the driveway. Maybe this was a step toward making a life for herself and Bailey here in Snoqualmie. Although it irritated her that Jake called Angie to check in on her like she needed looking after. If he was so worried, why had he taken off? And what was with the 'I love you'? That had thrown her off balance. She knew she had feelings for Jake, but she had no clue exactly what they were. And how was she supposed to figure it out on her own, with no Jake? She didn't even know where he'd gone or for how long. And she thought *she* had secrets.

The dishes clattered as she set them in the sink. The last thing she needed was another man in her life giving her nothing but grief, confusion and false promises. She had a place to live, a job of sorts, and enough money for the time being. She and Bailey would be fine. Now if she only had the backbone to stand up to Corinne Hastings. Maybe her starting point needed to be Mark. She would get a disposable phone the next time she went shopping and call him, tell him to get his wife off her trail or else. Or else what? She'd expose them to the world? The woman who had knowingly slept with a married man and gotten pregnant versus the beloved Governor of Missouri whose husband had cheated on her?

What if Mark played the innocent, grieving father who never got to see his child? They could make her into the villain so easily. They could take Bailey away from her. After all, she was the one who ran with the baby. And there were Mark and Corinne—a couple who could give a child everything, or so it would appear. Still, she had to know where Mark stood in regard to the baby.

The following afternoon, Shannon checked on Helen and asked Abe if she could use the car for a few hours.

"Be my guest. You don't have to ask." The old man waved her off. "It's a nice day for a drive. The rain finally let up."

"Is there anything you or Helen need? I'm driving down to the Wal-Mart in Covington."

"Not a thing. You have a nice afternoon."

"Thanks."

She went into her bedroom closet and dug under the stack of boxes to retrieve cash from her briefcase. She knew she should put that money in the bank, but she was still nervous about being tracked down.

Burying the briefcase once again, she gathered up Bailey and the diaper bag. She opened the car windows and drove slowly, enjoying the feeling of freedom. In the Wal-Mart, she first used an antiseptic hand wipe to clean the infant carrier in the shopping cart. Then she settled Bailey in the carrier and leisurely browsed the store, smiling when a few women stopped to comment on the baby.

After choosing two new outfits of clothing for Bailey, she shopped for something new to wear on Saturday night. It was only a girls' night out, but she wanted to feel new. Her last stop was in the electronics department where she purchased an AT&T disposable phone using her new 'official' identity as Shannon Chase to set up the account.

In the parking lot, she removed Bailey from the cart and placed her in the car seat, followed by their purchases. She sat in the car staring at the phone and her hands shook. When she punched in Mark's personal cell number, she half expected a message telling her the phone was no longer in service. Instead, he answered on the third ring. "Hello."

"Mark?"

"Yes. Who is this?"

"It's Heather."

A pause, then he said, "Hold on."

She could hear him talking to someone, then a door closed. "Where the hell are you?"

"I don't think that's something I want to reveal. And don't think you can trace this call, because you can't."

"Corinne is really pissed that you took off with the baby and her ten grand. What the hell were you thinking?"

"I was thinking that your wife has no rights to my baby and that I'm not sure what she might do to get her. Why would she want Ba…Amanda anyway?" Shannon closed her eyes and gritted her teeth at the near slip.

"Because she wants to rub this in my face for eternity. I told you to take care of it."

Anger coursed through her. "*It* is your child. How can you be so heartless?"

"No, she's *your* child. Believe me, finding you and that baby is not in my plan. But Corinne will not give up, especially since you took the money and ran."

"I had to. I had no way of providing for the baby once I got fired. And we both know who had a hand in that." She drew in a deep breath. "I only called to see where you stand in all this. I want you to have an attorney draw up papers giving me full custody of Amanda. I want you to give up any rights to her."

"Trust me, I'd love nothing more. But what do you think will happen once Corinne knows I've done that?"

"I don't care. You clearly don't want to be associated with this baby. So let her go. Let *us* go."

He let out an exasperated exhale. "I can't do that."

"Then we have nothing more to discuss."

"Heather, wait…."

She ended the call. Then she rummaged in her wallet and removed a slip of paper, dialing Brooke's office number. "Hi, it's me."

"Hey, this is a surprise."

"I figured your office phone would be safe and I'm using a non-traceable disposable. I just called Mark."

"You what? Are you crazy?"

Shannon expected the response and grinned. "No. I had to know what his part is in this search to find me and get to the baby. The last thing he wants is for us to be found. This is all Corinne's doing. Her best revenge on Mark's wandering would be to force his child into his life."

"Oh, sweetie. What are you going to do?"

"Stay here for as long as I can. Maybe that bitch will give up eventually."

"I hope so."

"How's my mom?"

"She's doing okay. She stayed in Uniontown with your aunt. I have the phone number if you need it."

Shannon reached into her purse to find a pen and scratched the number down on the Wal-Mart receipt. "Thanks." She paused. "I miss you."

"I miss you, too. Maybe when you're sure the trail's gone cold, I can come out there for a visit?"

"I'd love that. I don't know that I'll ever feel safe. I was hoping to get some insight while I spoke with Mark about how to end this, but he won't go up against Corinne. I actually entertained calling her and trying to make a deal."

"Now I know you've lost your mind. Hey, what about that guy who came to your rescue?"

"He's gone."

"Gone?"

"He just left town and I don't know if or when he's coming back." Her voice cracked despite her efforts at control.

"Uh-oh. You fell for him, huh?"

"No. He was a good friend. That's all."

"That's not all. I can hear it in your voice. Oh, shoot, hold on." Brooke returned. "I'm sorry. I have to go. Customers waiting. Call me again?"

"I will, I promise. Thanks for everything."

"Any time. Bye."

The third call was the hardest, but hearing her mother's voice was worth the heartache. "I swear we're both fine, Mom. I'm glad you're staying with Aunt Rita."

"I am, too. I may stay here until you're ready to go back home."

"I'm not sure that's going to happen, Mom. I might remain

here."

"Why can't you tell me where you are?"

Shannon took a heavy breath. "I will soon. The less you know, the better off you are for now. I'm so sorry about all of this." Tears spilled down her cheeks in hot tracks.

"Honey, it's okay. It'll all work out. Maybe you should come here to Aunt Rita's, too. You'd like it here."

"I'll think about it, Mom," she said, knowing it wouldn't—couldn't—be a consideration. "I have to go now. But I'll call you again soon. I promise."

"I love you, sweetheart. Kiss the baby for me."

"I will. Love you, too."

She ended the call and gave in to the grief, her shoulders shaking. Fumbling in her purse for tissues, she blew her nose and wiped her eyes. The other phone number tucked away in her wallet belonged to Jake's cell phone. She hastily punched in the numbers. The phone rang twice and, before he could answer, she stopped the call.

Rolling the phone around in her hand, Shannon wondered if she should dispose of it now and go back inside for another one. It wasn't supposed to be traceable, but fear raised doubts in her mind. Backing from the parking space, she slowed at the store's entrance, jumped out and tossed the phone into a trash receptacle, then headed back to Snoqualmie.

Chapter Twenty-Six

On Saturday, Shannon packed the diaper bag with plenty of diapers, formula and the baby food Bailey had just started to eat. She added two changes of clothing, just in case. "Okay, sweetie. Let's go."

At Dawn's house, she found Angie's SUV already parked at the curb. She pulled the Buick into the empty driveway and got out.

Angie came across the small yard. "Hi. Let me help you. If you're like me, you packed as if she was going to summer camp."

Shannon laughed. "You got it." She handed off the diaper bag, then removed Bailey and the car seat-slash-carrier. "I'll take this inside, too."

"You can if you want, but I'm sure Mom's got at least two carriers in there already. This place is Kiddie Central."

Inside, the TV blared in the living room where two boys and a girl who looked to be between the ages of six and eight, sat on the floor watching a cartoon. An older boy, maybe ten, sat on the sofa playing with an iPad. Dawn came from the kitchen with a toddler in tow. "Hi, Shannon. And there's that sweet baby." She reached out and took Bailey from her.

"Thanks for doing this. Let me know how much I owe you when we get back." Shannon set the carrier down.

Dawn waved a dismissive hand. "You don't owe me anything. I have the grandkids here anyway. One Saturday a month, I keep all the kids so the girls can have a night out."

Angie pointed. "That one is Sean and the girl is Amy. And this…" She picked up the toddler. "…is Raymond. They're mine. The other boys are David and Michael—the one with the iPad. They belong to my sister, Melanie, who's working tonight at the casino."

The front door opened and another woman came in herding two twin girls.

"This is Rachel and her two, Annie and Jessie."

The little girls raced past Shannon and fell to the floor in that boneless way children do, knees bent, legs behind them, joining the TV group.

157

"Are you sure you want to keep Bailey, too?" Shannon asked Dawn. "Looks like you already have your hands full."

"I'm sure. This is better than dinner and a movie for me. Now you girls go and have fun."

Shannon leaned in and kissed Bailey on the cheek. But the baby was already mesmerized by the silver and turquoise necklace Dawn wore. "You'll call if there's any problem?" Shannon asked, then added, "Oh, but I don't have a cell phone."

"I'll call Angie if I need you, but I promise we'll be fine."

Angie looped an arm through Shannon's and turned her toward the door. "Come on. It's time for the big girls to go out and play."

They piled into Angie's SUV and made a stop to pick up Lisa, another of Angie's friends. The women were welcoming and didn't press her with questions right away. When they reached Seattle, Rachel said, "Why don't we catch a movie first, then eat?"

Angie groaned. "If we're going to Quinn's, we need to get there early or we'll never get a place to park."

"We'll get a place to park. We're right near the theater," Rachel argued.

"But I'm hungry," Angie countered.

"So, get popcorn." Rachel turned in her seat. "What about you two?

Lisa shrugged. "Fine with me."

"I'm fine either way," Shannon said.

Rachel laughed. "Oh, we have a diplomat in our midst." She winked at Shannon. "So I'm counting that as a yes. Movie first."

Angie made a turn, drove a few blocks and pulled into the parking garage near the Majestic.

Shannon had seen previews of the movie they'd selected and knew she'd enjoy it. She needed to laugh. The movie didn't disappoint and she wiped away tears at some of the scenes.

"That was great," Angie said as they left the theater. "What did you think, Shannon?"

"I laughed until I cried."

When they reached the pub, Angie drove around the block twice before suggesting the rest of them get out and go inside to get a table.

"I'll stay with you," Shannon said. "That way you won't have to walk back by yourself."

They found a parking spot that Angie just squeezed into a couple of blocks from the pub. "I knew this would happen."

Shannon shrugged. "It's a nice evening for a walk. For once it's not raining."

Angie slid a glance at her. "Do you always see the glass-half-full side of things?"

"Definitely not. But you have to admit, it is a nice night."

"It is. So, are you having a fun? Rachel can be a bit overwhelming."

"She's fine. I like your friends and, yes, I'm having a good time."

They walked in silence for a block, then Shannon asked, "So, have you heard from Jake?"

"Nope. But I texted him that you were joining us tonight." Angie glanced over at her. "I hope that's okay. I should have asked."

Shannon shook her head. "It's okay."

It was Angie's turn to ask a question. "How did you and Jake meet?"

Unprepared for the question, she slowed her pace. "We just sort of ran into each other. He's a nice guy."

"He is. Though he's being very mysterious about this trip out of town."

They reached the pub and Angie held the door for Shannon to go ahead of her. They found Lisa seated at a table. Rachel stood at the bar, smiling and talking to a very good looking guy. Shannon stared and Angie leaned in, saying, "She's divorced since last April."

"Oh, I wasn't thinking...." Heat flooded her face. "Okay, I was wondering."

"We have one rule here. You can meet a guy, but at the end of the evening, we all go home together. No girl left behind."

"That's a very good rule," Shannon said. "But I'm not looking for a guy."

Angie grinned. "Already got one?"

"No. Had one. And now I have Bailey—and no guy."

Lisa nodded, then motioned toward Rachel. "Some women just can't live without them."

The pub was simple, but held a certain elegance at the same time. The menu offered an eclectic mix of fancy and traditional fare. Shannon settled on fish and chips and a Quinn's ale.

Rachel returned to the table, all smiles and flush. "That guy I was talking to is an architect. We're going out next weekend."

"Does he know about the twins?" Lisa asked.

Rachel glanced down at her rather impressive chest. "I think he noticed."

Angie laughed. "Good one."

Shannon liked these women. They had fun without being too obvious. They laughed at one another and themselves and, in the end, had each other's backs. She was reminded of Brooke and the good times they always had.

"Hey, Shannon? You still with us?" Lisa asked.

"I'm sorry. My mind was wandering." She stood. "Where is the ladies' room?"

Angie pointed and Shannon followed the direction. She used the bathroom and was washing her hands when Angie came in. "You okay?"

"Fine. I really like your friends. I was just thinking about a friend of mine I haven't seen for a while. We used to do things like this. I kind of miss her."

"Well, you're welcome to join us any time. We do this once a month, so mark your calendar."

They returned to the table as the waitress delivered their food. She'd also delivered a refill on Shannon's beer. "No, please. I can't have another." The rich ale had already begun to make her feel loose-jointed.

"Sure you can," Angie said. "I'm the designated driver tonight. We each take a turn."

By the end of the evening, Shannon was slightly wobbly from the beer as the women strolled back to the SUV.

Rachel put a hand on Shannon's shoulder. "I'm so glad you came out with us tonight. I hope you'll do this again."

"I will, thank you."

She had sobered by the time they reached Dawn's house.

"You sure you don't want me to drive you two home?" Angie asked.

"No, I'm fine now. And it's only a few blocks." Shannon followed Angie and Rachel into the house.

Dawn sat on the sofa looking like the crazy cat lady, except she had children draped everywhere. Bailey slept in her lap. Dawn smiled up at Shannon and whispered. "You want to just stay here tonight? I have room."

"No, thanks. I have to be up in the morning early to help Helen Swinson."

Easing her hands under the sleeping baby, Dawn lifted her and stood. "We had a great time tonight. She was an angel."

"Thank you." She strapped Bailey into the carrier. "I really appreciate this. I had fun tonight."

Dawn walked with her to the door. "You bring her by any time."

Angie followed Shannon to her car. "I'm glad you came with us. You have my phone number if you need anything. And most evenings, I work at Rusty's. That's a bar outside of town." She headed for the SUV.

"Aren't you forgetting something?" Shannon asked.

"What? My kids? They're staying with Grandma overnight. That's the only way I can sleep late in the morning." She waved. "Have a good night."

Her own mother would be just like Dawn, always ready to take her grandbaby for an evening or an overnight. Sadness gnawed at Shannon as she started the car. How would Bailey get to know her grandma if they stayed here in Washington? Maybe it would be best if she moved to Pennsylvania with her mother and aunt.

Shannon slowed as she approached the Swinson house. The streets were deserted except for one vehicle—a dark mid-sized car with tinted windows that sat idling at the curb just before the driveway. She considered continuing to drive, but where would she go? She had to come home sometime. Fumbling with the garage door opener clipped to the visor, she pressed the button. The door groaned open and then closed again behind the car. She sat until the overhead light went out, then got out of the car and stood on tiptoe to peer through one of the small block windows. She could make out the taillights and exhaust coming from the vehicle and she wished there were an inside stair entry to her apartment. She looped her purse over her shoulder, left the diaper bag behind, and hustled out the side door and up the steps with Bailey in her arms. Her heart pounded as she closed the door behind her and flipped on the kitchen light.

Bailey stirred but went back to sleep as soon as Shannon lay her in the crib. After changing and crawling into bed, she stretched and tried to relax.

The women she'd spent the evening with had been pleasant

and friendly. None of them had pressed her for information about where she came from or why she was here in Snoqualmie or what kind of work she did or who was Bailey's father. She'd told them she had a break-up shortly after Bailey was born and decided to find a new place to start over. She had met Jake and he had been very helpful to her in finding a place to live. And that led to a job of sorts. It had all been so easy. Maybe she was worrying too much about being found and about what other people would think of her.

Shannon leaned toward the window and split the blinds with two fingers, looking down at the street. The car was gone. She let out a breath she had not been aware of holding in and burrowed into the soft, cool sheets.

Chapter Twenty-Seven

Shannon jerked awake and listened. The wind had been building all evening, with reports of a storm moving in from the west. She split two of the slats in the mini-blinds and peered out, but saw no movement, other than the trees.

She got up to check on Bailey in her crib. The infant was sprawled on her back, sleeping soundly, her bow-like mouth making a sucking motion now and then. She had one arm wrapped around her stuffed lamb.

Just as she settled back into bed, Shannon heard a creaking sound. It was the sound made when anyone stepped on the second step from the top of her landing. Jake had mentioned replacing that step, but he'd never gotten around to it. Her heart pounded as she got out of bed and moved to the open bedroom door to listen. Now a scraping sound, like metal on metal. Like someone using a metal object on her aluminum storm door.

She hurried back to the night stand and removed her .38 from the drawer. With the gun aimed downward at her side, she crept up the hall as far as the kitchen, where she would have a view of the door. She would have to open the inside door to see anything or anyone on the steps or landing. Instead, she dashed across the room to the window and looked down at the driveway. No vehicle.

Breathing hard, she sat on the sofa, placing the gun gently on the coffee table. Her hands trembled and her mouth had gone dry. She went to the kitchen and got a glass of water, standing for a moment and listening. The wind whipped tree branches against the back and side of the apartment. Retrieving the gun, she went back down the hall, stopping first in the bathroom. Her heart raced and blood pounded in her ears.

When Shannon stepped back out into the hallway, something caught her eye and she looked to her left. A man stood with his back to her rifling through mail on the dinette table. She jerked her body back into the bathroom, stifling a gasp. Her heart nearly leaped out of her chest as she tried to not make a sound. She wanted to get to Bailey, but it was too risky that he might see her cross the hall.

She heard him moving about the living room. The baby chose that moment to waken and began to cry. She had to do something to keep him out there and not let him corner her or get near Bailey. The sound of shoes scuffing on the hardwood floor told her he was moving in her direction.

After taking in and releasing a deep breath, she steadied herself, swung out of the bathroom with a wide stance and aimed the gun using both hands. "Stop right there."

He held something in his hand, presumably a gun, and took another step toward her. She fired.

The sound ricocheted off the walls.

The man clutched his abdomen and dropped to the floor.

Bailey wailed from her crib.

Shannon's entire body shook. The man didn't move but, as she stepped closer, he groaned and his fingers flexed. Her only phone was in the living room. She'd have to get past him to get to it. She moved closer, aiming the gun. "Don't move or I'll shoot again." She inched along the wall, stepping around him. Keeping her eyes and the gun trained on him, she backed to the phone and pressed in 9-1-1.

"9-1-1. What's your emergency?" a woman asked.

"I j-just sh-shot a man. He b-broke into my apartment."

"What is your name and address?"

"Shannon Chase. 276 Falls Avenue, rear garage apartment."

"You said the person you shot broke in?"

Bailey wailed in the background.

"Is that a baby crying?"

"Yes, but she's fine."

"Is the man dead?"

"I d-don't know."

"Can you get out of the apartment until the police arrive?"

She stood staring at the body sprawled on the floor. "I c-can't. My baby's in the back room and I don't want to walk past him again. Please hurry."

"They're on their way. Is the baby okay?"

"Yes, I'm sure she's scared. I have to try to get to her."

She startled when the door opened and Abe Swinson peered inside. "I heard a gunshot. Everything okay up here?" He flipped on the overhead lights, breathing hard. Then he spied the body on the floor. "What happened?"

"He broke in. I have to get to Bailey. Can you hold this gun on him so I can go past him?"

Abe took the gun in his crooked fingers. "Sure. Go right ahead."

Sirens sounded nearby as she lifted Bailey from her crib and tried to soothe her. She shielded he baby's eyes and headed back to the living room. The man groaned, tried to raise up, then slumped unconscious on the floor.

She hurried past him and stood beside Abe. Feet pounded up the outside steps and a police officer appeared in the doorway. "Whoa, you need to put that gun down, Abe."

Abe lowered the gun and nodded, "Hi, Tim."

The officer looked at the man on the floor, then told his partner who had entered behind him, "Better call for EMTs."

He approached the man and felt for a pulse. "He's breathing." He turned to Abe and Shannon. "Want to tell me what happened here?"

"I shot him," Shannon said. "He broke in and he had a gun."

"Where is it?" the officer asked.

"I don't know. It went flying when he fell."

The second officer began to search. "There's something under the refrigerator. I can't get to it." He looked at Shannon. "You got a yardstick?"

"There's one inside the pantry cupboard in the corner."

He retrieved the yardstick and swiped under the fridge, making contact with an object that he slowly drew forward. "It's a cell phone."

Another siren announced the arrival of the EMTs. More feet pounded up the stairs.

"I swear he had a gun." Bailey's cry grew louder and Shannon swayed, trying to calm her. The thought that she'd just shot an unarmed man sent a wave of nausea through her.

The EMTs rushed up the steps and into the apartment. They knelt to attend to the man on the floor.

"Is he...dead?" Shannon asked.

One of the EMTs pressed a stethoscope to the man's chest. "Not yet, but he's lost a lot of blood."

The policeman asked, "Do you know the guy?"

Shannon shook her head. "I don't think so."

"Why don't you sit down and tell me everything that

happened?"

She jostled Bailey in her arms. "If I don't change her diaper, she's going to keep this up."

"Go ahead."

"I…um…have to go back there." She pointed down the hallway past the body where the EMTs were at work."

"Where are the diapers?"

"On top of the chest of drawers beside the crib in the bedroom."

"Hey, Greg, go back and get a diaper from the bedroom, would ya'?"

"Sure thing." The other officer returned and stepped around the EMTs to hand her the diaper.

Once she had Bailey changed and quieted, she sat on the sofa. "I swear I thought he had a gun in his hand. He broke in."

The EMTs announced they were taking the victim to the hospital as they loaded him onto a stretcher.

"Wait. Does he have ID on him? A wallet?" The officer reached into the man's back pocket and removed a tri-fold wallet. He glanced at the driver's license. "Says his name's Anthony Baker and he's from Jefferson City, Missouri."

"Baker?" Shannon asked.

"You know him?"

She hesitated. If she said yes, she'd have to explain a lot more than she wanted to. "No, I don't."

As the EMTs prepared to transport the man to the hospital, the second police officer said, "I'll ride along and stay with him."

The officer Abe had identified as Tim sat down beside Shannon and pulled out a notepad. "Tell me everything that happened."

"You going to be okay?" Abe asked Shannon.

"I'll be fine now. Thanks."

Abe excused himself to return to Helen. "You need anything from me, Tim, you know where to find me." He handed over the gun. "I suppose you'll need this."

"Is it yours?"

The old man shook his head. "No. It belongs to Shannon."

Shannon told the officer everything from the point of hearing something or someone outside the door to the point at which she shot the intruder.

"And you don't know him?"

"I don't. And I swear, in the dark I thought he was holding a gun."

The officer stared for a moment. "How long have you lived here?"

"About a month."

"Where were you before this?"

Her heart beat a rapid tattoo. Then she remembered the identity she'd been give. "Akron, Ohio. I don't know this man and I don't know why he would break into my apartment."

His gaze shifted to Bailey. "Cute baby. Where's her father?"

Heat spread into her face. "He's not in the picture. He wanted me to get rid of her. I couldn't do that."

The officer shook his head. "Any chance this Baker guy is connected to him?"

"I don't know. I left with Bailey so we could start over somewhere new, a place where we didn't know anyone."

"Okay. Abe vouched for you, the fact that you and the baby are here alone and that man is a stranger. Your storm door and lock were both picked. You should have a deadbolt installed in that door." He stood. "You're not planning to leave town, are you?"

"No. I work here. I take care of Abe's wife, Helen."

He nodded toward the gun. "Do you have a permit for this?"

Shannon felt as if someone had grabbed her by the throat. She swallowed hard. "No."

"I'm going to need to keep it for now." He glanced at the blood pooled on the hardwood floor. "You have anyone I can call to come and be with you, help you clean this up?"

She shook her head. "Not really. I'll be fine."

"I may have more questions later, after I have a chance to talk to Mr. Baker."

"I understand."

After he left, she stared at the blood and began to shake uncontrollably. That guy had to be related to Corinne Baker Hastings. She edged around the red pool, the odor creating a coppery taste in her mouth. Once Bailey was back in her crib, Shannon grabbed the stack of old towels and a pair of rubber gloves from under the bathroom sink. She unfolded the towels and spread them over the pool, watching them turn a deep crimson as they soaked up the mess. Gagging, she opened a plastic trash bag, balled up the

167

towels and stuffed them inside. Then she used a bucket of hot water and Pine Sol and a scrub brush to clean the rest as best she could. She tossed the scrub brush into the trash bag and raced down the stairs to put it all in the outside trashcan.

Abe called to her from his back porch as she turned to go back upstairs. "Shannon, you okay?"

"I will be eventually. I've never shot anyone before. I'm really sorry."

"No apology necessary. I'm just glad you were armed and could protect yourself. If anything like that happens again, you call me."

"I will. Thanks. I need to get back upstairs to Bailey."

"Tim Murphy is a good cop. You just tell him the truth and everything will be fine."

She nodded. The whole truth and nothing but? She was fairly certain that would all come out once Anthony Baker was conscious and speaking. If he survived. She shuddered thinking she might have killed a man.

Upstairs she lit a few scented candles and sat in the rocker. Thunder rumbled as the predicted storm rolled in. A flash of lightning brightened the sky followed by a loud boom. She blew out the candles, left one lamp burning, and checked the lock on the door—for all the good that was. In the bedroom, she sat with the pillows behind her listening to the storm outside and to her own terror. She could pack what they would need and drive up to Canada. Caleb had told her not to try to leave the country. He hadn't said she wouldn't be able to do so with the papers he had given her.

She was still sitting up in bed, staring at the opposite wall when the sun rose. The storm ended at some point in the previous few hours, but she'd missed it. Her mind had been busy entertaining three possible plans of action. And now, with the light of day, she knew what she had to do.

As she stepped out of the shower and turned off the water, she heard the phone ringing. She pulled on the over-sized terrycloth robe and padded down the hall. "Hello?"

"Ms. Chase, this is Officer Murphy. I responded to the call at your place last night?"

"Yes, I remember you."

"I was wondering if you could come by the police station and answer a few more questions."

"I…uh…suppose. If you need me to, of course."

"We do. I'd appreciate it. You know where we are on Douglas?"

"I'm not sure." She jotted down the directions he gave. "How is the man I shot?"

"He'll be fine. When do you think you can come by? Do you need me to send a car for you?"

"I'll be there in an hour or less. I have a car, thank you." She hung up and chewed on her lip. What questions could they have for her?

She called Dawn Kohler and asked if she could keep Bailey for a few hours, explaining what had happened the previous night.

"Oh, my. That had to be awful for you. Of course I'll keep her."

"Thanks, Dawn. I'll be there in about half an hour. I have to feed Bailey first." She hurriedly dried her hair and dressed, then packed up Bailey's bag and fed the baby. She stopped to tell Abe where she was going and that she'd be using the car.

"No problem. Let me know how things turn out," the old man said.

Shannon pulled into the parking lot of the Snoqualmie Police Department and into a space designated for visitors. Inside the station, she asked for Office Murphy.

Tim Murphy rounded the reception desk and greeted her. "Miss Chase, thank you for coming in. If you'd come with me, please."

He escorted her down a hallway and into a room marked 'Interrogation.' She didn't like the sound of that. A man dressed in a suit sat at a table inside the room.

"Shannon Chase this is Detective David Greer."

The suited man stood and nodded. "Miss Chase. Please, have a seat."

Shannon regarded him for a moment before sitting.

The detective nodded to Officer Murphy, who then left the room, closing the door.

"Miss Chase, I heard about what happened at your apartment last evening. And I've had an opportunity to interview Mr. Baker." He picked up a pen that sat atop a yellow legal pad in front of him. "Would you please recount the events of last night. Were you out earlier in the evening or at home?"

"I went to Seattle with some friends for dinner and a movie."

"Friends?"

"Yes, three other women."

"And what time did you return home?"

Shannon frowned. "I got to the sitter's around eleven forty-five and back to my place a little past midnight."

"Did you have drinks while you were out?"

"I had two beers with dinner. What's that got to do with anything? I wasn't drunk, if that's what you're asking."

He cast a cool glance at her. "I'm not suggesting you were. Just trying to get the full chain of events. Did you go home alone?"

"I…yes…well, me and my daughter. She's four months old."

"And what time were you wakened and discovered Mr. Baker in your apartment?"

"It was just past two. I thought I heard a sound and woke up, but then I didn't hear anything. I went out to the living room to investigate."

"With your gun in hand?"

"Yes. I didn't hear anything more, just the wind whipping the trees. I got a glass of water and then stopped in the bathroom. When I stepped back into the hall, I saw a shadow, a silhouette of a man looking through my mail. He had his back to me. So I went back into the bathroom. Then Bailey started to cry and I heard the man start down the hall. I stepped out into the hall and aimed the gun at him and told him to stop. He didn't, and that's when I shot him."

"He didn't identify himself?"

"No. He didn't say anything. He had something in his hand and he started to raise it. I swear I thought it was a gun."

"But it was, in fact, a cell phone."

"I found that out later."

The detective jotted a few notes then looked her in the eye. "Were you expecting anyone last night?"

"No. I don't really know anyone here. I just moved here a few weeks ago."

"From…" He riffled through his notes. "…Akron, Ohio."

"That's right." She gulped, wondering he knew the truth.

He sat back and tossed the pen onto the table. "We have a problem Miss Chase. As a matter of fact, we have quite a few problems."

Shannon's hands began to shake and she wound her fingers

together in her lap. "I don't understand."

"The man you shot is Anthony Baker. Brother of Governor Corinne Baker Hastings of Missouri. He admits you may not know him, but insists you do know Mark Hastings, the Governor's husband, quite well."

At the mention of Mark, Shannon's stomach clenched and bile rose in her throat. She swallowed hard.

The detective leaned forward, his arms resting on the table. "You do know Mark Hastings?"

"Yes." Heat rushed up her neck and burned in her face. "I know him."

"Mr. Hastings tells me he spoke with you earlier this week and that you were expecting him last evening."

Her head jerked up. "I…No, I was not expecting him. I did talk with him briefly, but…."

"Except Mr. Hastings knows you as Heather Carlson. He says the two of you have a child together."

Shannon began to shake all over. "I have a child fathered by Mr. Hastings. That's true."

"As a paid surrogate for Mr. Hastings and his wife, the Governor."

"What? That's insane." Shannon's heart pounded and she felt as if all the air had been sucked out of the room.

"And it seems you forgot one minor detail—to give them their baby. But you had no trouble accepting a payment of fifty thousand dollars. And then you got greedy, insisting on one hundred thousand. You thought Mr. Hastings was bringing the money to you last night, but he sent Mr. Baker who insists, by the way, that your doors were unlocked and that you didn't answer. Since you were expecting Mr. Hastings, Mr. Baker let himself in and called to you."

"None of that is true. Mark didn't even want me to have the baby. And I never received fifty thousand dollars. Governor Hastings came to my apartment and threw ten thousand dollars at me, but…." Something told her it was time to stop answering questions. She met the detective's gaze. "I think I'd like a lawyer now."

He stared at her, his mouth in a narrow, flat line. "Suit yourself." He stood and left the room, closing the door with a resounding thunk.

Shannon sat in the overly-cold room, shivering. *A paid*

surrogate? They were actually going to try to make her the villain? And how would that explain Anthony Baker breaking into her apartment?

Detective Greer returned with Officer Murphy. He placed a hand on Shannon's arm, forcing her to stand. "Heather Carlson, you are under arrest for extortion and for assault with a deadly weapon."

Chapter Twenty-Eight

Shannon sat staring at the telephone placed in front of her. One phone call. But who to call? If she called Dawn Kohler, she would know that Bailey would be cared for, but how would anyone know she needed help? She couldn't call her mother. Brooke. She picked up the vintage phone and punched in Brooke's cell number.

"Hello?" Brooke asked.

"Brooke, it's me. Look, I don't have much time. Something's happened here. I'm in jail."

"Jail? What's going on?"

"I can't explain everything. I need you to listen very carefully and write some things down. I'm being set up by Mark and Corinne. I shot a man who broke into my apartment and it turned out to be Anthony Baker, Corinne's brother. Bailey...Amanda is with a woman by the name of Dawn Kohler. I don't remember her phone number, it's in my purse and they took that. Her daughter's name is Angie and she works at a bar called Rusty's. Are you getting all this?"

"I got it."

"Good. I need you to call my Mom. I'm going to need her here. She can stay at my apartment. If you can reach Angie, I'm sure she'll pick Mom up at the airport in Seattle."

"I'm coming with her. I'll coordinate the flights so we both get there around the same time and I'll rent a car. My God, I can't believe this."

"The detective's name is Greer and the officer is Tim Murphy, in case you need to call here. I've asked for an attorney. Brooke...please hurry. And call Dawn."

"I'll be there as soon as I can, and I'll see that your Mom gets there."

"Thanks. I've got to hang up." She placed the phone back in the cradle and closed her eyes, drawing in a deep breath. She was shown to a small room where she was given an over-sized jumpsuit and a female officer watched while she changed, then took her clothing away. Next she was led to a small cell and ushered inside.

An hour passed in unnerving silence. She hoped Brooke had been able to locate Dawn's number and had called her. No one had told her what to expect, what came next. A few minutes later, she heard voices just beyond the door that separated the cells from the front office area.

"Oh, for Pete's sake, Tim. Do you think I'm bringing in a cake with a file? I need to see her now. My mother's babysitting her daughter."

Angie! Oh, thank God. Shannon stood, her fingers wrapped tightly around the cold metal bars. Waiting.

The door opened and Officer Murphy let Angie inside. "Ten minutes, Angie. That's the best I can do."

"Okay, okay." Angie stared at her. "I cannot believe this."

"Thank God you came. I was so worried about Bailey. Is she all right?"

"She's fine and Mom says not to worry. She'll take good care of her for as long as necessary. What the hell happened?"

Shannon gave a brief synopsis of the events. "I've asked for an attorney, but who knows how long that will take?"

"You don't want some court-appointed flunky. I got you covered. My ex-sister-in-law is an attorney in Seattle. I'll call her as soon as I leave here."

"She should know that I don't have much money. I'm not sure how I'd pay her."

Angie waved a hand. "Let's not worry about that now. Your friend called my Mom. She's arriving tomorrow and your mother will get here the next day. I'll go over to your place and make sure it's cleaned up for them. The police can leave such a mess."

"I cleaned up everything. The blood." She shivered.

"Yeah, but they searched your place while you were here. Abe told me when I called him. It'll be trashed."

"They searched my place? Why? They already had my gun."

Angie shrugged. "Who knows?"

Then it hit Shannon—the money. They would find the money and use that as evidence that she'd accepted a payment from the Hastings'. "Oh, God. This is a nightmare."

Angie wrapped her fingers around Shannon's. "Look at me. This is going to be okay."

"Why are you helping me? You don't really even know me."

"I'm a good judge of character, and I like you. I spoke with your friend, Brooke, and she told me the whole story. Besides, you're a friend of Jake's." She hesitated. "Do you want me to call him?"

Shannon shook her head. "No. Don't. Wherever he is, I'm sure he has enough to deal with. He can't do anything anyway."

Officer Murphy opened the door. "Time's up."

Angie held up a finger to indicate one minute. "Maggie Randolph, that's the attorney's name. She'll probably call you first to get the details. You hang in there."

Shannon nodded, feeling more alone than ever when the door closed behind Angie.

~ * ~

It was after six that evening and Shannon sat staring at the untouched dinner tray that had been delivered earlier. The door opened and a female officer came inside, unlocking the cell and sliding open the door. "Your attorney is on the phone."

"My attorney?"

"Ms. Randolph?"

"Oh, yes."

The officer held her by the arm and led her to a small conference room furnished only with a narrow metal table and two benches. A phone stretched from the wall and sat atop the table. "Pick up the receiver and press the blinking line. Knock on the door when you're finished." The officer snapped the door shut behind her.

Shannon tentatively picked up the phone and pressed a button. "Hello?"

"This is Maggie Randolph. Is this Shannon Chase, a/k/a Heather Carlson?"

"Yes, it is."

"Good. Do you prefer Shannon or Heather?"

"I...uh...Shannon, I suppose. For now."

"Okay, Shannon. I took the liberty of having the police fax me a copy of their report."

"Wait. Ms. Randolph? I hope Angie told you my situation. Financially, that is."

"She did. Let's not worry about that now. Okay?"

"Okay."

Papers rustled on the other end of the line. "According to the police report, you shot a man who broke into your apartment. The man turned out to be the brother of Governor Corinne Hastings. His story, not surprisingly, is quite different from yours. The police have charged you with extortion with regard to a surrogacy relationship with the Hastings and assault with a deadly weapon perpetrated on Mr. Baker."

"But I didn't...."

"I'm just reviewing with you what they've told me. Is this accurate so far?"

"Yes."

"You were brought in for questioning and, at that time, determined you wanted legal representation?"

"Yes. They.... Yes."

"Okay. Am I correct in understanding that you would like me to represent you in this matter?"

"I suppose.... I mean, I need an attorney and Angie recommended you."

"Yes, she did. But what do you want?"

Shannon hesitated.

"Ms. Chase, I've been practicing law for the past twenty-two years. I've won ninety-seven percent of my cases. I'm very expensive—usually. But you're a friend of Angie's and I do some pro bono work. So, let's put the checkbook aside and you tell me what you want me to do for you."

"I want you to represent me. Please."

"There, that wasn't so difficult. I'm in court tomorrow morning, but I'll be in Snoqualmie to meet with you after lunch. Is there anything you need?"

Shannon thought for a moment then said, "I'm probably going to need tampons soon."

Maggie Randolph chuckled. "Can do. Shannon, try to get some rest. Worry will do you no good, and I need you to be alert when we meet. Now, until you and I meet, I want you to talk with no one. Not a word to anyone about your case, your views on recycling, the weather. Nothing."

"I understand. Thank you so much, Ms. Randolph."

"Maggie. I'll see you tomorrow."

Maggie Randolph sounded like a no-nonsense person but with a hint of a sense of humor. Shannon felt relieved to have an attorney—an apparently competent one—in her corner.

She sat on the cot and glanced at the gleaming silver toilet attached to the wall in the corner. A four by four metal sheet offered little in the way of privacy. And she'd have to undo the one-piece jumpsuit to use the toilet. She was sure that, as soon as she had undone the suit and sat down, someone would come through the door. She squirmed with discomfort.

An officer came in later and took away the untouched dinner tray. Shannon kept only the cup of diced fruit and bottle of water. "Thank you."

When the lights dimmed and she lay on the cot in near darkness, she knew she couldn't put things off any longer. She undid the jumpsuit and squatted behind the sheet of metal on the cold toilet. Relief.

She lay on the cot, listening to a murmur of voices beyond the door. She appeared to be the only felon in captivity in Snoqualmie. She turned over the events of the past twenty-four hours in her mind. This time last evening, she was laughing and having a nice time with Angie and her friends in Seattle. It amazed her that Angie dove in to help without question. Then she thought of seeing her mother tomorrow, if they'd let her mother come in. Tears stung her eyes and trickled down her temples. Never would she have imagined her mother visiting her in jail. At least her mother and Brooke would be able to get Bailey and look after her. And what about Helen Swinson? Who would take care of her? If Abe had to get a new caregiver, then Shannon would be out of a job and a home.

She next thought of Jake, wishing he was there to reassure her, comfort her. But even Jake couldn't rescue her from this mess. The one thought that she'd held at bay came roaring through the darkness like an angry dragon—what if they actually convicted her of the crimes with which she'd been charged?

~ * ~

Maggie Randolph looked much the way Shannon would have expected—about five foot six, not thin but compact, with a determined walk and fiery red hair. She brought to mind one of those miniature Tonka dump trucks—bright, sturdy, and ready for work. Her handshake was warm and reassuring.

She spread out papers from her briefcase, glanced at them, then peered over the top of her glasses at Shannon. "I'm betting I already know more about this than you do. The defendant's always the last to know." She folded neatly-manicured fingers together in front of her. "According to the District Attorney, you entered into a legally-binding agreement with Mark and Corinne Hastings to carry their child and, upon birth of said child, to relinquish all parental rights of said child. You were to be paid the amount of fifty-thousand dollars when the child was given over to the Hastings'."

Shannon opened her mouth, but Maggie held up a hand to stop her. "According to the Hastings', you had been paid ten thousand dollars in advance and you subsequently refused to give them the child and absconded with both the baby and the ten thousand dollars. The police report shows that a search of your apartment yielded a briefcase with ten thousand seven hundred dollars inside." She removed her glasses and studied Shannon's face. "Okay. Speak."

"All of that is false. Well, almost all of it." She told Maggie about Corinne showing up at her apartment and tossing ten thousand dollars at her before walking out the door. "I never signed any agreement. The baby was completely unplanned, trust me. Mark never wanted a baby. He wanted me to get an abortion."

"Why do you think Corinne Hastings would come after you and your baby so aggressively? What woman would want a child that was born out of her husband's infidelity?"

Shannon winced. "I truly don't know. I never asked Mark for a thing. I was content to raise Bailey…Amanda…as my child, alone. Then Corinne found out about us and started pushing for me to let them adopt the baby. When I refused, she came to my apartment and pretty much threatened me that if I didn't just take the money and give over the baby, I'd be sorry."

Maggie nodded. "They also assert that you talked with Mark Hastings and told him if he wanted the baby, to bring a hundred thousand dollars to you and he could have her. He claims that he was unable to come himself and sent Anthony Baker, his brother-in-law on his behalf." She slid a stapled stack of papers across the table. "This, they claim, is the signed agreement."

Shannon took the papers in trembling hands and read. It all looked so legal, even down to her signature. "I did not sign this. I never saw this document."

"That's not your signature?"

Studying it closely, Shannon said, "It looks like my signature, but it has to be forged. I would never have signed this." Then she thought of the papers she had signed that first day she and Mark had met at the bank. "He forged my signature."

Maggie gathered up the papers and placed them inside the

briefcase. "Okay. I won't tell you this is going to be easy. We're going up against the Governor of Missouri. She's got a major pro-life constituency. But you know what?" She gave Shannon a grin. "I don't like bullies. And I believe you. The challenge will be to prove they're lying. That will be my job. Your job, for now, is to think of anything Mark Hastings said to you while you were involved that could dispute what they claim. Also, if you think of other women with whom he's been involved in the past, it would help. Nothing like a pissed off ex-girlfriend."

"I was only with Mark for two months, then I broke it off. I found out about the baby a week later. I also found out then about his reputation for philandering. I was so stupid." She took as shuddering breath. "Do you really think we can win this?"

"You know why I have such a great win percentage? Because I don't take on cases I don't *think* I can win. You do everything I tell you to do and stay calm and focused. You're scheduled for arraignment at three in Seattle. They're hurrying this along for some reason. We'll appear before the judge, along with the D.A. They'll read the charges and ask how you plead."

"I'm not guilty of this."

"Then that's how we plead. I'll try to get them to set bail, pleading the case that you're a single mother, but I'm not optimistic. Mainly because they'll argue that you're a flight risk. By the way, where is your baby?"

"She's with her sitter. But my best friend is flying in this afternoon and my Mom arrives tomorrow. They'll take care of her."

"Good. I'll see you later this afternoon. I have some work to do before the arraignment." Maggie walked to the door and knocked. "Shannon, thank you for letting me represent you."

"Wait. Maggie, would you call my friend, Brooke, and let her know what's happening?"

"Sure." She punched the number into her phone as Shannon gave it to her.

When the officer led Shannon back to her cell, he handed her a brown paper bag. "Your attorney left this for you. I had to check it first."

She glanced inside—a box of tampons, toothbrush, toothpaste, deodorant, a dark chocolate Godiva candy bar, and a paperback romance novel. Maggie had thought of everything. "Thanks."

179

As much as she tried to stay calm, her heart pounded and her breath came in short gasps. She sat in her cell and tried to imagine the arraignment, a judge hearing the claims of a respected Governor and then looking at Shannon—a woman with an alias, a gun, a lot of money, and no one to back up her story. And in the jumpsuit with her new blond, spiky hairdo, she looked the part of a felon. All she needed was a tattoo of a skull and crossbones on her neck and a silver stud piercing one eyebrow.

Chapter Twenty-Nine

Jake paced the hotel room. He had two hours before it would be time to head to the Federal courthouse to give his testimony. He stopped in front of the full-length mirror and stared. His black pants, jacket, and shirt, accented by the white tab at his throat, looked as foreign as the neatly-groomed man staring back at him.

In an effort to calm his nerves and distract his mind, he turned on the TV. Nothing on at this hour but the morning news. He opened a bottle of water and sat in the barrel-backed chair.

First a story about global warming, then a segment on the gun lobby battles. He got up to drop the empty bottle into a recycling bag the hotel provided. His head snapped around at the next news story.

"Breaking news from the Missouri capital. Governor Corinne Baker Hastings will hold a news conference later today. Apparently, she and her husband, Mark Hastings, had contracted with a woman to act as a surrogate mother for their child. The woman…"

Jake flinched as Shannon's photo appeared on the screen.

"…Heather Carlson, a former bank manager from Jefferson City, allegedly agreed to carry the child for the Hastings, then backed out of the deal and absconded with both the baby and the ten thousand dollar advance payment given her by Governor Hastings."

Jake slowly walked back to the chair and dropped down. *A surrogate?* She acted like the victim in the situation, and he had believed her. She wasn't much better than Crowley had been, selling children for a profit. The thought sickened him.

The commentator continued, "Ms. Carlson, who has been living under the assumed name of Shannon Chase, is currently incarcerated in Snoqualmie, Washington awaiting arraignment on a charge of attempted murder. This past Saturday night, she shot a man she claims was an intruder into her apartment. That man is Anthony Baker, the brother of the Governor. We're still getting all of the details, but one source tells us that Ms. Carlson contacted Mark Hastings last week to make a new deal for one hundred thousand dollars to turn over the baby girl. Unable to fly immediately to Washington state, Mr. Hastings asked his brother-in-law to meet with the woman. We'll have more details as they become available. Ms. Carlson is scheduled to be arraigned in a Seattle court later today."

Jake stared at the TV screen as the photo of Shannon faded and they moved on to another story. He picked up the remote and surfed channels, finding another displaying Shannon's photo as Heather Carlson and as she looked now with spiky blond hair. They showed a shot of Shannon sitting hunched in the back of a police car, crying.

His heart lurched for Bailey as he wondered where she had been, who would care for her now. She was the one victim in all of this. And to think he'd gone out of his way, put Caleb in a thankless position, just to get her proper documentation so she could live as Shannon Chase. "Damn." Jake felt like a fool. He owed Caleb an apology. And what about Abe and Helen Swinson? He'd delivered a felon to their doorstep. Jake had beaten himself up for failing to keep the promises he'd made. Meanwhile, Shannon or Heather—whoever the hell she was calling herself now—had promised a child and then failed to follow through.

His cell phone was buried in his duffle bag, since he couldn't take it with him into court. He needed to call somebody in Snoqualmie and find out exactly what was going on.

The phone on the night stand rang. "Yes?"

"Father Avery, it's Vince. We're waiting for you in the lobby. Time to go."

"I'll be right down." His phone call would have to wait.

At the courthouse, he was sequestered in a small private room until time for his testimony. It only gave him more time to think. The more he thought, the more idiotic he felt. And that soon transformed into anger. He had taken Shannon and her baby into his home, cared for them, helped her obtain identification and a place to live. And what thanks did he get? She lied to him about everything. She even came onto him, made it impossible for him not to act on impulse.

Jake shook his head. No, he couldn't put all of that on Shannon. He'd made love to her because he wanted to. She hadn't stopped him, but that didn't mean she was out to trap him, either. He'd told the Bishop to get his papers ready for his withdrawal from

Diocesan ministry. He was ready to break promises for Shannon—promises he'd made to God, no less.

The door opened. "Father Avery, they're ready for you."

As he walked with the marshal toward the court room, he had the feeling this was the last walk of Father Steve Avery. He'd been living as Jake Garber and, now that he'd made the decision to leave the priesthood, he couldn't go back to that name, that identity. He slid a finger under his collar and swallowed, straightened his shoulders and entered the court room.

It shouldn't have surprised him that no clergy were present—not a single priest in gallery. When he was called to take the stand, Jake walked briskly to the front to be sworn in, then took a seat in the witness chair.

The District Attorney stood in front of him. "Father Avery, will you recount for the court the events you witnessed at St. Damian's rectory on the evening of May sixteenth of 2011?"

Jake went through the events from the time he received the phone call from the parishioner's family and his return to the rectory to what he'd seen and heard there.

"And you have no doubt Louis Crowley was the man speaking with Father Martin at the time?"

"I'm certain. I not only heard him, but I saw Lou—Mr. Crowley—leave the rectory with a young child, a girl maybe six or seven years old. Lou wasn't happy because he said the couple was expecting a child of no more than three years."

"Did you question Father Martin about this later?"

"Not immediately. I went to the hospital to administer last rights to a parishioner. Later, when I asked about Lou being there, Alvin seemed nervous and said Lou just stopped by to say hello. I didn't mention the child."

"And you went to the police?"

"I did. I wasn't comfortable with what I'd heard and the fact that it involved a child. So I spoke with the police who put me in touch with the Bureau of Criminal Investigation."

The DA nodded as he paced, then turned to face Jake. "Is it true that you received death threats from the defendant?"

"I received threats, yes."

"Could you speak up, Father Avery?"

Jake leaned forward toward the microphone. "I received threats and the BCI thought they were coming from Mr. Crowley."

"Is it true that for the past two years and four months you have lived under a new identity and under the protection of U.S. Marshals?"

"Yes."

"And you are aware that Father Alvin Martin was murdered in his cell three weeks ago?"

Jake nodded. "Yes, I heard."

A muffled sob erupted from Sara Martin who was seated beside Lou Crowley and wearing shackles and handcuffs.

The D.A. returned to his seat at the prosecution table. "I have no further questions for this witness at this time, Your Honor."

The defense attorney, a short, squat man with thinning red hair and a belly protruding over his belt, stood. He approached Jake with a pensive expression on his face. "Father Avery, have you lived as a priest for the past two years and four months?"

The question seemed non-essential, but Jake leaned toward the microphone again. "No, sir, not if you mean in active ministry."

"Would you tell the court how your alter ego, Jake Garber, has lived then?"

The D.A. objected. "I don't see what this has to do with our proceedings. And we are not speaking of an alter ego. Father Avery was issued a new identity for his own protection."

The judge narrowed his eyes at the defense attorney. "I'll allow it, but be careful."

"Yes, Your Honor. Father Avery, describe your life in the past two years four months, please."

"I was given the identity of Jake Garber and relocated to Snoqualmie, Washington. I sustain myself working as a carpenter. I learned the trade from my grandfather when I was growing up."

"What about relationships?"

"Relationships? I…well…I have a few friends there. I pretty much keep to myself. I was told to be cautious, keep a low profile."

The attorney repeated, "Cautious. Would you say that a priest in exile taking up with a woman is being *cautious*?"

Lou Crowley snickered. Murmurs rolled through the courtroom and the D.A. was on his feet. "Your Honor…"

The judge smacked his gavel. "I'll have order in my court." He glared at the defense attorney. "Mr. Vance… Both of you approach."

"Your Honor, my line of questioning goes to the credibility

of the witness. He's been living a lie for the past month, maybe longer. How do we know he's not been lying from the start?"

The D.A. shook his head. "How my witness has chosen to live his life in the past few months has no bearing on what he observed two and half years ago."

Jake could see where this was going and he dreaded the questions that would come. Especially in light of the fact that the woman in this 'relationship' was just arrested for attempted murder.

The judge pointed to the defense attorney. "Do not cross a line here, Mr. Vance."

"Understood, Your Honor."

The D.A. cast Jake a questioning glance as he returned to his seat.

Jake could feel perspiration breaking out on his upper lip and forehead. He wanted to wipe it away, but didn't want to draw attention to the fact that the current line of questioning made him nervous.

"Father Avery, is it true that you have been involved in a relationship with a woman in the past few months?"

Was it a relationship? They were friends, but then they'd had sex. What was it called—friends with benefits? Jake glanced at the judge and then at the D.A., hoping one of them would intervene. Neither did.

"I have a few friends who are women."

"Oh, a few." Vance chuckled. "Quite the ladies' man."

"Objection," shouted the D.A.

"Granted. Mr. Vance wrap this up now, and you better have a point," the judge cautioned.

"Yes, Your Honor. I do have a point." He turned back to face Jake. "Is it true that you took in a woman and her baby, provided them shelter, lived with them before helping her secure her own place."

"Yes. She needed help…."

"And as a priest, you are still bound by vows, am I correct?"

"As a Diocesan priest, I am bound to my promise of celibacy. Yes." Sweat now poured down Jake's back and he squirmed. The movement wasn't lost on the attorney.

"Did you engage in a physical relationship with this woman?"

Jake swallowed hard. He was under oath. "I… Yes, I did."

The judge slammed his gavel again to silence the murmurings in the room.

"Well, then, why should we believe your testimony here today? Apparently you have little integrity in honoring promises and sacred vows. How do we know you even meant what you said when you were sworn in?"

The D.A. leaped to his feet, sending his chair scraping along the floor. "Your Honor, this is Mr. Vance's attempt to discredit our witness. But it's like comparing apples and oranges. Father Avery gave the police his account of what happened over two years ago when he was still active in the priesthood. His account has not wavered in all that time. His personal relationships have nothing to do with this case."

"It has everything to do with his credibility," the defense attorney said.

The judge scowled at both attorneys and then at Jake. "Move on, Mr. Vance."

With a smirk cast at Jake, the attorney said, "I have no further questions at this time."

"Your Honor, I request a brief recess to confer with my witness," the D.A. said wearily.

"I expected you would. Thirty minute recess." The judge stood and left the courtroom.

Jake stood shakily and paused before stepping out of the witness stand. How the hell had they found out? As he passed the defense table, Lou Crowley muttered, "Was she worth it?"

He stopped and glared at Lou, his hands curling into fists. The D.A. took him by the arm and tugged him along. Once they were back in the small private room, he whirled at Jake, "Any other little surprises you'd like to toss my way, *Father*?"

Chapter Thirty

The ride to Seattle in the back of the police cruiser seemed interminable. Just a few days earlier, Shannon had made the same trip with Angie and her two friends. She'd felt carefree and optimistic. She wasn't feeling particularly optimistic now.

Maggie stood waiting for her outside the side entrance to the courthouse, following as the deputy led her inside. They had half an hour to meet before the arraignment. Once they were secured in a small conference room, Maggie smiled at her. "How are you doing?"

Shannon exhaled. "I won't lie. I'm scared."

"I'm sure. I spoke with your friend, Brooke. She has picked up your daughter from the sitter. She and your mom will be staying at your apartment."

Shannon bit her lip, fighting tears. "Will I be able to see them?"

"Probably not before the arraignment."

She sat and stretched her arms out on the table, fingers knit tightly together.

Maggie sat opposite her. "I need for you to be calm and focused. The judge will ask your name. Legally, you are Heather Carlson. I don't even want to know how you got documentation as Shannon Chase. She will then read the charges. We're in luck that we drew Judge Rebecca Henniker. She's more likely to grant bail."

"It won't matter. I don't have any money. I don't know anyone…."

Maggie held up a hand. "That's already taken care of, if bail is granted. Look, we only have a few minutes. I want to run you through the procedures one more time. Okay?"

The question of who could afford her bail hung in the back of Shannon's mind as Maggie led her through what she could expect in the courtroom.

A knock sounded on the door before it opened. The deputy peered inside. "Judge Henniker is ready for you." He stepped inside and once again handcuffed Shannon before leading her to the courtroom.

Glancing around nervously, Shannon spied Abe Swinson sitting in the back of the courtroom beside Angie. Embarrassment warmed her face as Abe looked at her, then nodded.

Shannon's body shook as she stood beside Maggie and responded to the judge's questions.

"Would you state your name please?" the judge asked.

"Heather Carlson." She could now let go of Shannon Chase.

"Ms. Carlson, you are charged with extortion of Mark and Corinne Hastings and of assault with a weapon against Mr. Anthony Baker. How do you plead?"

"I never asked the Hastings for money. And I certainly I didn't intend to kill anyone. I was only protecting my daughter."

The judge held up a hand. "Ms. Randolph, please instruct your client on her response."

Maggie leaned close. "Just answer."

Heather nodded. "I'm sorry, Your Honor. Not guilty to both charges."

Maggie then said, "Your Honor, Ms. Carlson is the mother of a four-month-old child. We ask that bail is granted so that she may return to care for her child while she awaits trial. My client has never been in trouble before. She's never even had a parking ticket."

The District Attorney interjected, "Your Honor, Ms. Carlson has already shown herself to be a flight risk. The People ask that she remain incarcerated until her trial."

The judge paused and seemed to give consideration to both requests. "Will counsel please approach?"

Maggie and the District Attorney both stepped forward. Heather couldn't hear all that was being said but, at one point she heard Maggie say, "My client called the police herself after Mr. Baker broke into her apartment. She feared for her life after finding a strange man standing in her apartment in the dark."

"And that can be presented at trial," the D.A. countered.

The judge interrupted them. "I'm asking the questions here. Ms. Randolph, is your client able to post bail?"

The District Attorney raised his voice, "Your Honor, I strongly object. The victim in this case is the brother of the Governor of Missouri."

"I'm aware of that. But we are in Washington state. And do I have to remind you that this is my court and my decision?"

The D.A. murmured a response and stepped back.

When Maggie turned around, she gave Heather a slight wink.

"Ms. Carlson, I am going to grant bail in the amount one hundred thousand dollars and I am going to release you on your own recognizance. You have no prior criminal record and it seems there's some uncertainty about why Mr. Baker entered your apartment." She stared at Heather. "I'm doing this for your child and at the disagreement of the District Attorney, as you no doubt heard. Do not make me sorry."

"Yes, Your Honor. Thank you."

"A hearing will take place twelve days from today." The judge stood and left the courtroom.

Heather turned to Maggie. "What does this mean? What happens now?"

"You'll be returned to the Snoqualmie police. They'll process you and then you'll be released to go home. I'll be gathering information for the initial hearing and we'll need to meet. I'll come to you."

"Thank you. What about the bail?"

"Abe Swinson."

"Mr. Swinson? But, he doesn't have that kind of money, does he?"

"Apparently he does." She paused, then said, "Heather, do exactly what they tell you to do. Don't even think about leaving town. You'll end up back in jail for good and Abe will lose ten thousand dollars."

"I understand. I just want to go home with my baby. I won't leave the apartment until it's time to come back to court."

The deputy came to escort Heather from the court room and to the waiting police car.

Two hours later, she waited for Brooke to pick her up at the police station. She stood when Brooke came through the door. Her friend presented identification to the desk officer and then wrapped Heather in a tight hug. "Thank God. I was so afraid they'd keep you locked up."

"Just get me out of here." She signed for her personal items and walked unsteadily toward the door.

In the car, Heather hunched over and sobbed.

Brooke rubbed her back. "Oh, honey. That had to be awful for you."

"It was. And this is only the beginning." She looked up at

Brooke. "Why are they doing this to me? I didn't ask for a thing from Mark."

"This isn't about Mark. It's Corinne getting even with both of you and, at the same time, making a pro-life statement and pretending to want a child. It's about votes." She started the rental car and backed out of the parking space. "Let's get you home. Your mom's going crazy wanting to see you."

All Heather wanted to do was to sink into her mother's embrace and hold her own daughter. When they pulled into the drive, Heather saw Abe Swinson come out his back door. She got out of the car and walked to him. "Thank you so much. Why would you put up bail money for me?"

He shrugged. "Why not? You didn't do anything wrong."

"I didn't but how would you be certain of that?"

He smiled. "I'm a good judge of character. That man was no more invited into your house than he was invited to the White House. You were protecting yourself and that sweet baby. And I'm not going to stand by and let some power hungry politician railroad you."

Heather wrapped her arms around him. "God bless you. I promise I won't disappoint you."

He patted her back. "I know you won't. You come down tomorrow and let Helen see you. She's napping now, but she was worried."

"I'll be down to help her in the morning. I need to do something normal."

"Okay, if you change your mind, we'll be fine." He went back into the house.

She took the steps two at a time. Her mother sat in the rocker, feeding Amanda. Heather blinked back tears at the sight. "Hi, Mom."

"Heather, come here."

Relief washed through her at the realization that there was no longer a need to continue the charade as Shannon Chase. She knelt and kissed Amanda's cheek then her mother's. "I'm so glad you're here."

Once Amanda was settled in her crib, Heather stepped into her mother's open arms and wept.

"It's going to be okay," her mother reassured, rocking her.

Heather almost believed it. "I need a shower."

"You probably haven't eaten, either. I'll have something ready for you when you're finished," her mother said.

"Thanks, Mom."

She lingered in the shower until the water began to cool, trying to wash off the past few days. Her thoughts turned to Jake, wondering where he was, if he knew what was going on. Would he believe everything they'd say about her on the news? How would she ever face him again?

When she emerged from the shower and dressed in a pair of comfy jeans and a tee shirt, she joined her mother and Brooke in the kitchen. "Grilled cheese and tomato soup. Comfort food."

Her mother ladled soup into a bowl and set it on the table. "Sit down and eat, then you can fill us in on what happened and what's going to happen."

The creamy grilled cheese and rich tomato soup warmed her, made her feel safe and at home. When she'd finished her second bowl, she pushed it away and sat back in the chair, telling them the whole story.

"So, do we call you Heather or Shannon now?" Brooke asked.

"Everyone here knows me as Shannon and the baby as Bailey. But there's no point in pretending any more, now that my life has been splayed across every news channel. I'll explain to Abe and Helen tomorrow." She looked at her mother through a sheen of tears. "I'm so sorry for the shame this bring to you. I'd understand if you told me to continue as Shannon Chase."

"Nonsense. You're my daughter, Heather, and I'm proud of you." Her mother reached for her hand. "What about your attorney? Is she good?"

"She's great. I don't know what she said to the judge to get me out on bail. And Mr. Swinson paid my bail." Tears stung her eyes.

"The Swinsons are a wonderful couple," her mother said. "I took them some dinner earlier."

"Thanks for doing that." She looked around the apartment. "We'll have to figure out sleeping arrangements."

Brooke pointed to the darkened corner of the living room. "Nope. All taken care of. Your friend, Angie, brought over an air mattress. I figured you and I can camp out here and your mom can have the bed."

"I don't know how I got so lucky with the people here. They don't even know me."

"Well, they must know all they need to, because they sure have rallied around you," Brooke said. "What about Jake? Will we get to meet him? Sounds like he's the real hero in the story, rescuing you after the accident."

She shook her head. "He's gone out of town. I don't think he'll be back any time soon." She stood and stretched. "I'll do these dishes, then I think it's time to turn in. I'm exhausted."

"I'll inflate the air mattress," Brooke said.

Heather got her mother settled into the bedroom and carried out sheets, blankets and two pillows to the living room. She made her bed on the sofa. "I haven't told you yet how much I appreciate all you've done."

Brooke smiled. "Wouldn't do anything less, you know that. We're best friends, always." She hesitated, then asked, "What didn't you say in your mother's presence about Jake?"

"What do you mean?"

"I saw the look on your face and heard the disappointment in your voice when you said he'd gone away." She propped herself up on one elbow. "Spill."

"There's nothing to tell. He's a nice guy who helped us out. That's all."

Brooke studied her for a moment. "Okay, I'll buy that for now. You've been interrogated enough this week. Sleep tight." She turned over and pulled the sheet up to her shoulder. "I will get the rest of the story."

Heather turned off the lamp and sank into the sofa. But when she closed her eyes, it was Jake's arms that wrapped around her and held her there. It was his mouth leaving a hot trail down her neck and across her breasts. It was his image looming over her, looking at her with such tenderness. And then she remembered his hasty departure after their night of lovemaking. It hit her like a glass of ice water tossed into her face. His words through the phone, "I love you" echoed in the hollow of her heart. Would he still feel that way now that the story of Heather Carlson had hit the national news? Did he already know? The thought that he'd heard the accusations against her and might draw his own conclusions without hearing her side of the story made her sick. It wasn't as if she'd fallen in love with him. But she knew she could and she had a sense he felt that way, too. One moment of poor judgment had delivered to her both her greatest blessing—her baby—and her greatest curse, and that would possibly cost her a chance at happiness.

Chapter Thirty-One

Jake walked into the hotel bar and scanned the dimly lit space. He spied Caleb at a table off to his left. He reached up and removed the white tab from his collar and unbuttoned the top two buttons of his shirt. The feeling was one of removing a too-tight dog collar.

Caleb nodded as Jake approached. "So, it's over?"

Jake stuffed the collar tab into his jacket pocket. "It's over." He sat down and, when the waitress came by, ordered a scotch.

"I'm glad. You deserve to get back to your life," Caleb said.

Get back to his life? He couldn't go back. "I need to ask you something. If I choose to continue with the identity of Jake Garber, is that a problem?"

Caleb's eyebrows lifted, his forehead wrinkling. "Not a problem. The FBI has closed the case and concluded that there's no one else on your trail. But you might need to explain your reasons."

The waitress delivered Jake's drink and he took a sip. "I've learned a few things in the program, the life I've lived for the past two years. I'm not suited to return to Father Avery's life."

"Does this have anything to do with Shannon?"

"You mean Heather. It might have, once. Not now." Jake downed the rest of the drink and held the glass up to signal the waitress for a refill.

"You saw the news, I guess."

"I did. I owe you an apology. You went out on a limb for her, for me. I actually trusted her."

Caleb sat for a moment, staring at him. "Things aren't always what they seem, Jake. You should know that better than anyone."

"Are you saying I should give her a chance to explain? Explain what? She lied to me from day one."

"Well, I'm not a relationship counselor. I've been married and divorced twice. But let me ask you one thing."

Jake nodded. "Go ahead."

"You love her?"

The words hit him in the pit of his stomach. Yes, he loved

her. He loved her enough to walk away from his former life, from who he was, and reach for a future with her. But that was before. "Doesn't matter now, does it?"

Caleb shook his head. "Despondency doesn't suit you. Neither does self-pity." He stood and tossed some bills onto the table. "Drinks are on me. Your independence celebration." Before walking away, he grasped Jake's shoulder. "Don't let your pride get in the way. You've kept secrets, too. You had your reasons, she might have hers." He slapped Jake's shoulder. "Have a good life, Jake Garber."

Jake turned and watched Caleb walk out of the bar and out of his life. No more watch dog. No more support from the U.S. Marshals. Tomorrow he would go to the Bishop's office and sign papers that would release him from the priesthood. Then he'd fly to Florida and see his father for the first time in over two years. He'd already called his sister. She and her family would meet him there. After that, he wasn't sure. He liked life in Snoqualmie, but he needed to hear the truth from Shannon—or Heather—before he made any decisions.

The next morning, Jake arrived at the Bishop's office wearing khakis and a white shirt. He sat the desk and reviewed the papers slid over to him, then signed Steven Avery to the document that released him as a priest.

"What will you do now?" the Bishop asked.

"I'm going to visit my family, then I'll return to Washington state."

The Bishop stood. "May I give you a blessing?"

Jake extended his hand. "Just wish me well, as I do you."

Shaking his hand firmly, the Bishop nodded. "I hope you have a full and happy life."

"Thank you." Once outside, Jake stood and drew in a deep breath, letting it out slowly. Doubt hit him like a tidal wave. What had he just done? Had he truly thought the decision through? Should he have given himself more time once the drama of the trial was over?

His entire adult life, all he knew was being a priest. Even though he'd lived the past two years as someone else, under the surface he still knew himself as a priest. Sure he'd crossed the line with Heather. He was still a man. That didn't make it right on any count. But making love to her was not unforgivable. At least not with God. His faith was built on the dynamic of forgiveness.

Instead of hailing a cab, Jake began to walk. He needed to clear his head. If he believed in a God that would forgive him for breaking a promise, how could he refuse to forgive Heather? If she was guilty of the charges leveled against her, he didn't see a future for them, but he had to at least listen and to forgive her. If he were to be honest, he had to admit he owed her an explanation as well.

But first he needed to find out exactly what was going on. He pulled his cell phone from his pocket and called Angie.

~ * ~

"Heather, come here quick." Brooke waved her toward the living room. "CNN is talking about this town."

Having just come out of the shower, Heather wrapped a towel around her hair and hurried to the TV. What she saw made her jaw drop.

"The FBI has been working to capture Crowley for the past two years. Following the death of Father Alvin Martin in a New York prison, Father Steve Avery remained the only witness to seal the fate of Crowley and his accomplice Sara Martin. Another odd twist to the story is that Sara Martin is the sister of Father Alvin Martin. She was an adoption worker for a private New York adoption agency."

The camera zoomed in close on Father Avery as he left the courthouse. Heather gasped. "That's Jake."

Brooke turned to look at her. "That's your hero?"

Pointing at the TV, she repeated, "That's Jake. That's the man who rescued us when I crashed my car." Then she glanced down at the sofa, remembering being in his arms. "Oh, my God. He's a priest?"

"You didn't know that already?" Brooke asked.

"If I'd known, I never would have…." Heat washed over her. "Where's my mom?"

"She took some of the banana bread she baked down to the Swinsons."

Heather stood and moved closer to the TV. "I can't believe he…he and I…right here on that couch."

Brooke stared at her wide-eyed. "Are you telling me he slept with you? The priest?"

"Slept with me? No. He didn't stay long enough to sleep. That lying bastard!"

"Shhh, they'll hear you all the way downstairs." Brooke stood and put a hand on Heather's arm. "I'm so sorry."

Heather moved toward the sofa, then veered away and sat in the rocker. "I'm such an idiot. I thought he was a nice guy, you know? One of the good guys. And I had no intention of getting involved with him. It just kind of happened. What the hell is wrong with me? First Mark and now Jake."

Brooke motioned to the TV. "Looks like he's got plenty of trouble of his own."

Heather whipped her head up. "The biker!"

"Biker? What…?"

"There was a guy on a motorcycle. I thought he was after me. I'll bet he was after Jake the whole time. And that son-of-a-bitch didn't even have the decency to tell me. I was scared to death. That's why he stayed here in the first place, because I was terrified. And he just let me believe I was in danger."

"But you were in danger, just from someone else."

"He didn't know that. He had everyone in this town fooled. I wonder if he really thinks he'll be welcome here after this. Surely everyone in town knows the truth by now." She snatched up the phone and pressed in one of the numbers on the list she kept on the table.

"Angie, have you seen the news today?"

"Today? No, did something else happen?"

"Did you know Jake was here under witness protection?"

"What?"

"I just saw him on CNN. He's in New York testifying on this big child trafficking case. The thing is, he's not Jake. He's a priest— Father Steve Avery."

Silence hissed through the phone. Then Angie said, "Can you hold for one second? I have another call."

"Just come over if you can or call me back." She hung up.

Brooke waited a moment before asking, "Did she already know?"

"Didn't sound like it. She had to take another call. She'll either call back or come over here." Overwhelming sadness hit her then and tears rolled down her face. "I feel so…so dirty. God, Brooke, I had sex with a priest."

From the door, her mother gasped. "What did you say?"

~ * ~

197

Half an hour later, following an embarrassing confession and explanation to her mother, Heather sat across from Angie at the dinette table. "He called you?"

"Yep. Right after you did. He was the other call I got while we were talking. He told me everything."

"Everything?"

"I guess now he can talk freely about what happened because the trial is over and the bad guys—and girl—are all in jail. You have to know he wouldn't have deliberately deceived you. He was more concerned about what's happening to you."

"When you talk with him again, tell him he needn't be concerned. I have a good lawyer and I'll be just fine."

Angie narrowed her eyes and stared at her. "You seem kind of angry with Jake. Is there something more to this?"

"No, not at all."

"You sure about that? Because I got the same feeling when I was talking with Jake, that there was something more he wasn't saying. Shannon, if there's…."

"Heather. You can call me Heather. I don't need to hide behind a fake identity any longer. I have no secrets now."

Angie laughed. "We all have secrets." Then she sobered. "Look, I want you to know I don't believe what they've said about you. Neither does my mom or other folks in town who've met you. So you tell me what you need me to do to help."

Heather's throat tightened with emotion and she swallowed hard. "You've done so much already. Maggie is a wonderful lawyer. I couldn't believe she convinced the judge to let me out on bail."

"Oh, she can be very convincing. I just hope she can find the evidence she needs to clear you altogether."

Heather slumped back in her chair. "That might be asking a lot. Did you see the oh-so-tearful interview last night with Corinne Hastings? You'd think I kidnapped *her* baby. She's making it sound like that's exactly what I did. You have to know I'd never give up my child. I did not agree to turn the baby over to them."

"I saw it, and I believe you. What I didn't see was her husband looking all that grieving. What's up with him?"

"Mark? He never wanted the baby in the first place. He likes the life he has as the Governor's husband. She works sixteen hour days and he screws around and spends her money. A child would only interrupt his routine."

"That's a shame that he never wanted to know Bailey. Should I call her that?"

Heather shook her head. "No. Her name is Amanda."

Angie smiled. "That's a beautiful name and it suits her. Where is she?"

"She's napping. My mother and Brooke went shopping. We were out of groceries and I just can't bear to leave the apartment, except to go down to help with Helen."

Standing, Angie gave her a hug. "I've gotta run. But you have my cell number and the number at Rusty's. You need anything at all, you just call."

"Thank you. Mostly for believing in me. I'm sorry I lied to you."

"Hey, you did what you had to do to protect yourself and the baby. I'd have done the same thing." She opened the door to leave, then paused. "You have Jake's number?"

Oh, she had his number all right. She had no intention of calling him and no intention of arguing that point with Angie. "I have it."

"Okay. I'll talk with you soon."

Heather watched until Angie reached the bottom of the steps. Then she went back to the bedroom to check on Amanda—sound asleep. She was still standing there, staring at her daughter, examining her features when she heard footsteps coming up the stairs. She headed down the hall, figuring her mother and Brooke could use some help with the groceries.

When she rounded the corner, she stopped in her tracks. "What are you doing here?"

"Now, Heather, is that any way to talk to the father of your child?" Mark Hastings filled the doorframe wearing a suit, a menacing look, and holding a gun. "Where is she?"

"Sleeping." Heather backed away, trying to get to the kitchen where she could at least arm herself with a butcher knife.

"Don't think about it. Just get the baby. I want to see my daughter."

"No. I told you, she's sleeping."

He sauntered into the center of the living room, the gun trained on her. His face twisted with rage. "Get the damned baby. Now!"

She stumbled as she backed down the hallway. "What are

you going to do?"

"What I should have done in the first place. Take care of this mess."

He nudged her into the bedroom and shoved her onto the bed. Then he turned and stared down into the crib. "They're so cute when they're sleeping."

"Mark, that's your daughter. Surely you can't think about hurting her."

"Shut up. Get over here and pick her up. We're going for a drive."

Her entire body shook as she reached into the crib for Amanda. She bent to pick up the diaper bag.

"Leave it. Just the baby. And don't even think about calling for help. You wouldn't want the old folks downstairs to get hurt." He moved her toward the door. "Here's what you'll tell the old man if he comes outside. I'm your brother, just came by for a visit and we're going for a drive so you can show me the area. Got that? And say it with a smile, like you're happy to see me." He gave her a push through the door and onto the landing at the top of the steps. "One wrong move and I'll kill the brat first, then you."

The coldness in his voice left her no doubt he was serious. Dead serious. Predictably, as they reached the bottom of the steps, Abe stepped out onto his porch. "Nice day, isn't it?"

"Beautiful." Heather fought to keep the tremor from her voice. "Look who stopped by—my brother. Quite a surprise, so we're going out to see the area."

Abe stared hard at her, then at Mark. "I see. Well, nice day for a drive."

Mark already had a car seat in the back of his Mercedes and stood right behind her while she got Amanda fastened in, then waited for her to latch her seatbelt before he closed the door. He turned right out of the driveway and then headed north on Route 203.

"Where are you taking us?" she asked.

"Like I said, for a drive. It's a beautiful day to see the mountains, don't you think?"

"You won't get away with this, you know."

"Maybe. Maybe not. But if you think I'm going to let you testify in court, you're crazy."

She turned to face him. "I don't understand. I'm the one on

trial here. Your wife has seen to that. I don't get what it is you think you have to lose, other than being exposed as a cheat, which everyone pretty much knows already."

"And yet that reputation didn't stop you."

"I must have been insane to get mixed up with you." She breathed, then tried a different approach. "Mark, I haven't asked a thing of you for Amanda. You're not even listed on her birth certificate. All of this mess is Corinne's doing, not mine."

"My wife is apparently obsessed with getting her hands on this baby. She and I agreed early on that we would never have children. We both have careers."

Heather couldn't stop herself. "Yes, I know. She's in politics and you're a professional leech."

His arm shot out and the back of his hand connected with her mouth. Her head snapped sideways, hitting the window. "I warned you to shut the hell up."

She tasted blood and touched her lip. A slick smear appeared on her fingertips. Instead of wiping them on her jeans, she reached down and wiped the blood on the side of the leather seat. If she was going to die, she was certainly going to leave evidence.

They were approaching the hairpin curve by Jake's cabin. She wondered if Jake was home yet and would he possibly see them. Not likely. The cabin sat too far up from the road. At his current speed, Mark was likely to hit the same tree she had, unless she warned him. She weighed out which could be worse, slamming into that tree or continuing on with Mark. A glance at the baby sleeping in the back seat decided for her. "Be careful. There's a hairpin turn coming up."

He barely eased off the gas and the tires squealed as he took the curve.

Heather tried pleading. "You don't have to kill Amanda. Just leave her somewhere—a gas station or someone's doorstep. We could leave her at that cabin we just passed. Take me instead."

"You're not the problem. *That's* the problem," he said, jerking a thumb toward the back seat.

Anger over-rode any sensibility she had. "*That* is your daughter and her name is Amanda Grace. She's only a baby and none of this is her fault. What I don't understand is what you're so afraid of. This fight is between me and Corinne."

He laughed. "And you're dumb enough to think you can

201

win?"

"I think when the court has all the facts, they'll see exactly what happened."

"And that's why I can't let you testify."

Exasperated, she exhaled. "What exactly do you think will come out in court that can possibly harm you?"

"There's a little matter of ninety-thousand dollars."

"What? I didn't take...."

"Relax. I know you didn't. I told Corinne you needed fifty thousand to give over the kid. Corinne gave you ten grand. So, I told her I talked with you and you were insisting on a hundred thousand now." He chuckled. "For a smart woman, she can be incredibly naïve. She actually gave me the cash to take care of the matter and get the baby. Anthony was supposed to snatch the kid and bring her to Corinne, but he fouled that up. The idiot."

"You're going to kill me and the baby so you can keep ninety-thousand dollars?"

"So I can look like the grief-stricken father and supportive husband and keep my *career* going." He glanced at her. "I never said I was a good guy. I don't really care what your opinion is of me. I have a good thing going with my marriage to the honorable and quite wealthy Governor Hastings. And I don't plan on letting you or your brat destroy that for me. Once you're out of the picture, the legal case goes away, Corinne punishes me for a while, then forgives me—as usual—and life goes on. For some of us."

Chapter Thirty-Two

Doris and Brooke turned up the driveway. Doris approached the policeman talking with Abe.

"I'm sure the guy isn't her brother," Abe said. "Look, Tim, something wasn't right. She was nervous."

"This is her mother. She'll tell you. The girl doesn't have a brother and she was not going willingly with that guy."

"Abe, what's going on?" Doris asked.

"A man was here about thirty minutes ago. Heather and the baby went with him, but I don't think she wanted to go. Tell Officer Murphy here if Heather has a brother."

"No, she doesn't. She's an only child." She looked back to Abe. "Who was the man? Do you know him?"

Abe shook his head. "Never saw him before. He was all dressed up in a suit. Tall, maybe six feet, light brown hair."

"Oh, my God," Brooke said. "I think that's Mark."

The officer turned toward her. "Mark?"

"Mark Hastings. The husband of Governor Hastings of Missouri. Mark is the baby's father."

The officer asked Abe, "What kind of car was the guy driving?"

"A late model silver Mercedes."

"If we go upstairs, I can pull his photo up on the computer," Brooke said, already heading for the steps.

Once she had the Missouri Governor's site open, she clicked on a photo of Mark Hastings and called Abe over.

He studied the picture, then said, "That's the man."

"Can you copy that photo and send it to my email," Officer Murphy asked.

"Can do." She right clicked on the photo and asked for his email address. "It's sent."

Doris slumped on the sofa. "Isn't there someone you can call? We've got to start looking for her."

"Mrs. Carlson. Your daughter is out of jail on bail pending serious charges. Is there any chance she fled to avoid prosecution?"

"Absolutely not. She wouldn't do that and she certainly wouldn't put Amanda in danger." Tears filled the woman's eyes. "If she's with that man, it's against her will."

"Can you tell me if she took her purse or cell phone?" he asked.

Brooke did a quick search of the apartment. "Her purse is on the floor by the sofa. Her cell phone is on the kitchen counter. And she never goes out with Amanda without taking a diaper bag. It's still in the bedroom."

"Okay. Let me call this in to the Chief." He stepped outside to make his call.

"I'm sorry I couldn't stop them," Abe said, sitting down beside Doris. "But Tim's a good cop. He'll get the ball rolling and they'll be found. I'm sure of it."

"I hope you're right. Thank you for picking up on the fact that Heather doesn't have a brother."

"I remembered her telling us she wished she'd had a brother growing up. And then she stressed the word when she told me who the man was. Maybe if I'd put the pieces together faster, but this old brain of mine...."

Doris patted his hand. "Don't blame yourself. You did what you could."

Abe stood. "I have to get back to Helen. But please keep me posted on what's happening. I'd hate for anything to happen to your daughter. She's a good girl."

Officer Murphy came back inside. "The Chief's making a few calls. I'll let you know if we find anything. In the meantime, please contact me if you hear from your daughter." He handed Doris a business card.

"In other words, you're all going to walk on eggshells with this because it involves Mark and Corinne Hastings," Brooke said.

The young officer flushed. "I know you're upset, but we do have procedures to follow."

Abe turned to him. "I hope they're not right about that, Tim. You can't wait too long to start searching just because that guy's married to a governor."

"I promise you I'll do everything I can, Abe. You know the Chief—he wants all the facts first. And the girl is out on bail right now. It's not uncommon for someone to think they can outrun the law."

"She's not like that. And I can tell you, judging from the look on her face, she was not going willingly with that man. Please just find her before it's too late."

"I'll do everything I can." He waited for Abe, then followed him down the steps.

~ * ~

Brooke glanced out the window to see the officer speak once more with Abe, then get into his cruiser and drive off. "I feel so helpless."

Doris sat on the sofa, her arms wrapped around her middle. "Oh, sweet Jesus, please protect my girls."

Brooke returned to the computer and then punched in a phone number.

"Who are you calling?" Doris asked.

"The one person who can stop this. Governor Hastings."

A young woman answered the phone, "Hello, Governor Hastings' office. May I help you?"

"My name is Brooke Jamison. I need to speak with Governor Hastings immediately regarding an urgent matter."

"I'm sorry," the woman said cordially, "but if you leave your name, phone number and the nature of your call, I'll pass that on to the Governor's assistant and someone will call you."

"Fine. I'm Brooke Jamison, a friend of Heather Carlson. Mark Hastings kidnapped Heather and her baby this afternoon from her apartment and is probably going to kill them." She paused, taking a breath. "I'll hold now while you get the governor on the line."

"I...uh... Yes, please hold."

Classical music intended to be soothing irritated Brooke as she waited. Finally, a man came on the line. "This is Eric Lindstrom, Governor Hastings' personal assistant. How may I help you?"

Brooke repeated to him what she had stated to the first receptionist.

"Is this some kind of joke?"

"It's not a joke," Brooke shouted into the phone. "I have to speak to..."

"This is Corinne Hastings. Who is this?"

Brooke once again identified herself, noting she was Heather's friend. "Your husband has apparently come to finish the job your brother couldn't do. He forced Heather to go with him, along with the baby, and I'm sure it's not because he planned a little family picnic. You need to find him before he does them both harm."

"That's ridiculous. My husband's in St. Louis to speak on my behalf at a conference."

"No, he's not. The police are already involved and have his photo and a description of his car. My next call with be to the news media."

"Give me your phone number," the Governor demanded.

Once Brooke recited the number, the line went dead. "Well, that should get someone looking for them."

She went to the sofa and sat, putting an arm around Doris. "They're going to be okay. Heather's smart and she's protective of Amanda. She won't let Mark or anyone hurt that baby."

"He had to have a gun. She would never have walked out of here willingly unless she feared for their lives."

Brooke suspected as much, but didn't want to be the one to say it. "Don't worry. The last thing the good Governor wants is to have this spread all over the news. If the police can't find Mark Hastings, I've no doubt she will."

~ * ~

Corinne Hastings paced her office. She stopped at her desk and buzzed for Eric, "Get in here." When he opened the door, she asked, "What time is Mark's speech in St. Louis?"

"At seven-thirty, ma'am."

She glanced at the clock—six-fifteen. "What hotel?"

"He's staying at the Ritz Carlton, the same place as the conference."

"Get him on the phone now."

"Yes, ma'am."

Eric left, then returned shortly. "I'm sorry. They said he never checked in."

She stopped pacing and stared out the window at the dusky sky. "Thank you. You can go."

Eric paused. "Is there anything I can do? That woman on the phone earlier said Mark had kidnapped someone?"

Corinne shook her head. "No. That was a crank call. It's fine."

The minute Eric closed the door behind him, Corinne picked up her cell phone and punched in Mark's number. Her call went to voicemail. She had to be careful of the message or she could be implicated later. "Mark, you missed the conference and I'm worried about you. You need to stop what you're doing and call me right away. I'm sure it's a misunderstanding that we can work out."

With her brother hospitalized, Corinne had nothing to do but wait for Mark's call. She couldn't trust anyone else with this information. She buzzed Eric again. When he came into her office, she pointed to a chair. "Sit down, please."

He complied.

"What exactly did that woman say to you earlier?"

He repeated Brooke's message.

Corinne forced a laugh. "I swear some people will do anything to try to make trouble. Turns out she's a little crazy and a pro-choice advocate. I spoke with Mark and everything is fine. You don't have to worry any more about her. If she calls again, let me handle it."

"Are you sure you want to deal with her?

"I said I'll handle it." Her voice was sharper than she intended. She softened her tone. "It's late. You should go home."

"But the report…."

"Tomorrow's another day, Eric. Mark got delayed. Car trouble. So he's heading back here and I'll be joining him for dinner. I'll call the conference people in the morning and explain." She stood behind her desk. "Goodnight."

A moment later, Eric was at the door again. "I'm sorry. I was just leaving when the phone rang and I answered. It's the Washington State Police on the line. They insist on speaking with you."

Chapter Thirty-Three

Jake picked up a rental car at Tampa International. He headed for the causeway that would take him to Clearwater where his father lived. The temperatures were in the upper seventies and a nice breeze blew across the harbor. He opted for open windows rather than air conditioning. He'd first called his sister, then spoken with his father on the phone so the man wouldn't keel over from shock when his deceased son showed up on his doorstep.

He had told his dad he would stay only a few days, but now that he was here in the fresh air and sunshine, he might spend a week or two. He had a lot to sort out. The beach might just be the place to gain perspective. Angie had called twice, but he didn't even retrieve the messages. He needed to step away from his life in Snoqualmie and he knew she'd understand.

After a tearful reunion with his father and with his sister and her family, Jake settled on the deck of his father's home, gazing out at the Gulf. The sun had dropped low over the water, a crescent of orange glowing on the horizon. Jake felt a hand on his shoulder.

"You okay?" his sister asked.

He turned and looked up at her. "I will be."

She sat on the chaise beside his chair and turned sideways to face him. "So we really have to call you Jake now?"

He grinned. "You don't have to. But it's easier for me to keep that identity."

"No problem. Look, I know you've been through a lot, especially these past few months. I want you know I'm here for you if you need to talk. Or come and stay with us for a while. Charlie would love to spend time with you again."

Stephanie was his fraternal twin. He could see himself in her eyes and her smile. "Thank you. He's a great kid, you know. I wish I could have told you all the truth back then. I hate that you thought I was dead, mourned me."

She smacked his arm playfully. "Yeah, well, just don't expect me to do it again. I made a nice speech at your memorial mass. Nick probably taped it, but I don't think you want to see it."

"Probably not. But thanks for the kind words."

She turned and sat back in the chair, staring out at the water. "What will you do now?"

He shrugged. "I need to go back to Washington. I have a life there, work."

"Anything else?"

He fixed his gaze on the water. "I don't want to scandalize you."

She sat up. "Oh, my God, there is someone. I knew it."

"What do you mean you knew it? You thought I was dead."

"All through dinner, you were distracted."

He turned his head to face her. "It doesn't bother you that I got involved with someone while I was still a priest?"

"Heck, no. When you say someone, you do mean a woman, right? And you were never meant to be a priest. Nick and I had a running bet on how long you'd last."

"What do you mean?"

"I just never saw you that way. I watched you with Charlie when he was little and always thought you should have kids of your own. You're a good man. You have a big heart. But that whole celibacy thing? Seriously, that is a waste on you. You and the right woman will make beautiful kids."

He thought of Bailey, how beautiful she was, the feelings she elicited in him just by smiling at him.

"What are you grinning about?" Stephanie's eyes widened and she lowered her voice. "Don't tell me you have a baby."

"No. Heavens, no. But you're right. There is someone."

She sat up and turned toward him. "Tell me."

He told her about Shannon and Bailey, including the fact that Shannon was now free on bail pending a hearing and possible trial. "Although now her cover's been blown. Her real name is Heather Carlson and the baby's name is Amanda."

"Oh, bro, you sure don't know how to pick 'em."

"I don't think she's guilty. I got to know her and saw her in action as a mother. She's a good person. She just got mixed up with the wrong guy and got into a mess."

Stephanie gazed at him for a moment, then said, "You love her."

He nodded. "Yes, I do." It was a hard admission because he wanted not to love her, not to care. His life had been crazy enough for more than two years. The last thing he needed right now was more chaos.

"Then help me understand why it is that you're here."

"I needed to see you and Dad, let you know I was alive and okay."

She patted his knee as she stood. "And now we know. Tell me one thing—does this woman deserve you?"

"Probably not. She's deserves better."

"Well, maybe you should let her decide that. I can't wait to meet her." She bent and kissed his cheek. "We're taking the kids to the hotel before they get cranky. See you tomorrow."

"Goodnight. And Steph, the kids are great. My new niece is just gorgeous. She's going to be a heart-stopper when she's older." Throughout the day, every time he looked at his one-year-old niece, Julie, he saw Bailey.

"Thanks. And, yes, Nick's already setting up his rules for dating. Mainly that she can start dating when she's thirty-five."

Jake laughed. "Sounds like a plan." He stood and gave her hug. "See you tomorrow."

He remained out on the deck long after the sun had dipped below the horizon. Lights from various water craft sparkled on the darkened waters of the Gulf. A part of him wanted to stay here until all the drama was over and he could resume his quiet life in the Northwest. Another part of him wanted to get on the next flight to Seattle so he could be there for Shannon or Heather, whichever name she was using now. He thought about her choice of paint for her bedroom—heather green. A hint? Maybe a way to subconsciously connect with her past.

He stretched and yawned, then went back inside. His father sat in a recliner, remote in hand, sound asleep. Jake lifted the remote and set it on the table beside the chair. He walked down the hall to the den that doubled as his bedroom. A computer sat on the desk in the far corner. Jake turned it on and paced while it booted up. He first checked his email which never amounted to much. Then he went to the website for the Snoqualmie Valley newspaper. He found the story about Shannon or, rather, Heather being arrested and then released on bail. The photograph on the front page must have been taken at the police station. He could see the fear in her eyes and. as much as he wanted to believe her, the accusations were also believable.

A glance at his cell phone revealed that Angie had tried twice more to reach him. He hit reply and waited.

"About time. Jake, where the heck are you? Do you know what's been going on up here?"

"I'm in Florida reconnecting with my family. I guess you've seen the news and know all about me, huh?"

"Yeah, yeah. Look, Mark Hastings has kidnapped Heather and the baby. We think he's intent on disposing of both of them."

Jake felt as if someone had punched him in the gut. "You can't be serious. Would he really think he'd get away with it?"

"Apparently so. The man is a sociopath."

He thought about Heather and Amanda in the hands of a crazed killer and his stomach plummeted.

"Jake?"

"I'm here. I'll be on the first flight I can get tomorrow. I'll let you know once I'm on my way to Snoqualmie from Seattle. I'm sorry I ignored your calls. I won't do that again."

"I got the guys from Rusty's forming a search party. They're going up into the mountains in the morning. That's got to be where he took them if he intends to…well, to not be found."

Jake was already doing an online search for a flight. "Damn, I don't have my truck at the airport. Can you send someone to meet me? I'll email you the flight info."

"I'll pick you up myself."

"Thanks, Angie. I'll see you tomorrow."

He found a flight that would get him into Sea-Tac at eight a.m. and booked it. Then he went to the living room to waken his father. "Dad, an emergency's come up. I have to fly back to Seattle first thing in the morning."

"What happened now?"

Jake explained the situation with Heather. "I have to be there, Dad."

His father studied him for a moment. "This woman's more than a friend, isn't she?"

A flush warmed his face. "She is. Or, at least, I hope she will be." He grinned. "You know, in a way she reminds me a bit of Mom."

"Well, then, she must be special."

He glanced at his father. "You're not upset with me? I mean, having been a priest and getting involved like this?"

"All I ever wanted was for you to have a fulfilling life. You go to her. I'll explain everything to your sister when she arrives for breakfast."

"She'll swear this was my way of getting out of cooking."

"She knows already about the girl?"

Jake nodded. "She does."

"Then she'll understand. What time do you have to leave?"

"Now. But I'll call you once I get there."

His father stood and hugged him. "I only ever wanted for you to be happy. The way you talk about this girl, she makes you happy."

Jake nodded. The implications carried both anticipation and terror.

~ * ~

Amanda's cry escalated from a whimper to a full-out, non-stop wail.

"Will you shut her up?" Mark demanded.

"I can't. She's hungry and she probably needs a clean diaper. You wouldn't let me bring anything."

"Dammit." He slammed a hand on the steering wheel. "Where's the damned road I need?"

Minutes later they came to small gas station with a convenience store. Mark pulled over. "Tell me what she needs."

"I can go in, just give me money."

"Yeah, right." He got out of the car, took the keys and rounded to the back door on her side. Opening it, he reached inside. "Dammit. How the hell do you get her out of this seat?"

"Where are you taking her?"

"I'm going inside and she'll be my insurance that you don't try to run." He stepped back. "Get her out of there."

Heather released the baby from the car seat and bounced her in her arms, cooing in a soothing voice. But Amanda was not about to be soothed.

Mark snatched the baby from her arms and then ordered her back into the car. "What does she need?"

"I doubt they have formula. Get milk and a baby bottle if they have them. Which I also doubt. Otherwise, get rice cereal and some jarred food—bananas, sweet potatoes, green beans. Any of those. Be sure to get a spoon. Why don't you just let me come with you? I won't say a word, I promise."

"Stay in the car." He slammed the door shut and juggled the

baby in his arms.

Mark returned a few minutes later and tossed a grocery bag to her. Then he thrust the baby into her arms. "She stinks. You need to change her."

Heather laid the baby in her lap and removed the dirty diaper, setting it on the floor. "I need wipes or something to clean her."

"Use another diaper, dammit. And hurry up. We don't have all night." He choked. "Jesus, that stinks."

Heather resisted a smile. She noticed the diaper that was soggy and full had leaked on his suit jacket. *Good for you, baby,* she thought. She used a diaper to clean Amanda as much as she could, then put a clean diaper on her. "Do you want to hold her while I throw the dirty diapers away, or would you like to do the honors?"

"Give them to me."

She complied, making sure she handed the diaper over with a loose grip. As he climbed out of the car, the diaper dropped open and some of it's contents splattered onto his leather seat.

"Shit."

"Yep." She had opened a jar of the bananas and was spooning them into Amanda's mouth. She glanced sideways to see Mark trying to clean the seat without touching the excrement.

He flung the diapers into a trashcan and hurried back to the car, starting the engine.

"You can't drive until I've fed her and she's back in her car seat."

"You're kidding, right? You do know I'm going to kill you both, so I think we can take that little risk."

Heather struggled not to gasp. She couldn't let him see her fear now. "And if the police spot us, they'll pull you over. You know, on second thought, just drive."

"She's had enough. Put her in the car seat and let's get going."

It was Heather's one chance. If she could make a dash for the convenience store with Amanda before Mark got out of the car, maybe they'd have a chance. But as she opened her door, the lights of the business went out and the clerk came out a side door and got into a pickup truck. Screaming now would only result in an immediate death for herself, Amanda and the innocent clerk.

She got out, fastened Amanda into the seat, then got back into the car. "It's getting dark. Where are we going?"

"There's an old logging road not far from here. Leads to a deserted logging camp. They'll never find you there." He reached out and ran a finger along her cheek. "You were so sweet, so willing to please. Maybe we'll give things one more go for old time's sake. You just might die smiling."

Her stomach twisted and she batted his hand away. "You're disgusting."

He laughed. "Now, now. No need for name-calling." He started the car and pulled from the darkened parking lot.

Headlights shone in the side mirror as another vehicle approached from behind.

"Get the hell off my ass, jerk," Mark complained. "I can't see for shit with those headlights glaring." He slowed and opened his window, flagging the other driver to go around him.

Heather recognized the vehicle as the truck from the convenience store. At least it looked the same. She wished the driver would have stayed behind them so someone would know where Mark had taken them. But the truck passed and the taillights faded into mist that had begun to form.

Mark slowed, watching the side of the narrow road. "Finally." He cut the wheels hard to the left and onto a rutted dirt path. The Mercedes bounced over the ruts, the bottom scraping every so often.

"This can't be good for a Mercedes," Heather said.

"Shut up."

The headlights swept across a clearing where two small buildings sat in a state of disrepair. "Honey, we're home."

He stood with a flashlight, waiting for her to get Amanda out of the car. Popping the trunk, he removed a canvas bag. Then he led the way to one of the buildings.

"How did you find this place?" Heather asked.

"A little research. Brilliant, isn't it?" He forced the door open and flashed the light around the inside. "Sorry I didn't have a chance to clean."

He removed two battery-powered lamps from the bag and set them on the filthy desk. His cell phone bleated, indicating a message. "What do you know? I have a signal all the way up here." He put the phone to his ear, then began to laugh. "I guess someone called the wife on me." He turned on the speaker so she could hear the message from Corinne Hastings. "Looks like I'll have some explaining to do when I get home."

Heather knew she had to buy time, keep him talking. "Why does Corinne want the baby?"

"Who the hell knows. Probably so she can rub my nose in my indiscretion every day. And there's her pro-life stance. What could be better for an election than holding up a baby—one your wandering husband fathered—and loving it as your own? Dumb bitch. I'm sick of her politics and her pretences and her holier-than-thou attitude. I might be going down for this, but I'm taking her with me." He stopped moving and faced her. "If you'd just stayed put a while longer, we could have worked this all out. And she'd never had to have known about the money. But, no, you had to run."

"I'll give you back the money. I have it."

"You're really clueless, aren't you? Do you have any idea how much of Corinne's money I've siphoned off over the years? And she would never have known. But, now, you'll go to court and testify and she'll start asking all kinds of questions. You've heard the expression take the money and run? Well, that's what I fully intend to do. I think I'll like Brazil."

He snapped the cell phone closed. But she noticed he hadn't turned it off. She wondered if anyone would think to track the GPS.

Amanda began to cry again.

"Now what's wrong with her?"

"She's probably wet."

"Well, change her."

"The diapers are in the car. Will you get them?" She feigned laying the baby on the filthy desk.

"And you wonder why I don't want the brat." He paused in the doorway. "Don't even think about trying anything. There's nowhere to go up here."

Her thoughts raced as she frantically scanned the shabby cabin. The windows were boarded over. Mark slammed through the door. His eyes followed her gaze. "Don't even try." He tossed the package of diapers to her. "Change her and shut her up."

"I can't lay her on this desk. It's filthy. Give me your jacket."

He removed his jacket and threw it toward her. "You're a pain in the ass, both of you."

She spread the jacket on top of the desk and laid the baby down. Keeping on eye on Mark, she felt the pockets for the car keys. Nothing.

Mark paced the room, his agitation growing.

Heather picked up Amanda, soothing her. She fought to keep her voice calm. "Mark, it's not too late to stop this. If you leave now, you'll be in Canada before I can get to a phone. I'll stay here until morning."

"Shut up! Just shut up."

She bounced Amanda in her arms when the baby whimpered. "If you're leaving the country, there's really no need to kill us."

"Maybe I just want to clean up the mess and start over. No one will know I was even here. My loving wife has been the one tracking you down. Her brother will have to testify to that fact." His smile and the wild look in his eyes made her tremble. "It's perfect. I get rid of you and take down the great Governor Hastings at the same time."

"So why don't you just do it? Get it over with."

He whirled and strode toward her. "This is my party. You're a guest. I'll decide when it's over." He grabbed her arm and dragged her toward a closet.

Heather clutched Amanda with her free arm. When he opened the closet door, she balked. She hated small, enclosed spaces. "There's no need for this. We can't go anywhere."

"I have something to take care of. I want you here when I get back. That's when the real party's gonna start." He shoved her inside the closet and a lock clicked.

His footsteps faded as he crossed the room, then the door closed leaving her in the dark and in complete silence. Her body shook and she tried the doorknob. She turned and something covered her face causing her to step back and gasp. Her arms protectively covered Amanda who now slept peacefully.

Heather kissed the baby's head. "I'll get us out of this somehow. I promise."

When Mark returned and released her from the closet, light had begun to break outside.

"I need to use the bathroom. And then I need to feed the baby again."

"Give her to me."

She turned to keep him from taking Amanda from her.

"I'll hold her while you use the bathroom." He took the baby in his arms. Amanda took one look at his face and wailed. "Hurry up. It's behind that partition."

Heather rounded the corner to find a rusted and blackened toilet devoid of water. Her stomach rolled and she fought down nausea as she undid her jeans and relieved herself. She noticed something in the back wall of the cabin. A door. Did it lead outside or just to another room or closet?

Amanda shrieked and Mark shouted, "What the hell are you doing?"

She jerked up her jeans and hurried back to Amanda. "You were gone a long time. Where were you?"

His cold stare sent shivers through her. "Digging a grave."

Chapter Thirty-Four

Jake raced through the airport and out to the curb where Angie waited. He tossed his bag into the back of her SUV and climbed in the front. "Any news?"

"No. They've got everyone up on that mountain—local police, states, and the FBI. I'm scared for her, Jake."

"Let's go to my place. I need my truck."

"What are you going to do?"

"I'm going up there and find her."

She pulled from the curb. "They won't let you through. I was up there most of the night. They have a command center set up at the gas station and the road blocked to traffic."

"I don't plan to stop and ask permission. I know that mountain. I've hiked there often."

She sighed and cut into the passing lane, jamming her foot down on the gas. "Then I'm going with you."

"No, you're not."

"You seem to forget that I'm driving. And I know that mountain, too."

Once they were out of traffic and heading toward the mountain, Angie said, "So, I have to ask—do we call you Father Steve now? Boy, that was a shocker."

"I can imagine. No, I'm still Jake. I left the priesthood."

"You're sticking around here then?"

Jake knew what she was trying to ask and figured he may as well tell the whole story. "I've learned some things about myself in the past couple of years. I'm not sure I was ever cut out to be a priest. The reasons I had for choosing that vocation weren't enough. There are a lot of ways to help people, to make a difference."

"There are."

"I imagine the news was the topic of discussion at Rusty's?" he asked.

"Oh, yeah." She laid on the horn and tore around a slow-moving pickup truck.

Jake braced himself. "Do you believe Heather's innocent,

that she's the victim here?"

"Don't you? C'mon, Jake. That guy is crazy and he kidnapped her and the baby."

"His baby."

"If you don't believe her, why are you charging up the mountain to rescue her?" When he didn't answer, she continued, "The only thing she's guilty of is having poor taste in men. Well, in one man, at least."

Jake stared forward at the roadblock ahead. "Pull into the gas pumps."

"I don't need gas."

"Just pull up there and get out."

She headed into the parking lot and motioned to one of the policemen that she was pulling up to the pumps. She slid down from SUV. "I'll see what I can do, but I'm pretty sure they're not going to let us go any farther."

"That's why I'm not asking." He moved behind the wheel and gunned the engine. Gravel sprayed out behind the vehicle as he sped around the roadblock and up the mountain. In the rearview mirror, he saw two uniformed officers scramble to get into a car to give chase. He floored the gas pedal.

The narrow, winding mountain road was treacherous and his heart pounded as the SUV fishtailed around a curve. Angie had told him the gas station attendant followed them the night before and that Mark must have taken one of the old logging roads. A glance in the mirror told him the police car hadn't caught up yet. He slowed in the thick fog as he came to a rutted road that disappeared into the woods to his left. Cutting the wheel sharply, Jake turned and tried to avoid some of the deeper ruts. This had to be the right place. It had to be.

~ * ~

Mark had paced and rambled for more than an hour. But he hadn't touched her or taken Amanda from her. For that, Heather was grateful. She needed to distract him, break the escalation in his train of thought. "I need the rest of the baby food. It's in the car."

He stopped and whirled around to stare at her, looking almost surprised at her presence. "What?"

"She's hungry. I need her baby food. If you want, I can go and get it."

"Yeah, right. I'll let you just walk out the door. I'll be right back." He lifted the gun and pointed it at her. "Don't try to run. I won't miss."

The second he was out the door, she picked up Amanda and hurried to the door she'd seen in the back of the cabin. It opened to the outside. Holding Amanda tightly against her, she ran, following a narrow path deeper into the woods, trying to hold onto a sense of direction toward the road they'd turned off from. Morning fog masked the light, made it difficult to see more than a few feet ahead. It was still a better option than staying and waiting to be shot.

"Heather! You can't go anywhere. If you're not careful, you're going to kill yourself out there."

His shrill laugh sent chills up her spine. She huddled behind thick overgrowth and shushed Amanda. She could hear him moving closer. He would find them soon enough if she stayed there.

She looked to her left. A path cut back through the trees and toward the dirt road. She clutched Amanda in her arms and made her way along the path. She could hear Mark moving deeper into the woods, calling to her.

She broke into the clearing and reached the Mercedes. As she'd hoped, the keys dangled from the ignition. Ripping open the driver's door, she placed the baby on the passenger's seat, slid into the driver's seat and started the engine. No time for a car seat. She hit the gas and spun the car around, one hand on Amanda.

Mark swore as he raced from the trees and into the clearing. A bullet dinged off the hood of the car. She sped up, careful not to bottom the car out and have it stall.

She rounded a turn and slammed on the brakes, veering off the road. A black SUV headed straight toward her. It came to a stop in a cloud of dust. Terror filled her. What if Mark had an accomplice? Her only desire was to protect Amanda. She crawled across the console, threw open the passenger side door and clutched the baby, prepared to run back into the woods.

"Heather?"

The familiar voice brought her to a halt. She looked over her shoulder. "Jake?"

He rushed toward her. "Are you both okay?"

"We have to get out of here. Mark's crazy. He has a gun and I'm sure he's headed this way." The words were barely out of her mouth when a bullet zinged by and exploded in the trunk of a pine.

"Get in the SUV." Jake took Amanda from her arms and shoved her toward the idling vehicle.

A police car with lights flashing and siren blaring pulled in behind them. The two cops jumped out, guns drawn.

Jake lifted one hand, palm out. "I'm not armed. But he is," Jake said, motioning to the man who now stood in the center of the road, gun aimed.

"Drop the gun, Hastings," one of the officers shouted.

"I don't think so."

A second later, a loud bang was followed by silence.

Jake put his arm around Heather, drawing her against him. "It's over."

She clung to him, burying her face in his chest.

"Come on. Let me take you home. Are you hurt?"

She shook her head. "No, we're okay. I just want to go home."

He helped her into the SUV and handed Amanda to her. "I'll be right back."

Jake strode to where the police officers stood over Mark Hastings. He said something to them, motioned to the SUV, then nodded and walked back to her. "They'll need a statement from you. We'll go down to the gas station where they've set up camp."

He turned the SUV around and headed back to the mountain road.

"How did you know what was going on?"

"It was on the news. I was in Florida with my family."

She hugged Amanda close and rested her chin on the baby's head. "You probably saved us both by showing up when you did with the cavalry."

"I ran the roadblock and they were chasing me."

"How did you know where to look for us?"

"The kid from the gas station followed you last night. The police were waiting for the fog to clear enough to move in."

"But you didn't wait."

He glanced at her. "All I could think of was you and Amanda alone with that maniac."

Two police cars screamed past them, heading up the mountain.

"So, you know about us. You called her Amanda."

"I saw the news."

She nodded. "I saw the news, too. We've both been keeping secrets."

221

They reached the gas station and Jake pulled into the parking lot. Angie and two police officers all raced toward the vehicle.

Angie pulled the door open and reached for the baby. "Oh, sweetie." She looked up at Heather. "Are you okay?"

When her feet hit the ground, reality hit her brain and she began to shake. Angie pulled her close. "Oh, honey. That had to be terrifying."

Heather leaned into her and cried.

A female officer waited a moment, then said, "Miss Carlson, I can take you and your baby to the hospital to be checked out."

"We're okay. I just want to go home."

"I'll take them home, officer." Angie kept an arm around Heather's shoulders.

"We'll need to get a statement, Miss Carlson," the police woman said.

"Can't it wait? She and the baby have both been through an ordeal," Angie said.

The officer spoke with a detective, then returned to them. "Someone will come by in a few hours unless you want to come to the station."

"I'd appreciate it if they'd come to my house. I'm exhausted and I need to see my mother," Heather said.

Angie held out her hand to Jake. "Keys."

"I'll drive."

"Fine." Angie climbed into the passenger's seat.

"I'll ride in the back with Amanda. Take it slow," Heather said.

In the car, Heather held the baby in her lap and let her head fall back against the headrest, closing her eyes. Tears trailed down her cheeks.

When they pulled into the driveway behind Abe's house, Brooke raced down the steps and pulled Heather into a hug. "Oh, thank God. We were so scared."

"I was, too." She leaned into her friend and cried.

Her mother stood at the bottom of the steps, tears streaming down her face. Heather broke free and ran into her mother's arms.

Angie walked by them. "I'm taking Amanda upstairs and giving her a bath."

"Thanks," Heather said.

"Let's all go upstairs," Brooke said.

Jake hesitated, "I…uh…" He looked to Heather. "Can we talk for a minute?"

She nodded.

"We need to talk about everything. So much has happened."

"This isn't the time, Jake. Or is it Father Steve?" She started to walk away, then turned back to him. "You should have told me. I told you the truth, and you… You slept with me, let me believe you were someone else. I can't begin to tell you how that hurts. How that shames me."

"Heather…."

But she was already hurrying up the steps.

Chapter Thirty-Five

Heather wakened to sun streaming through the bedroom window. She had slept for hours. A nightmare replay of the events had jarred her from sleep once, screaming. Her mother had crawled in with her and held her until she was once again able to sleep. Now she lay alone in the late afternoon light. Voices drifted toward her from the living room. She sat up and stretched, touching fingertips to her swollen lip and remembering Mark's slap. She shuddered when she thought of Mark, the demonic look in his eyes, then the realization he'd taken his own life rather than be captured.

She padded down the hall toward the voices. Her mother sat in the rocker with Amanda while Brooke did dishes. Heather's stomach rumbled and she remembered she hadn't eaten since lunch the previous day.

"Hey, sleepy head. You ready for dinner?" Brooke asked.

Heather rubbed her eyes. "Maybe coffee first. And breakfast?"

"Sit. I'll get it for you."

Heather sat on the sofa. From her grandmother's lap, Amanda grinned and gurgled at her. Tears filled her eyes as she realized what was nearly lost. Brooke set a mug of coffee on the table in front of her, then sat down and rubbed soothing circles on her back. "Hey, it's okay. You're both okay now."

Heather drew in a shuddering breath. "I know. But that doesn't mean everything's over. Corinne Hastings could still push to take Amanda from me if she can convince a judge I signed that surrogacy agreement."

"That reminds me. Maggie called. She'll be here in about an hour to meet with you. She has news. I was about to come and wake you when you came out here."

"Good news or bad news?"

"She didn't say, but she sounded upbeat."

Heather sipped her coffee. "I need to shower. I'll take this with me."

"You should eat something," her mother said.

"I will after I shower."

Moments later as she stood under the warm stream from the shower, she let go of the tears she'd been holding in. Her body shook and she wrapped her arms across her bare breasts. It would take some time before she'd feel safe again.

She dressed in jeans and a sweatshirt, despite the seventy-plus degrees outside. She couldn't stop the chill that rattled through her. She was sitting at the table eating pancakes and bacon when Maggie arrived.

The attorney embraced Heather, then gravitated to the baby. "Oh, she is just precious."

"Thank you."

Maggie took a seat opposite Heather at the dining table. "So, I have news."

Heather pushed her plate away and waited.

"Suddenly both Corinne Hastings and her brother, Anthony, are insisting that Mark Hastings was behind everything. Corinne says it was Mark's idea to push you to give over custody of the baby, that he concocted the idea of creating a false surrogacy agreement with a forgery of your signature. And she claims she only came to see you and gave you the ten grand because Mark told her that's what you wanted. According to Anthony, Mark sent him here to get the baby with the understanding that you knew he was coming. He's being magnanimous and saying he doesn't hold you responsible for shooting him, that he did enter the apartment without your knowledge."

"In other words, they're pinning everything on Mark and they'll walk away scot free," Heather said.

Maggie frowned. "Unfortunately, you're probably right. The good news is, I've already filed for a dismissal of all charges against you. If they're going to claim that Mark was behind everything, then that leaves you in the clear. And since he's deceased, there's no one else to claim any rights to Amanda."

"Are you serious? This nightmare could come to an end?" Heather said.

"We have to meet in Judge Henniker's chambers tomorrow morning at ten. She already has my filing, as does the District Attorney."

Doris Carlson asked, "How likely is the judge to dismiss the charges without a trial?"

"I'd say more likely than not, given the circumstances." Maggie glanced at her watch. "You might want to turn on the TV. Governor Hastings is scheduled to give a press conference in a few minutes. I'm sure it's made national news."

Brooke turned on the television and surfed through channels until she found one announcing the press conference. A few moments later, Corinne Hastings, wearing a black suit—the grieving widow—strode to a podium. She took a sip of water and cleared her throat. "As you all know, my husband suffered a mental break in the past few days. He was a very troubled man for some time, but I never believed he would become violent." She took another sip. "I'm ashamed to say he got involved with a young woman and, when she became pregnant, Mark became obsessed with the idea of obtaining full custody of the baby in hopes I would raise the child with him." She lifted her eyes to look directly into the cameras. "You all know my stance on pro-life and there was no way I would hold this innocent child responsible for the sins of her parents. So, of course, I agreed."

"God, she's politicking standing on the body of her dead husband," Brooke muttered.

"I was never aware of my husband's illegal activities in his effort to convince the woman to give over the baby. I want to clarify, also, that my brother, Anthony Baker, was equally duped by Mark into acting on his behalf. The alleged break-in at the home of Heather Carlson was a mistake, a matter of miscommunication between Anthony and Mark. I spoke with my brother earlier today. Neither of us holds Ms. Carlson responsible for her actions in believing she had to defend herself and her child when she shot Anthony. I would, no doubt, have acted in a similar defensive manner to protect my own child, had I been so blessed."

"And there it is—the tug of pro-life heartstrings," Brooke said.

"I want to apologize to you, my supporters, for allowing my husband's mental health issues to cast a shadow over this office and over the great State of Missouri. You deserved better from us. I wish to announce that I will not be running for re-election in the coming year. I will finish my current term and serve the people of Missouri to the best of my ability. Thank you."

Brooke's eyes widened. "She's not running? Wow, I thought that speech was a set-up for another term."

"She's afraid she'll lose. And Corinne Hastings hates to lose. By choosing not to run, she has the control," Maggie said. "And there is the matter of the Senate seat that just opened up." She smiled at Heather. "Well, after that speech, I'd say my petition for dismissal of the charges against you will be a shoe in." She stood. "I have to get back to Seattle. I'll see you at the courthouse tomorrow morning."

Heather walked Maggie to her car. "Thank you so much for everything you've done."

"It's my pleasure. See you tomorrow."

When she returned upstairs, Brooke grabbed her in a bear hug. "It's over. It's really over."

"Just about. I won't breathe easy until the judge finalizes everything." She sat beside her mother on the sofa and hugged her close. "Mom, I'm so sorry for all of this."

"It's not your fault." She tightened her hold. "I'm grateful both you and Amanda are okay." Easing away, her mother asked, "Will you move back to Jefferson City now?"

"I don't know, Mom. I kind of like it here. It's a beautiful place, the people are great. It might be nice to raise Amanda here. But if you need me...."

Her mother shook her head. "No. You have to make a decision that's best for you and Amanda. I kind of like it here, too. Your Aunt Rita wants me to move in with her in Uniontown, but I don't want to be that far away from my granddaughter."

Heather broke into a smile. "You'd think of moving here?"

"Wait a minute," Brooke said. "You're both going to leave me?"

"You can visit any time," Heather said. "I'm going to run downstairs and give Abe the good news. I hope he gets all of his bail money back."

Upon hearing her news, Abe hugged her as if she were his long lost granddaughter. "That's wonderful."

"I should be back on schedule in a day or two and be of more help around here."

"We've managed okay. We can do so for a few more days. You need to get some rest."

As she stepped out onto Abe's porch, a pickup truck pulled into the drive. She watched as Jake got out.

~ * ~

Heather descended the three steps from the porch and stopped. "Hi."

Jake stood by the truck. "Hi. I know you don't want to talk to me. But I hope you'll at least listen."

She opened her mouth to respond, but closed it again, crossing her arms over her chest and waiting.

"You know everything?"

"I don't know that I know everything. I saw you on the news. It explained why you had some pull with Caleb to get documentation for me and the baby." She studied him for a moment. "I would never have guessed you were a priest. I'd say you hid that pretty well."

He glanced away from her gaze. "I'm really sorry. You have to understand why I couldn't tell you the truth."

"Oh, I understand. What I don't understand is the fact that you made love to me. You let me think there could be something between us."

"There can be."

"I don't see how."

"If you'll just let me explain."

Anger flashed in her eyes. "There is no explanation, is there?" She pulled away and started up the steps.

Jake raced after her. "Shannon!"

She reached the landing at the top and whirled around. "I'm not Shannon. She doesn't exist. She was as much fiction as you are." She went inside and slammed the door.

Jake climbed the few remaining steps, his feet heavy and his heart heavier. He stood there, weighing his options. If he walked away now, there would be no second chance. He knocked. An older woman opened the door. "Yes?"

"I'm Jake Garber. May I please speak to Shann... to Heather?"

"You were on the news. You're the priest, aren't you?"

"I was."

She stepped out onto the landing, closing the door behind her. "She's pretty upset right now. And I don't want you to upset her even further."

Jake dragged a hand through his hair. "I only want to explain."

"I'm Doris Carlson, Heather's mother. I was raised Catholic, so you'll understand when I say I'm confused and disappointed."

"You're not the only one who's confused."

She stared at him. "This is very bad timing for you. She's just been through an ordeal with the last man she trusted."

"I know. I don't want to hurt her. I—I care about her and about Amanda."

Doris Carlson studied him for a long moment. "What do you want from Heather?"

"I just want to explain some things. Do you think she'll ever talk to me?"

"That depends. What do you want to talk with her about?"

What had Angie said to him—'get out of your head and into your heart. That's where the answer lies.' Jake drew in a breath and exhaled. "I want to tell her that I'm no longer a priest, that this is where I belong, and I think it's where she belongs, too. With me. I want to tell her I love her."

Doris stared into his eyes as if searching for a hint that he might be lying. "You mean that?"

"With all my heart. I love her and I love Amanda. I'd like to see if Heather feels the same way and if we can have a future."

She opened the door. "Wait here. I'll see what I can do."

While he waited, he noticed someone peeking between the curtains of the small kitchen window. A moment later the door opened and Heather stood before him. "My mother insists I listen to you."

"Can we go somewhere and talk? Privately."

"Where?"

"Will you come with me to the falls?"

"We can talk right here. The last time I took a ride up the mountain, it didn't turn out so well."

"Heather, please. Just come with me. It's beautiful up there and what I have to say…."

"Fine. Let's go." She pushed past him and descended the steps in a rush. She was in his truck before he caught up with her.

He climbed in and got the truck moving before she could change her mind. They rode in silence until he pulled into the parking lot at Snoqualmie Falls. He removed the key from the ignition, then faced her. "Before we have this conversation, there's something you should know. I asked to be released from the priesthood."

"Good for you."

"I'm also no longer being hunted, so being with me won't put you in danger. That worried me. The biker was looking for me, not you."

She nodded, but said nothing.

He couldn't read her face. "Walk with me?"

She got out of the truck as quickly as she'd gotten in and strode purposefully to one of the observation platforms overlooking the falls. She leaned on the railing. The evening light glinted through the trees and shone like diamonds in her hair.

Jake leaned beside her. "I often come up here when I need to think something through. It's so peaceful."

She turned, staring up at him, her jaw set hard. "Why did you say you loved me when you left that message and took off?"

"Because I do love you. I didn't expect this. I don't know what I expected. For two years, I've just gone through the motions of living. And then you showed up, literally crashed into my life, you and Amanda. It wasn't long before you both had my heart tangled around your fingers."

"You could have trusted me, Jake. Or am I supposed to call you Steve?"

"I'm Jake. I can't go back. I want to move forward." He met her gaze. "But I don't want to do it without you."

"How do I know this isn't temporary, like your attraction to the priesthood? Will you decide in ten years that Amanda and I aren't right for you?"

He flinched. "That's a fair question, I suppose. I think I always knew I wasn't meant to be a priest. I was good at it, but it was work."

"Relationships are work."

"I know. The thing is, being with you makes me want to work harder. You brought some part of me to life that I'd denied. I'm not talking about sex, either. Being with you and Amanda made me feel whole, complete."

She pressed her lips together and he saw the struggle in her eyes.

He forged ahead, hoping to take advantage of her struggle. "Whatever happens, I want us to be together. That is, if it's what you want, too."

Turning her back on him, she leaned once again on the

railing. "My charges will likely be dismissed. We have a meeting with the judge tomorrow."

Jake wanted to touch her, to pull her into his arms, but knew he had to wait and let her give him the signal that it would be okay. Everything around him felt so fragile, he tried not to breathe.

"I'm not returning to Missouri," she said. "I'm staying here." Then she turned around again to face him. "There can never be secrets or lies between us again. Not even the little ones."

"No secrets or lies. Ever."

"And I need time. I won't rush into something when I have Amanda to consider." Then she flushed. "What happened that night at my apartment was a mistake. It was wonderful, don't get me wrong. But it shouldn't have happened yet. I want to slow down, savor us getting to know one another."

"I can do that." He fought to keep his voice even.

"Okay, then." She stared down and when she lifted her face, a smile tugged at the corners of her mouth. "God isn't going to be mad at me, is He?"

Jake laughed. "God will dance at our wedding. Some day." He drew her into his arms, his lips claiming hers. Her arms closed around him, deepening the kiss.

When they parted, she gazed up at him. "Do you think you can get used to calling me Heather?"

He traced a finger along her jaw. "It's a pleasure to meet you, Heather."

She laughed and narrowed her eyes. "Haven't we met before—Jake?"

"Briefly. But now we'll have a lifetime to get to know one another." He kissed her again.

They stood for a while, silent, watching the sunset. Jake stood behind her and wrapped his arms around her. "I'm in love with you, Heather Carlson."

She dropped her head back into the crook of his shoulder. "I love you, too," she said.

~ * ~

When Jake escorted her into Rusty's the following evening, she was astonished to see a small group of friends and acquaintances, along with her mother and Brooke stand and applaud.

"You did this?" she asked Jake.

"Not me. It was Angie's idea," he said.

Angie came out from behind the bar and hugged her. "Congratulations on being a free woman. I thought it was something worth celebrating."

"It is. Thank you."

Angie glanced at Jake, then back to Heather. "Maybe a time to celebrate a whole new beginning."

She grinned. "Could be."

"What do you mean 'could be'?" Jake draped an arm around her shoulders and pulled her close.

"Okay, everybody, it's an open bar and buffet. Let's get this party started." Angie headed back behind the bar.

Once everyone had their turn at congratulating Heather, they sat at tables and booths, enjoying the spread and chatting.

Jake stood in front of the vintage jukebox. He dropped in coins and pressed buttons, then turned to Heather. "Dance with me?"

The song began—*Just the Way You Are* by Bruno Mars.

"A man who can cook *and* dance?" she marveled.

He drew her into his arms. "Come here."

"That isn't a slow dance."

"It is if we make it one. Just listen to the words." They stood in the same spot, molded to one another, swaying until the song ended. Jake smiled down at her. "Amazing." He lowered his face to hers, planting a firm kiss on her lips.

Whistles and applause sounded from the men at the bar. Someone called out, "Go for it, Choirboy."

Jake laughed. "I'm trying, trust me."

Heather raised an eyebrow. "What exactly are you trying to do?"

"Sweep you off your feet."

"Well, why didn't you say so?" She wrapped her arms around his neck, standing on the tips of her toes.

Jake tightened his hold, supporting her. "I'll never let you down."

She regarded him for a moment, then smiled. "I know."

The End

About the Author

Linda Rettstatt likes to know what makes people tick and she loves a good story. This combination fuels her passion for creating stories that capture your mind and touch your heart. Her writing garnered the 2012 EPIC eBook Award in Mainstream Fiction for her novel *Love, Sam.* Linda grew up in SW Pennsylvania and suffers a bout of homesickness every October when she thinks of the fall leaves and trails at her beloved Ohiopyle State Park. She now lives in NW Mississippi with her cat, Binky, who only allows her to share the apartment because she brings home the Fancy Feast.

If you enjoyed PROTECTION, visit Linda's website
http://www.lindarettstatt.com
where you can find links to more of her books.

Made in the USA
Charleston, SC
15 October 2014